THE WOUNDED WHOLE

THE WOUNDED WHOLE

A Novel

CAROLYN LAWSON

iUniverse, Inc.
Bloomington

The Wounded Whole
A Novel

Copyright © 2013 by Carolyn Lawson.

All rights reserved. No part of this book may be used or reproduced by any means, graphic, electronic, or mechanical, including photocopying, recording, taping or by any information storage retrieval system without the written permission of the publisher except in the case of brief quotations embodied in critical articles and reviews.

This is a work of fiction. All of the characters, names, incidents, organizations, and dialogue in this novel are either the products of the author's imagination or are used fictitiously.

iUniverse books may be ordered through booksellers or by contacting:

iUniverse
1663 Liberty Drive
Bloomington, IN 47403
www.iuniverse.com
1-800-Authors (1-800-288-4677)

Because of the dynamic nature of the Internet, any web addresses or links contained in this book may have changed since publication and may no longer be valid. The views expressed in this work are solely those of the author and do not necessarily reflect the views of the publisher, and the publisher hereby disclaims any responsibility for them.

Any people depicted in stock imagery provided by Thinkstock are models, and such images are being used for illustrative purposes only. Certain stock imagery © Thinkstock.

ISBN: 978-1-4759-8745-4 (sc)
ISBN: 978-1-4759-8746-1 (ebk)

Printed in the United States of America

iUniverse rev. date: 04/26/2013

CHAPTER ONE

A strong, cold, whistling wind blew outside the windows of the small, dilapidated wood-frame house, forcefully knocking tree branches against the walls while the shrieking sound of a newborn's cry cut through the dim light. Was the tempestuousness of that February night in 1946, when she was born in the small town of Salem, Georgia, an omen for Bay McQueen's future? Growing up at a time when being colored with very dark skin was considered a curse, Bay quickly developed a poor self-image. Yet she possessed all she needed to soar above society's illusory constructs. Would she become aware of her power? Living in a world where the rules were already set, part of a family she had no control over, made life difficult. Trouble seemed to follow her like a hungry baby crying for Mama's milk. The infant soon grew into a cute, thin little chocolate girl with a head full of long, thick hair and the prettiest light brown eyes you ever saw. Bee, her mother, would braid her hair every Sunday, and Bay would wear it that way all week. Bay had a lot of potential, but she didn't know it. Her parents weren't around much. They didn't know anything about raising children. They just had them.

Five years passed, and Bay and her family were still living in that same wood-frame house she was born in, as chillingly poor as ever. Still, Bay loved the beauty of nature. It made her feel accepted despite her skin being dark as a blackberry. One very pleasant, misty fall morning, Bay struggled to open the fragile window in the bedroom she shared with her sisters, and then she placed a stick under it to keep it from closing so she could inhale the fresh air and watch the yellow, orange, and brown leaves on the trees and the ground. *Sho wish I kin stay here 'n' watch dis putty sight!* she thought to herself.

Suddenly, she heard Sadie call her. "Bay, don'tcha be foolin' 'round too much 'n dere. Ya need ta git reddy fur school. We all goin' ta be late!"

"I'm comin'." Bay stood in front of the mirror. She dreaded getting dressed; looking at herself, she felt nothing but sadness. *I wish I wuz de color of Mama, Sadie, 'n' Carrie. I'm blacker den ev'rybody, ev'n ma teach'r. Dat's why she hate me!*

Bay was in the first grade and hated it as much as hearing about the fires of hell and brimstone—and Mrs. Stone, her teacher, didn't help the situation. She was a mean old crow who had a reputation for yelling so loud she could be heard by teachers and students throughout the huge brick building. "You'd better do it over and get it right, now! That's wrong! Erase that!" How could a child learn anything with a voice as loud as a siren blasting in her ears?

After school that day, Bay decided she'd had enough of that monstrous teacher. *I'm goin' ta tell ma mama*, thought Bay. She patiently waited for her mother, Bee, to come home from work. An hour later, Bee walked through the door and went straight to her room to change clothes.

Bay followed her. "Mama, Miz Stone yelled at me real loud 'n' hit me on ma back as hard as she could," said Bay. "She hurt me!" Tears filled Bay's eyes and rolled down her cheeks.

"Bay, I know how lazy ya kin be. Miz Stone jus' want ya ta do ya work," replied Bee.

"Ev'rybody is lazy sometime, but dat ain't why she hit me. She jus' mean 'n' hateful!" shouted Bay, running out of the room crying. "I hate school! I hate Miz Stone!" It seemed as though nothing in the entire universe was big enough to hold her tears.

Mrs. Stone was a stout, light-complexioned woman with huge hands. While Bee was alone in her bedroom, she thought, *Mayb' I do need ta talk ta Bay's teach'r, but what kin I say ta a schoolteach'r?* Bee never did talk to Mrs. Stone. A few weeks later, the family moved to the other side of town.

Life is a constant flow, and where it goes nobody really knows. One Sunday morning, while some folks slept and others were rising to prepare for the day so they could go to the Lord's house to repent or pacify an angry God for their sins during the previous week—which were in their own minds, not God's—LC and Bee packed all their stuff and waited patiently to start loading it, and it didn't matter to them about it being Sunday. They had a certain date to be off the property, which was to be expected when you didn't pay the rent. You had to move on until you learned to play by the rules. Mr. Taylor, their neighbor, volunteered to move them and didn't charge anything. Early that morning, LC and Bee put all their belongings on Mr. Taylor's truck. He cautiously drove the beat-up brown vehicle up the dusty dirt road, Lane Street, that led to the projects. Bay and Sadie rode in the back, which gave them a chance to see the scenery and feel the warm breezy air blowing against their faces and through their hair. As Mr. Taylor drove his truck over the bumpy road, Bay noticed that the left side of the road was nothing but a line of juke joints or nightspots for partying. During the fifties, the projects weren't considered the ghetto, especially by those who lived there; they were brick homes, warm and safe, with large playgrounds for children's play.

When Bay saw their new home, she was so excited. "Gee, ain't never ever seen or liv' 'n a house like dis before!" cried Bay.

"Look at de walls, so putty 'n' green!" said Sadie.

They walked down the hallway, and Bay opened a door to the bathroom. "Look at de tub! It's real nice!"

Sadie walked over and turned the water on. "It's hot! It's hot!" cried Sadie, clapping her hands. "Now we don' hafta boil water on de stove 'n' take a bath 'n dat big grey tin tub!"

"Dat's good! De closest I come ta seein' a real one wuz 'n dem magazines Mama brung home frum her job at de white ladeez house," said Bay.

"I sho like dis house 'n' wish we could live here furever 'n' ever."

"Mayb' we will. Didya see de playground? Let's go play 'n' haf some fun!" said Bay.

A year later, Bay and Sadie's happiness was history. For some reason, Bee and LC began fighting every weekend. After their parents returned home from the neighborhood juke joint late one Saturday night, smelling like they'd been bathing and sleeping in moonshine for weeks, Bay and her sisters were awakened by very loud noises that sounded like broken glass splattering everywhere. Bee was throwing plates, cups, spoons, and anything she could get her hands on. All kinds of horrible profanity was being used, none of it fit for children's ears. The girls jumped out of bed, ran into the kitchen, and saw their father slap and knock their mother on the floor, with blood all over her face and on his hands. Blood was everywhere!

The girls began yelling, "Stop it, Daddy! Stop it, Mama! Daddy, please don' hit Mama no more! Somebody help!" Sadie, who was only ten years old, grabbed the broom and began swinging. Little Carrie used her small fists, but Bay just stood there crying. She loved both her parents and just wanted them to stop. However, she knew there would be more fighting as long as they continued to drink whiskey at the juke joints and shot houses.

Suddenly, Bay heard loud knocks at the door. Blue lights were flashing through the window. Bay rushed to open the door, because she knew it was the law and her parents would have to stop fighting. Two officers grabbed LC, handcuffed him, and took him to jail. They told Bee to clean herself up and go to bed to get sober. Sadie and her sisters went to their room.

"Sadie," said Bay, "I don' like ta see Mama 'n' Daddy drunk, 'specially Mama; she look bad!"

"Ev'rybody's talkin' 'bout us. Dey says we bringin' de ghetto ta de projects. Seems like we raisin' ourselves," exclaimed Sadie.

"Dat ain't so, we ain't no ghetto girls," replied Bay.

"Ya know what, Bay? Sometime I feel like we 'n de world all by ourselves."

"I'm scared. How we goin' ta make dem stop?" asked Bay.

"Don' know, but I'll find a way," answered Sadie, hugging her sisters.

Most nights, Bay would look up at the moon and count the stars. This night was different. She wanted to talk to God. Where she learned about Him is a mystery, because her parents didn't know what the inside of a church looked like. Bay went outside into the very warm summer night, sat on the concrete curb beside the garbage can, and looked up at the dark sky. "Mr. God, ain't never met ya 'n' don' know dat much 'boutcha, but I heard ya haf power ta help people, so could ya please help me? Would ya please stop ma mama 'n' daddy frum drinkin' whiskey 'n' fightin'? I be mighty happy 'n' t'ankful! Amen."

A month later, Bay and her family had a surprise visitor: Bee's Aunt Lottie from Florida. Everybody called her Big Mama. Someone had written her about the fighting between LC and Bee. Big Mama arrived on Bee's front porch early one Saturday morning about nine o'clock. Bay and Carrie were looking out the window and saw a taxi drive away. Then a tall, slender, dark-complexioned woman about sixty years of age with two suitcases walked up on the porch, set her bags down, and began knocking.

"Somebody's on de porch! A lady is on de porch!" yelled Bay.

Bee got out of bed, half asleep. "Whoever is at de door, I oughta jus' let dem stay dere, 'cause dey ain't got no respect!" she shouted. When Bee opened the door, she got the surprise of her life. "Big Mama, whatcha doin' here? Why ya didn't let me know ya wuz comin'?"

"Aren't you going to invite me in?"

"Sho, come on in," replied Bee, hugging her aunt.

Bay, Carrie, and Sadie were standing next to an old blue sofa beside the door. When Big Mama saw them, she thought they were such pretty girls. *Bay looks shy, but there's a subtle determination about her. Carrie is just a sweet little four-year-old, friendly and mischievous, and Sadie is like the little mother of the house—wise beyond her years.* After clearing her mind, Big Mama introduced herself to the girls, and then she took three beautifully wrapped gifts out of her big green bag and handed them out. Sadie received a pretty red-and-white dress. She had never had such a beautiful dress! Bay had always desired a doll and a blue sweater, and that's exactly what she got. Big Mama gave Carrie a tiny doll and a new pair of shoes. The girls were so happy!

"Thank ya, Big Mama," said Sadie. "Ain't never had a dress as fine as dis."

Bay walked over to Big Mama, looked up at her, and said, "Thank ya, Big Mama!" with a wide smile on her face. Carrie was playing with her new friend and shoes without saying a word.

During all the excitement, Bee waited in awe. She knew Big Mama hadn't come this distance just to give the girls some gifts. And soon, Big Mama told the children to take their gifts to their room so she could talk to their mother.

Now the women were alone in the living room. LC was still asleep, or pretending to be. "Bee, I'm here because it's clear that you and that man you married are having problems," said Big Mama.

"Who tol' ya dat lie? Me 'n' LC is doin' jus' fine!"

"If you're doing so fine, why do you fight every Friday and Saturday night? Folks in the projects don't have to use a calendar to tell when it's the weekend. All they have to do is wait on you two to fight," exclaimed Big Mama. "Tell me, Bee, don't you think your behavior is affecting the children?"

"I tol' ya, LC 'n' me ain't havin' no serious problems."

"You're lying, girl! Where is that man you call a husband?" asked Big Mama, walking toward Bee's bedroom.

Bee ran behind her and grabbed her by the arm. "Wait a minute, Big Mama, wait a minute! Don' wake LC up. He'll start yellin' and cussin'!"

"Well, he can't cuss or yell louder than me! Why don't you stop trying to protect him and tell the truth?"

Bee began crying. "Who tol' ya 'bout me 'n' LC?"

"It really doesn't matter. I'm here because I love you and want the best for you."

"Big Mama, I'm tired of livin' like dis 'n' I know deep 'n ma soul dat life is s'posed ta be betta, but I don' know what ta do!" Bee said, burying her face and tears in Big Mama's chest.

"Hush, honey, it's going to be all right." Big Mama held Bee until the tears stopped. "Bee, listen to me. If you want better, you must ask God to help you be better."

Suddenly, LC walked out of the bedroom with a mean look on his face, slamming the door behind him, and saw

Big Mama comforting Bee. "Big Mama, whatcha doin' here, 'n' how long ya plan on stayin'?" he asked.

"I'm here because somebody wrote me about you and Bee fighting every weekend," replied Big Mama. "Now, to answer your second question, I'll be leaving in a week. I just want to make sure Bee is all right and to let her know she doesn't have to take a beating from you or anybody else!" said Big Mama firmly.

"I ain't been beatin' on Bee. I jus' wanta be respected as de man."

"I see. So that's how you think a man is supposed to act when a woman doesn't behave the way he expects?"

LC walked closer to Big Mama and looked her straight in the eyes. "De Bible says a man is de head of his house, 'n' I'm jus' tryin' ta do de right thang!" he said with a loud voice.

Big Mama looked at him in pure amazement. "From what I understand, you never go to church, read a Bible, or pray. If you did, there would be evidence somewhere. You sure wouldn't be beating your wife!" stressed Big Mama. She turned and looked at Bee. "You and the girls can come live with me. Anytime a man mistreats you and thinks he's doing God's will, you're in serious trouble."

"Mayb' he'll change. He's tryin' ta do betta," replied Bee.

"I don't hafta lissen ta dis. Ya know what? I'm goin' over ta de café!" said LC, walking out the door.

"Bee, it's not just about LC changing," said Big Mama. "You've got to change too. Why are you holding on to something that doesn't exist? You've got to work this out for yourself. I can't do it for you."

The week ended, and Big Mama returned to her home in Astoria, Florida. Bay and Sadie really missed her. For the first time in their lives, they had felt loved. Their feeling of love and stability soon ended.

Two weeks later, while Bay and her sisters were in their bedroom playing, Bee nervously walked in with some disturbing news.

"Girls, I hafta tell ya somethin'." They walked toward her like three helpless pets, full of doubt, fear, and uncertainty. "We got ta move," said Bee.

"Again?" cried Sadie. "I'm tired of movin'! I like it here!"

"I jus' kin't pay de rent no more," replied Bee. "I fount a putty li'l grey house on Cane Street by de railroad tracks."

Sho don' sount dat good ta me, thought Bay.

Bay and her family packed their stuff and moved to the house on Cane Street. It was not nearly as nice as the projects. It was a big, gray, ugly house, and while they were moving in, the train passed by—rolling down the tracks with the squeaking sounds of the wheels slowing down, smoke rising and blowing in the air, and then moving faster down the tracks. Bay walked through the front door and said, "I hate dis house. I don' wanta live here!"

Bee looked at her. "Gal, ya ain't got no choiz, so put dat stuff 'n de kitchen! Ya gittin' mighty grown, tellin' me whatcha don' wanta do!"

Sadie followed Bay into the kitchen. Bay was crying. "Sadie," she said, "I'll be glad when I git big 'n' don' hafta be led 'round 'n circles by grown folks. If ya ask me, dey don' know what ta do frum one minute ta de nex'."

"Dat's 'cause dey ain't really dat smart. I kin take care of a whole house betta dan mos' grown folks!" Sadie said proudly.

A year later, in 1953, LC's sixteen-year-old brother, R. Lee, came to live with Bay and her family, and he brought trouble with him. One night, Sadie was staying overnight with a friend, and Bee was in her bedroom asleep with Carrie beside her. Bay, seven at the time, was in her room asleep when R. Lee sneaked in and closed the door. He quietly sat on the edge of Bay's bed, pulled down her panties, and began moving his fingers around in her genital area. Bay slowly awoke as she felt his finger trying to penetrate her vagina.

Without warning, Bee burst through the door. "Whatcha doin' ta ma chile?" shouted Bee.

"Ain't doin' nothin'!" replied R. Lee.

"I oughta call de law. Git outa here, ya low-down dirty bastard! Git ya stuff 'n' git out, now!" yelled Bee.

Bay, now fully awake, knew that R. Lee could never be trusted. What he did to her left a scar in her soul.

Bee continued yelling, "Git out!"

"Whatcha goin' ta tell LC?" asked R. Lee, moving toward the door. "I ain't got no place ta go."

"Live on de streets!" replied Bee.

R. Lee left, but Bee never talked with Bay about what happened. Both were products of the times, the fifties, when to openly talk about sex—whether consensual or not—was shameful. In the colored community, indulging in sex outside of marriage was known as "doing the nasty," so Bee kept quiet about the crime against her daughter, thinking it would be forgotten. It never was. It went underground within the recesses of Bay's mind and became a festering sore, blossoming outwardly in various negative forms.

As the saying goes, time waits on no one. Six years later, 1959, three months before the exhilarating sixties burst on the scene bringing many challenges and accomplishments, Bay's life became part of that puzzle. Now thirteen, she felt all grown up. She not only started noticing boys but wanted a nice sweet-potato of her own, and she was willing and ready to do whatever it took to get one.

Looking in the mirror was no longer an unhappy experience for Bay. As she moved from side to side, and then turned with her back facing the mirror and looked over her shoulder, she thought, *I see how dem boys always lookin' atcha. Ya mus' be a mighty fine-lookin' girl. Mayb' ya oughta wear a tight skirt ta make dem thirst!* She *was* a very beautiful girl, five feet five inches tall, with the prettiest and smoothest black skin, black shoulder-length hair that was thick and wavy, and a figure that was envied by many. Bee knew what she was up against with her girls, so she tried to keep them on the right track by taking them to church.

That's right, Bee was a Christian now. It had happened four years earlier, around 1955, two years after she caught R. Lee with Bay. One summer afternoon, the girls were outside playing, and a group of women from Calvary Holiness Church stopped in front of their house, singing and playing drums and tambourines. "Is your mama home?" asked the tall lady with a small drum in her hand.

"Yes, ma'am," replied Sadie.

"Go tell her we'd like to come in and pray with her."

"I'll git her," responded Bay gladly. A few minutes later, she returned. "Mama say come on 'n."

While the women went inside, the girls continued to play. Twenty minutes later, they heard their mother crying and the sound of loud drums and tambourines. "Sadie, what's happenin' ta Mama?" asked Bay.

"She gittin' religion. When people git religion, dey stop doin' bad thangs 'n' go ta church."

Bay beamed with joy. "Do dat mean Mama won' cuss, drink whiskey, 'n' fight wit' Daddy no more?"

"Dat's how it's s'posed ta be. Sometimes folks git mighty weak. Dey say de devil make dem dat way," exclaimed Sadie.

"Mayb' de devil won' bother Mama 'cause she wuz a real faithful soldier when she wuz 'n his army," said Bay, giving a soldier's salute.

The women left, and the girls excitedly ran into the house to see if Bee had changed. Bay looked at her mother. "Mama, ya got religion?"

Bee stood up with her hands raised above her head and tears rolling down her cheeks. "I'm saved! Thank ya, Jesus, I'm saved!"

Bay and Sadie looked at each other. They happily danced around the room shouting, "Thank ya, Jesus! Thank ya, Jesus! Mama is saved!"

The girls didn't realize that their mother getting saved would change their lives too. Bee began taking them to church just about every night, even during school. Bay and Sadie started to resent it.

On that evening in 1959, while they were getting dressed for Bible study, Bay was just as mad as a rattlesnake. "I'm doggone tired of goin' ta church," she cried. Bay sat on her bed and folded her arms. "I ain't goin'!" she continued as she crossed her legs.

Sadie stopped, fastened her belt, walked over to Bay, and said, "Bay McQueen, de las' time ya had a birthday, ya wuz only thirteen." She leaned over, whispering in Bay's ear with a smile. "Dat means ya ain't grown yet! Ya think I like goin' ta church all de time? Dere's otha thangs I could be doin'." Sadie pranced over in front of the mirror.

Bay jumped off the bed with a cheap grin and went over to stand next to her big sister. "I guess ya do haf otha thangs ya could be doin', such as kissin' round-head, bumpy-face Junior Payne!" shouted Bay. She knew Sadie didn't like to be teased about Junior Payne, so Bay ran out the room with Sadie chasing her.

Fifteen minutes later, the sisters reached the front door of the church out of breath, settled down, and walked inside. Bee was already there, sitting in the mothers' corner and watching her girls as they entered. She wasn't the only one. There were three or four boys about Bay's age or a little older sitting in one of the pews. They were looking at Bay and Sadie like they were a cool drink of water and the church was a parching hot desert. Sadie and Carrie sat in the very back, but Bay loved attention, so she walked past the boys so they could see her walk from behind. She did have an air of class and elegance about her. When Bee saw what was going on, she came over and made Bay sit next to her and Mother Max, who jumped up and down every five minutes. There was a story going around that five years ago the woman shouted so hard, her bloomers fell off.

Finally, all the dancing and testimony ended. The preacher got up and preached for about an hour and a half. Bee and the girls got home at eleven o'clock. They could barely get up the next morning for school. Bay didn't like school, so she felt that she had an excuse to stay home. Of course, this was Sadie's last year, and she didn't want anything to prevent her from graduating. She decided to talk to Bee about allowing her to spend more time on her assignments and less time in church.

Saturday morning was the perfect time to talk to Bee about her schoolwork. Everybody except LC was eating breakfast. Bee had baked a large pan of hot biscuits and country-fried bacon, with syrup on the side. Sadie looked at Bee. "Mama, ya know I'll be finishin' school 'n six months?" she said.

"Course I do, 'n' I'm so proud of ya," replied Bee, touching her daughter's hand. "Ya be de first McQueen ta finish high school. Den ya kin go ta college."

"Well, I won' be goin' nowhere if I don' study more. I kin't keep goin' ta church ev'ry night 'n' graduate," said Sadie.

"Honey, we hafta do God's will. He so good ta us," responded Bee.

"Mama, I don' b'lieve God goin' ta put us 'n a lake of fire 'cause we don' go ta church ev'ry night," interjected Bay, with a piece of biscuit in her mouth.

"Amen, it sho don' take goin' ta church ev'ry night ta git God's approval," said LC, entering the door to the kitchen and closing it loudly as the girls raised their heads in disbelief.

Daddy don' know nothin' 'bout dis house 'cause he ain't never here. He always wit' Betty Jean. If he been home, R. Lee wouldn't of messed wit' me, thought Bay sadly.

Bee got up from the table and walked over to LC. "How would ya know whether I'm 'n church ev'ry night or not? You ain't never here. Go back where ya slep' las' night!" she yelled angrily as LC left the room.

"Mama, what 'bout me, do I hafta go ta church ev'ry night?" interrupted Sadie.

"Jus' on weekends," Bee agreed.

"What 'bout me 'n' Carrie?" insisted Bay.

"Bay, I want you 'n' Carrie 'n church ev'ry Wednesday night *and* weekends," said Bee.

"Dat ain't fair," muttered Bay softly. She pretended to be disappointed but was quietly thrilled. *At least I be gittin' attention frum de boys,* she thought. When they noticed her, it made her feel really good. There was nothing and no one in life that made her feel valued.

Wednesday-night prayer meetings and Bible study brought no guarantee that the devil would leave you alone. Mother Max's handsome grandson, who was sixteen, walked up to Bee one evening. "Sister McQueen," he said nervously.

"Yes, Billy," she responded.

He struggled to get his words out. "Can I walk Bay home tonight?" he asked.

Bee looked him over for a moment, thinking, *He seems ta be a nice boy 'n' he come frum a very nice churchgoin' family.* "All right, go on," she said.

Bay and Billy left Bee outside the church talking. When they reached the McQueen's porch, the light was off. It was very dark. Billy and Bay began having strange feelings in their bodies. He grabbed her, and they pressed their lips together and began kissing clumsily.

"Billy, wait a minute. Yer pullin' ma tongue too hard!" cried Bay.

"Bay, I'm so sorry. I got so excited. You're so fine."

"Good grief, I ain't never been kissed before, but if it's anything like dis, I'll never be again!" shouted Bay, leaving Billy standing on the porch. She immediately went into the bathroom and looked in the mirror at her tongue. She saw blood. *Ma goodness, ma tongue is bleedin'! I mus' be pregnant! I'm really 'n trouble.* She didn't want to talk to her mother. Bee would only make her start going back to church every night. Instead, she decided to tell Sadie.

"Sadie, I done somethin' mighty bad tonight," said Bay, closing the door of Sadie's room behind her.

Sadie raised her head from her book. She was sitting in a chair next to her bed. "What didya do?"

"I kissed Billy Max tonight. He pulled ma tongue so hard it wuz bleedin'! Sadie, am I pregnant?" asked Bay seriously.

Sadie could hardly stop laughing. "No, Bay, ya ain't pregnant." Sadie took Bay by the hand, and they sat on the bed. "Mama never tol' me nothin' 'bout sex or how a woman gits pregnant neither. Sister, it takes more dan a kiss. Jus' sit back 'gainst dat pillow, 'n' I'll tell ya all 'bout it." They talked until they both fell asleep.

Six months quickly passed, and it was June 1960, and Sadie's graduation day. Everybody, including LC, was going. They had to be at the auditorium at four o'clock. "Hurry up, y'all. We goin' ta be late. We ain't goin' in dere on cp time!" said LC firmly.

"I'm comin'," replied Bee, walking out of the bedroom wearing a beautiful pale-blue dress with a wide-brim hat to match. LC looked at her from her head to her feet, put his hands in his pockets, and moved so close to her that she felt the heat from his body. "Bee, ya sho lookin' good. Think I jus' might need ta start followin' ya ta church!" said LC excitedly.

Bee dropped her head. Quickly she turned, walked away, and called the girls. LC, still watching Bee, couldn't understand why the change in her had not helped their marriage. Sadly, he didn't realize he needed to change too.

Finally, the girls came out of their room. They couldn't believe how wonderful their parents looked. "Mama, Daddy, y'all look good!" cried Bay.

Carrie didn't say anything. She just stood there proudly with her chest stuck out and both hands behind her back.

Sadie was equally delighted. "Dis is de happiest day of ma life!" she said.

Off they went to the graduation. Bee cried during most of the program. Of course, she didn't realize that more tears were coming. A week after graduation, Sadie was sitting on the front porch, anxiously awaiting the arrival of the mail. She had applied to a college in Florida to study education. When she saw the postman coming, she ran to meet him. "Mr. Saxon, ya haf a letter fur me?"

"Yep, I sure do!"

Sadie could tell by the return address that the letter was from Astoria State University in Florida. She was nervous about opening it, so desperate was her desire to attend college. She sat down on the porch steps, closed her eyes, took a deep breath, and opened the letter . . . and then she jumped up, screaming, "I made it! I made it! I made it!" Bay and Carrie came running out of the house. Bee was just walking into the yard from work. "Mama, I've been accepted ta Astoria State University!" shouted Sadie. "I can live with Big Mama. She'll be glad!"

"Dat's wonderful. I know she won't mind. Ya goin' ta make a much betta life fur yourself!" responded Bee enthusiastically.

Carrie began singing, "Sadie's goin' ta college ta make us proud. I kin too! Yes, I kin too!" Everyone was excited, except Bay. She pretended to be happy, but she wasn't. It was the very day of Sadie's departure before Bay let her true feelings out.

Sadie was packing. She busily walked from the bedroom to the living room, carrying boxes and suitcases. As she reentered the bedroom, she noticed Bay sitting in an old straight-backed chair, somberly looking out the window. "Bay, ain't ya goin' ta help ya big sister finish packin'? The taxi will be comin' soon," she said, looking at the watch Big Mama gave her for graduation.

Bay got up from the chair. Her hands were stretched out and tears filled her eyes as she began pleading in a low, pitiful voice, "Sadie, please, please don' leave me. If ya go, I won' haf nobody!"

Sadie took her by the hand and sat on the bed. She affectionately put her arms around her sister. "Bay, please don' cry. I promise I'll write." Bay cried louder and louder.

Bee rushed into the room along with Carrie. "What's da matter?" she asked.

"Bay don' want me ta leave," answered Sadie.

"Bay, ya need ta stop actin' like a baby. Ya know Sadie got ta go ta college!" shouted Bee.

Bay's buried anger came to the surface as never before. "Sadie's de only one who cares 'bout me. Mama, ya ain't never been here fur me!" yelled Bay as loud as she could. Now Bay was on the floor, on her knees. "Sadie, please don' go!" she begged.

Sadie looked at Bee. "Mama, let me talk ta her alone." Bee, with tears in her eyes, took Carrie and left. Sadie took a handkerchief out of her pocket and began wiping Bay's face. "Bay, do ya love me?"

"Yes."

"Sister, when ya love someone, ya ain't afraid ta let de person be free. Bay McQueen, I love ya. Jus' 'cause I'm 'n another state don' change nothin'. Ya could ev'n visit me," exclaimed Sadie.

"Ya really mean it?"

"I cross ma heart 'n' promise ta lay ma hands on de Bible," replied Sadie, smiling. They walked out of the room hugging.

"Sadie, ya taxi is here!" cried Carrie. Everybody helped Sadie put her bags inside the taxi. Sadie sat in the backseat and waved good-bye as the taxi drove off. Her family kept waving until she was out of sight.

CHAPTER TWO

After Sadie went off to college, the McQueen family became somewhat unsettled; she had provided the balance in her sisters' lives, and their mother becoming a Christian didn't change things as far as Bay was concerned. Bee had a challenge ahead of her; she knew she'd never be able to make up for lost time, but she desperately wanted to be in their lives now.

Two weeks had passed since Sadie's departure, and Bay felt so lonely. It seemed as though her whole world had collapsed. *How kin I ever feel close ta a silent mother I don' know?* thought Bay as she walked onto the front porch to join Bee and Carrie. A pleasant soft breeze moved against Bay's beautiful dark skin and hair as she watched the lightning bugs fly briskly in the darkness.

"Bay, we sho glad ya 'cided ta sit on de porch wit' us. Ain't nothin' like sittin' out 'n de nice fresh night air," said Bee, rocking back and forward in her brown rocking chair. Bay didn't say a word, just walked over and took a seat on the steps while Carrie lay on a blanket reading a book. Suddenly, everything became too quiet for Bee; she couldn't take it anymore. "More folks goin' ta be 'n hell dan ya kin 'magine," she said, just to break the silence. Bay looked at her mother, wishing she'd shut up.

"Mama, how ya know it's a hell?" interrupted Carrie.

"The Bible says so, and dat's anough fur me," replied Bee sternly.

Bay could tell Bee was uneasy about Carrie's question. She couldn't wait to throw a curve. "Mama, is dat hell goin' ta be big anough ta hol' ya church?" asked Bay. "I heard dat ya pastor, deacons, 'n' mothers is havin' sex all over town!" she said, laughing.

"Bay, yer jus' makin' dat up! Anyway, what ya know 'bout sex?" asked Bee.

"I know plenty!" said Bay, beaming with pride.

"Bay McQueen, one thang I know is dat ya betta keep ya dress down! Since ya so experienced, you 'n' Carrie git reddy fur Bible study 'n' prayer meetin' tomorrow night," Bee snapped as she got up out of the chair and went inside.

Seven o'clock Wednesday night, Bay and Carrie were seated together in the second row of the middle aisle of the church. Deacon Sumner began doing what folks call "raising a hymn." He'd say a few words, and the congregation would join in singing the same words. Bay and Carrie could barely keep their composure. The deacon was a very funny-looking man. His head was as round as a pumpkin. He wore the same black tight-fitting suit every Wednesday night. That particular night, Bay and Carrie were about to die from repressed laughter. Still standing, Deacon Sumner, with his hymnal in his right hand, leaned back and kicked his left foot forward, almost falling. Bay and Carrie laughed loudly. Bee, appearing to be embarrassed, came over and marched the girls outside. They just knew they were in deep trouble. After Bee closed the door behind her, she laughed so hard tears rolled down her cheeks. Purged of their repressed laughter, the three of them went back inside, but the prayer meeting was over. Bee and the girls went home to prepare for the next day.

During the summer, there wasn't much for Bay and Carrie to do. Bee and LC worked every day and left the girls home alone. Carrie spent her time reading everything she could find. Bay sat around looking at magazines, watching TV, and primping. She was growing up. Many nights she cried herself to sleep. She felt such emptiness inside. She decided to try to talk to Carrie, who had just turned twelve. She found her sister in the bedroom, lying on the bed, reading a book.

"Carrie, why ya always readin' books?"

"'Cause dey take me places I kin't go, 'n' meet people who help me b'lieve 'n maself," replied Carrie.

"I wish I felt dat way, but mos' of de time I feel lonely. Carrie, dere's somethin' missin' 'n me. I won' ever be happy till I find it," said Bay sadly. "Carrie, do ya ever feel dat way?"

"No, I don'."

Abruptly, Bay got up off the bed and walked over to the window. "It's out dere somewhere."

"Bay, dat's why I read. I know life is s'posed ta be betta. Dere is somethin' in me dat tell me ta keep goin'."

Bay walked over to Carrie. "I'm glad we talked. I feel much closer ta ya."

"Me too."

The following day, a beautiful summer morning, Bee let Bay and Carrie know before she went to work that they were allowed to visit the YMCA. By twelve-thirty, Bay was all dressed. Her white pedal-pushers were really fitted. Bee wouldn't ever have allowed her to leave the house with pants that tight. She was wearing a low-cut pale blue shirt and white sandals. Bay turned around in front of the mirror, her long black hair hanging down her back. "Girl, ya sho look good!" she said.

Carrie walked into the bedroom and made a circle around her sister in amazement. "Bay, ya sho look good, but Mama ain't goin' ta be happy wit' dem clothes 'n' lipstick," said Carrie seriously.

"It's 1960, not 1940. Anyway, Mama ain't here!" snapped Bay.

"Mama might not be here, but nosy Mother Caine nex' door always tell on us."

"By de time Mama finds out, de excitement will be over!" cried Bay with a sly grin on her face as she walked toward the door. "Carrie, ain't ya comin' wit' me?"

"Yer not goin' ta get *me* 'n trouble."

"Okay, Miss Chicken, I'll give ya all de juicy news when I git back," said Bay, and she walked out the door.

As Bay was walking down the street from her house, she heard a boy yell, "Hey, baby, kin I go?" She pretended not to hear him, holding her head in the air and swaying from side to side.

In a flash, he caught up with her. Now he began walking beside her. "Whatcha name?" he asked.

"It's Bay McQueen. What's yours?" she asked, trying to be all proper and refined.

"I'm Sam Ellis, and I'd sho like to get to know you."

Whether it was the truth or not, Bay liked what she heard. He made her feel like a million dollars. As she looked in his eyes, she thought to herself, *He is a fine sweet-potato!* Sam was about five feet eleven, 165 pounds, with a medium-brown complexion.

"Where you headed?" Sam asked, interrupting Bay's thoughts.

"I'm on my way to the YMCA," she said, being careful to talk properly.

"Can I walk with you?"

"Sho . . . I mean, *sure*."

After reaching the Y, they stood outside the fence, watching children dive and swim. When the boys looked over at Bay, they tried awfully hard to impress her. One of Sam's friends came over to speak, but his eyes were mainly focused on Bay.

"Sam, who is this?"

"This is Bay McQueen," replied Sam proudly. "Bay, this is my teammate, Buster Brown. We call him Slam 'cause he's real good on defense."

"Sam, I didn't know ya play football. How old are ya?" asked Bay.

"I'm sixteen. What about you?"

"I'm fourteen."

"For a fourteen-year-old, you're well put together!" said Sam.

"Lordy, have mercy!" responded Buster Brown, walking off.

Bay loved all the attention. She and Sam hung around the Y for a long time. Five o'clock came swiftly. Bay needed to get home before her mother did. "Sam, I had a nice time, but I've got to get home."

"I'll walk with you."

"I don't think so. Mama and Daddy didn't tell me that boys can walk me home," replied Bay.

"I'll just walk you halfway."

"I guess so."

When Bay reached her house, she started to go through the back door, but stopped. Instead, she decided to peep through the window to see if Bee was in the kitchen. Bee's back was turned. She was busy stirring something in a big pot on the stove. Bay quietly eased around the house to go through the front door. As she tried to softly open it, Bee yelled, "Bay McQueen, come in here dis minute!" Bay stood in the doorway of the kitchen. "Whatcha doin' wit' dem tight-fittin' pants on?" asked Bee. "I done tol' ya not ta leave dis house showin' ya behind!"

"Mama, I ain't showin' ma behind. I jus' want ta look putty 'cause folks notice me, 'n' it makes me feel good, like I'm somebody."

"Chile, ya already somethin' without wearin' lipstick 'n' tight clothes," said Bee. "Who wuz dat boy ya wuz wit' today?"

"Sam Ellis."

"Bay, ya ain't takin' company, so don' start gittin' friendly wit' boys," stressed Bee, walking over to put plates on the table.

"Mama, Sam is a nice boy."

"All boys 'n' men is nice till dey git 'n a female's private parts. After dat, dey move on ta somebody else, always on de prowl. De truth is, dey lookin' fur de Lord 'n' don' know it. When dey goin' ta learn dat dere ain't no eternal power 'n a woman's coota?"

"Ah, Mama!" laughed Bay loudly.

"Chile, don' think ya is top prize, 'cause ev'ry woman dat look good is top prize till he done been through de whole town!" said Bee, chuckling.

Bay sat down at the table, and Carrie walked in. Bay looked at her sister. "I know ya tol' Mama on me," said Bay.

"I did no such thang. Before Mama could git 'n de yard, nosy Mother Caine met her at de fence," exclaimed Carrie.

"Bay, Salem is a very small town. Ev'rybody knows ev'rybody," interrupted Bee.

"Bay, did Mama tell ya dat we received letters frum Sadie today?" asked Carrie excitedly.

Bay quickly stood up. "Where is it? Where is it?" Bee reached up on a shelf next to the stove and handed Bay her letter. "I kin't wait to read it. I'm goin' ta wait till bedtime," said Bay.

Finally, Bee and the girls enjoyed their supper. They ate hot homemade chicken vegetable soup with delicious crackling cornbread.

The next morning, before leaving for work, LC told Bay not to leave the house. He'd heard on his job about her provocative clothing.

Daddy kin't tell me what ta do. He don' do right himself, 'n' he ain't never home, she thought, laying in bed, thinking about how bored she was. *I wish we had a telephone. Sho be glad when school starts. Jus' three weeks away.*

Carrie awakened and turned over in the bed next to Bay. "Did ya ever read Sadie's letter?"

"Yeah, Sadie is havin' lots of fun 'n' made lots of friends too. She goin' ta try ta come home nex' summer," said Bay.

"I miss Sadie a lot," said Carrie, with tears filling her eyes.

Bay got out of bed, went over and sat on Carrie's bed, and held her. "Carrie, it's okay ta cry. I didn't know ya missed Sadie too. Guess I thought dat, 'cause ya always got ya head 'n a book, ya don' notice nothin' else."

"I know I'm de youngest 'n' sometime I feel invisible, but I do haf feelings 'n' a heart, too!" replied Carrie passionately.

"Yes, ya do haf a heart," Bay said softly, with tears in her eyes. For the first time, Bay realized that she was not the only wounded soul, and she felt helpless comforting Carrie. *Mayb' returning ta school will help both of us*, thought Bay.

Bay and Carrie welcomed the return to school with open arms. They walked to Carver High and Middle School, which was about six blocks from their house. Both were excited and apprehensive, wondering about their teachers and classmates. As soon as they reached the school, Carrie went in one direction and Bay in the other.

Bay went through the double doors of the main entrance and found herself in a crowded hallway. Students were busy pushing their way through the crowd and looking on classroom doors, trying to find their names. While Bay was passing through the crowd and looking on a door, someone yelled, "Hey, Bay!" She turned and looked over her shoulder. It was Sam Ellis and a pretty, light-complexioned girl. He came over, and the girl followed him. Deep inside Bay felt worthless, seeing Sam and this girl together.

"What happened to you during the summer? I used to look for you at the Y," said Sam.

He didn't look too hard, thought Bay. "Mama and Daddy made me stay away from the Y because you and I were together, and my pants were too tight," responded Bay, trying to speak correctly.

The girl with Sam laughed. "Sounds just like my mother!"

"I forgot my manners. This is my cousin Savannah," said Sam.

Bay's eyes lit up, and with a refined smile, she extended her right hand. "Pleased to meet you."

"It's nice to meet you too. Why don't you come over to my house sometime?"

"That sounds great," said Bay, smiling.

"Hey, I have to find my class. We'll see you later," said Sam.

He and Savannah left Bay standing alone. She walked over to the next classroom, and there was her name on Mrs. Peterson's door. *I hope she's nice. Anyway, deep breath, here goes*, thought Bay, opening the door to walk in.

As Bay sat in the classroom, surrounded by classmates and listening to Mrs. Peterson give instructions about class schedules and activities, she realized that high school was quite different from elementary. Students were treated with respect and were expected to act responsibly. Bay liked that. At least she didn't have to sit in a classroom petrified, not knowing when she would be yelled at or walloped in her back with a big fist.

The day went by quite swiftly. Everyone was tired and anxiously awaited dismissal. Finally, the bell rang. Everyone exited the classroom and scattered.

Bay had left the building and was walking home when she heard Sam and Savannah calling her, so she stopped to wait for them. Finally, they caught up with her. "Bay, wanta go to Mr. Jake's Teen Club with us?" asked Sam.

"When?"

"Now!"

"I ain't . . . I mean, I've never been to a club. Besides, I can't dance a lick. If I did, Mama would skin me alive!" said Bay seriously.

"Are *you* going to tell her?" interrupted Savannah.

"I don't have to. Everybody in town will."

"Bay, come on, we'll have a good time," prodded Sam.

"Please?" Savannah said.

"I sure would like to go, just to see what it's like!" responded Bay excitedly.

Mr. Jake's Teen Club was a very popular place. When Bay, Sam, and Savannah arrived, it was packed! Teens were dancing, eating, and talking. Bay had never seen anything like this before. She felt right at home. Sam led Bay and Savannah through the crowd to find seats. After they were seated in a booth, a waiter came over to take their order.

"Hey, DJ, how's it goin'?" asked Sam.

"I'm just working and studying hard. Ready to order?"

"Nothing for me," interrupted Bay. She knew she didn't have any money.

"I'll have two chili dogs and two milkshakes," said Sam. "I'll have chocolate. Bay, what flavor would you like?"

For a moment, Bay was speechless. "Ah . . . ah . . . I'll have strawberry."

"I would like a cheeseburger and a Coke," said Savannah.

Afterward, they settled back to listen to the music on the jukebox and watch the movements of the many dancers on the floor. As Bay watched and listened, her body yearned to move.

Sam, sensing her desire to dance, took her hand. "Let's dance!"

Now Bay and Sam were on the dance floor. "Just do what you see me do," said Sam.

First, she felt a little clumsy and strange. A few seconds later, she was doing the twist, round and round and up and down. Bay was having the time of her life. "Sam, this is so much fun!" she said, laughing.

"Let's do it again, round and round and up and down!" shouted Sam.

All at once, the music stopped. They began laughing. Before they could catch their breath, everybody on the dance floor began yelling, "Do the jerk! Do the jerk!"

Someone hurried over to put money in the jukebox. Now everybody in the building was doing the jerk!

Bay looked up at the clock on the wall. It was five o'clock. Much as Bay hated to leave, she realized it was time for her to go home. "Sam, it's five o'clock. I'd better be going home."

"Yeah, me too," responded Sam. "Let me go get Savannah."

He immediately returned with his cousin, who said, "Bay, I had the best time ever. What about you?"

"It was super. I hate to leave!"

"Bay, Savannah and I will walk you halfway home," said Sam.

"No, Sam, I'll get into deep trouble. Mama will make me go to church every night and weekends!" They all laughed. "Sam, thanks for the chili dog, milkshake, and lots of fun. Savannah, I enjoyed you too. Hope to see you soon."

They said good-bye and went in opposite directions.

Bay nervously arrived home about five-thirty. As always, she peeped through the kitchen window to see if her mother was cooking supper. If so, she would try to sneak through the living room.

Tonight was different. Surprisingly, Bee was not there—only Carrie, peeling white potatoes. *Somethin' is wrong,* thought Bay. *Mama is always home by now.* She opened the door. "Where's Mama?"

"She over at Mother Caine's house. She had an emergency call frum Astoria. I think it's 'bout Big Mama," exclaimed Carrie seriously.

"I hope she ain't sick."

"Mayb' she ain't," replied Carrie, walking over to the sink to wash more potatoes.

"Oh, Carrie, let me tell ya 'bout today," said Bay, turning around in a circle. She stopped turning and went over to the sink, where Carrie was still washing potatoes, to make sure she looked her sister dead in the eyes. "Carrie, if I tell ya somethin', will ya promise not ta tell Mama or nobody?"

"I promise, promise, promise, a million times I promise," replied Carrie, curious.

"Ta make it really official, hol' ya right hand up 'n' repeat after me: 'What Bay is 'bout ta tell me is top secret, 'n' I'll never tell nobody.'"

Carrie repeated every word. "Bay, I kin't stand it no more. What happened?"

"I went to Mr. Jake's Teen Club today after school. I danced 'n' danced 'n' danced! Sam and I did de twist 'n' de jerk, 'n' ate! He bought me a delicious chili dog 'n' milkshake!"

"Bay, didya really do all dose diff'rent dances?"

"I sho did," replied Bay proudly.

"Will ya teach me how ta do dem?" Suddenly, Carrie became worried. "What if Mama finds out? We'll be 'n big trouble."

"Mama ain't home all de time," responded Bay mischievously. They both smiled, laughed, and began singing, "Round 'n' round 'n' up 'n' down." They stopped quickly and became quiet when they heard someone at the kitchen door. It was Bee, and she was crying. Mother Caine was with her. The women walked into the living room and sat on the sofa.

Bay and Carrie looked at each other and rushed over to their mother. "Mama, what's wrong? Big Mama is goin' ta be all right," said Bay. Bee's tears continued to fall. Bay became alarmed. It brought back old memories and insecurities. "Mama, please don' cry. Ya kin tell Carrie 'n' me."

"Big Mama is dead. She died suddenly," responded Bee, wiping tears from her eyes.

Bay was stunned. A deep sadness welled up inside her. She had never had anybody close to her to die before. Tears began to fill her eyes. "I didn't git ta spend lots of time wit' Big Mama, but de first time I met her I really liked her, 'n' she felt de same 'bout me too. She made me feel loved."

"Me too," said Carrie, handing Bay a tissue to wipe her face. "I'll never forget de beautiful shoes 'n' doll she gave me when she visited us fur de first time," continued Carrie, now crying.

"Tears won't bring Big Mama back," said Mother Caine.

"I've got ta go be wit' Sadie ta make plans fur Big Mama's funeral," said Bee, getting up off the sofa. "How 'n de world am I goin' ta git dere? I don' haf a dime ta pay our fare."

"Bee, I'll let you have the money," Mother Caine assured her. "You can pay me back when you can."

"Mother, thank ya so much," replied Bee, hugging the older woman around the neck. Mother Caine left so Bee could finalize her plans.

Before Bee had left Mother Caine's house, she had checked the train schedule to Astoria. "Girls, we will leave Salem Friday mornin' at ten o'clock 'n' arrive 'n Astoria 'bout three o'clock," said Bee. "Bay, git me some writin' paper so I kin write excuses ta y'all's teachers, 'cause we won' be back till Monday evening."

Bay hated to miss school. At the same time, she was anxious to see Sadie and Astoria. Bay and Carrie quickly forgot school and their new friends. They became very excited about their trip. "Bay, we only haf one more day of school," said Carrie excitedly.

"Tomorrow is Thursday, and we won' go back to school till Tuesday. I kin hardly wait till Friday!"

That Friday, August 19, 1960, Bay awoke at six o'clock, stretching like a rubber band and looking over in Carrie's bed. Her sister was sound asleep. "Carrie, wake up! Today is de day we goin' ta Astoria on de train!" cried Bay enthusiastically.

"Girl, it ain't ev'n daylight yet. I ain't ridin' nobody's train in de dark!"

Bay jumped out of bed laughing. "Ah, Carrie, plenty folks ride de train 'n de dark. We leavin' at ten o'clock. Besides, we haf lots of work ta do. We got ta bathe, dress, eat breakfast, 'n' fix lunch ta take on de train!"

Bay's excitement rubbed off on Carrie, who rolled out of the bed onto the floor and jumped up singing, "We goin' ta haf a wonderful time. We will see Sadie 'n' lots of new thangs, la, la, la!"

"Carrie, dere's one problem," said Bay, smiling.

"What?"

"We kin't be dis happy 'round otha people. We goin' ta a funeral," reminded Bay, walking over to the mirror. "We need ta be sad."

Carrie walked over and stood beside Bay with a sad look on her face. Both began laughing. Suddenly, they heard Bee calling.

"Rise 'n' shine!" she yelled.

The morning swiftly passed. By 9:45, Bee and the girls were out of the taxi at the train station when they heard the conductor yell, "All aboard!" Mr. Lacy, the taxi driver, shouted, "Mrs. Bee, let's grab your bags. Hurry, or y'all gonna miss your train!"

They ran toward the train, and Bee handed the conductor their tickets. "Thank you, ma'am. Watch your step," he said. "Second and third row on your left."

"Thank ya," said Bee, waiting on Bay and Carrie to walk ahead of her. Bay and Carrie sat next to each other on the third row behind Bee.

"Dis is de mos' excitin' time of ma life. I kin't b'lieve I'm on a train!" said Bay.

Bee turned around, holding her finger to her lips. "Bay, don' talk so loud. Dere is otha folks on de train," she whispered.

"Okay, Mama."

"Gosh, dis is jus' like 'n books 'n' de movies!" interrupted Carrie excitedly.

Soon Bee and the girls were settled comfortably in their seats. After all the excitement, they were ready for lunch. Bay reached into her bag and pulled out a chicken sandwich, an apple, and a large tea cake. She bit down on the sandwich with her eyes closed. "Um, um, I do love chicken. Dis is so good!" she said. "If heaven is like dis, I don' mind goin'!"

"Jus' look at all dat water!" said Carrie, looking out the window.

"You 'n' Bay quiet down!" cautioned Bee.

A few hours later, Bay and Carrie were sound asleep with full stomachs. Bee could barely relax, much less sleep. She was thinking about Big Mama. Tears began welling up in her eyes. She thought about her own mama, who died when she was only ten years old. Since that time, Big Mama had taken care of her. Now both were gone. Next, she started thinking about LC and how unhappy her life had been with him. "He don' love me. If he did, he'd come home at night 'n' treat me wit' some respect," mumbled Bee, her tears flowing heavily.

Hoping nobody noticed her tears, Bee pulled a tissue out of her purse to wipe her eyes. Suddenly, a new passenger sat next to her. She didn't want this gentleman to see her crying. The stranger didn't say a word. A few minutes passed, and then he handed her his handkerchief. "Take this, it's better for tears," he said.

"Thank you," replied Bee politely.

The man extended his hand. "My name is Jack Albertson."

"I'm Bee McQueen."

"Nice to meet you, Bee."

"Likewise," said Bee softly. Bee wasn't an educated woman by society's standards, but she had worked around enough rich white folks' homes and lived long enough with Big Mama in her younger days to know how to exhibit good manners and talk correctly when necessary. *He's a very dignified-lookin' man 'n' quite handsome too,* thought Bee.

"Where are you from, and where are you headed?" asked Mr. Albertson.

"I'm going to Astoria, Florida, to my aunt's funeral. I live in Salem, Georgia. Where are you going?"

"I'm originally from Austin, Texas. I'm on my way to Astoria too," responded Mr. Albertson, smiling.

"Well, I declare!" said Bee in a soft southern drawl.

"I live in Astoria. I'm the pastor of St. Paul's Baptist Church."

Before they could finish their conversation, the train began slowing down. Finally it made a complete stop. "Astoria, Florida!" cried the conductor.

Bay awoke, stretching and looking around. "Are we here already?"

"Yes, we are. You and Carrie slept all the way here," said Bee.

Bay poked Carrie in the side. "Wake up! Wake up! We're in Astoria!"

As quick as a flash of lightning, Bee and the girls were off the train. Pastor Albertson walked over to them. "Mrs. McQueen, it's so nice meeting you. Hopefully we'll meet again. You made my trip quite pleasant," he said, looking at Bay and Carrie. "Who are these beautiful young ladies?"

"These are my daughters," replied Bee.

"Girls, you're as pretty as your mother!" he said, smiling. Now he looked at Bee. "Please stop by St. Paul's before you leave."

"If I can," replied Bee. She and the girls watched him as he walked away.

"Mama, I think de pastor wants ta git ta know ya betta!" teased Bay.

"Hush, Bay, dat ain't true. He's a servant of God. He's jus' bein' kind," Bee said nervously.

"Mrs. McQueen," interrupted Carrie in a deep masculine voice, extending her right hand to her mother. "Please stop by and worship with us before you leave!" Bay and Carrie roared with laughter.

"How 'n de world we goin' ta git ta Big Mama's house?" asked Bay.

"One of her neighbors s'posed ta pick us up," responded Bee.

"Sho wish he'd come on. Ma feet hurt, I'm hungry, I'm sleepy, 'n' I wanta see Sadie!" said Bay, walking over to sit down.

"Me too," said Carrie.

"Anyhow, how we goin' ta know him 'n' he know us?" asked Bay.

A tall, dark-skinned, good-looking man walked up to Bee. "Hello, Mrs. McQueen, I'm Mack Martin, Big Mama's neighbor. Sadie sent me to pick you up," he said.

"Thank ya so much."

"Let me help you with the bags."

Eventually, they loaded all their bags into his fancy red Thunderbird. "Gee, I ain't never seen a car so fine!" said Bay excitedly.

"Mr. Martin, you mus' be rich. Dis is a beautiful car!" interrupted Carrie.

"What kind of car is dis?" asked Bay.

"It's a Thunderbird," replied Mack proudly.

Bee didn't show any emotion but felt like a queen riding in such a beautiful car. As they approached Heights Park where Big Mama lived, Bee and the girls were amazed. "I never seen such putty houses!" said Bee.

"I seen dem 'n magazines," responded Bay.

"You didn't see no colored people 'n dem," replied Carrie.

"Sadie never tol' us 'bout dese houses," said Bay.

"Sadie is busy wit' school," responded Bee.

Mr. Martin turned a corner and made a right turn into the driveway of a pretty, moderately sized brick house trimmed in gray. Bee looked at Mr. Martin as he turned off his ignition. "Is dis Big Mama's house?"

"Yes," replied Mack. He'd enjoyed every minute of their company. Most of all, he enjoyed their response regarding the house. "Ladies, let's unload!"

While they were unloading the luggage from Mack's car, Sadie opened the front door of the house. Carrie and Bay dropped their bags and ran toward her. "Oh, Sadie, I'm so glad ta see you. I miss ya so much!" said Bay, crying and hugging her.

"Sadie, I love ya 'n' miss ya too," exclaimed Carrie, hugging and kissing her on the cheeks.

Sadie began crying. "You two is ma babies. It's hard bein' away frum ya. I'm so thrilled ta see ya. I need ya more dan ever, 'cause I don' haf Big Mama no more."

The girls had never seen Sadie so brokenhearted. "Sadie, it's goin' ta be all right," said Bay.

"It really is," reassured Carrie.

Bee walked over to Sadie and pulled her close so her head rested on her mother's bosom. "Honey, it's goin' ta be all right. God is wit' ya. Jus' ask Him ta help ya," said Bee.

"Mama, it hurts so bad!" replied Sadie, holding her mother as tight as a helpless baby in pain.

"I know, I know."

The girls and Mr. Mack followed Bee as she escorted Sadie into the house. After Mack had finished taking the bags inside the house, he went into the living room, where Bee was seated next to Sadie. Bay and Carrie were busy inspecting the surroundings. "Mrs. McQueen, if y'all need me, just call. I live next door, and Sadie knows my number. Sadie, sweetheart, Big Mama loved you very much. Everything is going to be all right. Now you have your mother and sisters with you," said Mack.

"Mr. Martin, thank you so much for meeting Mama and my sisters at the station," replied Sadie, tiptoeing to kiss him on the cheek.

"I loved Big Mama too," he said as he turned and walked away.

"Sadie, mus' be mighty nice livin' in a house like dis. Never thought Big Mama had such a putty house," said Bay.

"Mama, haf ya ever been 'n dis house before?" asked Carrie.

"No, I ran off wit' ya father when I wuz eighteen. Big Mama didn't haf dis house. She wuz so good ta me. After ma mama died, she did all she could fur me. I wanted somethin' else but didn't know what. I jus' felt empty inside, like a part of me wuz missin'. When LC came along, I thought he wuz it. How wrong I wuz!" exclaimed Bee.

Bay quietly listened as her mother talked. She could understand those feelings. She felt the same way most of the time.

Carrie had become very tired of all the excitement. "Sadie, kin ya show me where I'm goin' ta sleep?"

"Sure, come on, li'l sister!" replied Sadie, putting her arms around Carrie.

"I'm comin' too!" said Bay.

They left Bee standing in the living room, looking around and wishing she could turn back the clock. She looked above the fireplace and saw an old high-school picture of herself. She was just sixteen. She looked a lot like Bay. The difference was, Bee was light-skinned and Bay was as dark as a blackberry. She walked away from the picture. *If I had stayed wit' Big Mama, I'd've gone ta college 'n' made somethin' outa maself*, she thought.

The doorbell rang, interrupting her memories. Bee walked over and opened the door. Two women were there, loaded down with food and drinks. "Come on in!" said Bee. "I'm Big Mama's niece and Sadie's mother."

"How do you do?" said the tall, dignified woman. "I'm Leona Payne."

"I'm Frances Swain," said the other lady as her eyes darted about, looking at Big Mama's beautiful antiques.

"Where's Sadie?" questioned Miss Payne.

"I'll get her." While Bee went to get Sadie, the women put the food in the kitchen and made a beeline back to the living room.

When Sadie entered the living room, both women rushed over and gave her a big hug. "We are so sorry to hear about Big Mama," said Leona. In the same breath, she asserted, "I know you're going to sell all Big Mama's crystal, china, and furniture. Well, Sadie, dear, I'd like to be the first person to make an offer."

"Once Big Mama told me I could have that beautiful wicker rocker in her bedroom," interrupted Mrs. Swain.

Sadie looked at Bee, and then she turned to the two women with a cold and stern expression on her face. "Nothing Big Mama left is for sale. Anyway, I don't remember either of you visiting her when she was sick. She told me to watch out for you scavengers!" said Sadie firmly.

Both women walked quickly to the door and didn't look back. Sadie set them on fire! Bee watched them leave with great delight.

"Didya see dose hussies git outa here?" asked Sadie, laughing and holding her stomach. "Old biddies is sho brave, comin' here wantin' ta lie 'n' bargain fur Big Mama's stuff!"

"You gave dem a earful. I'm real proud of ya!" said Bee.

Sadie looked at Bee in a very professional manner. "Mama, come with me," she said. Bee followed her to Big Mama's bedroom. Sadie walked over to a beautiful antique desk and pulled out a large envelope. "This is Big Mama's will." Bee looked stunned and a little nervous. She hadn't thought about who would inherit Big Mama's estate. Her aunt wasn't rich but had done quite well in real estate over the past years. While Sadie opened the document, Bee sat on the bed. Then Sadie took a seat next to her and read. "'I, Lottie Raines, leave my house, car, insurance, and contents to Sadie, my beloved great-niece. To my niece, Bee, I leave fifty thousand dollars, to be held in a trust to purchase a home for her and the girls and for their education. Bee, hopefully you will begin to live the life God planned.'" Now tears were rolling down Bee's cheeks. Sadie could barely finish because of her tears.

Bay and Carrie walked into the room. "We been lookin' ev'rywhere fur y'all," said Bay. Then she noticed both were crying.

"What's de matter?" asked Carrie.

"We wuz readin' Big Mama's will. She lef' me de house, car, 'n' contents," said Sadie.

"Great smokin' Joe!" cried Bay. "What did she leave us?" Carrie nudged her in the side, reminding her that when someone died, she was supposed to be sad. Bay regained control. "Dat's awfully nice of Big Mama," said Bay.

"I know she's 'n heaven wit' de Lord," interrupted Carrie.

"Bay, ta answer ya question, Big Mama lef' ya . . . no, kin't tell ya," responded Sadie, smiling with her hands on her hips. "Guess, Bay."

"She lef' me lots of shoes 'n' clothes!" said Bay excitedly.

"Nope!"

"I know! I know! She lef' money fur education!" cried Carrie. Bee was enjoying the game.

"Since ya kin't guess, I'll tell ya. Hold ya breath. You too, Carrie," continued Sadie.

"Shall I close ma eyes?" asked Carrie.

Sadie was really enjoying this. She hadn't had so much fun since she left home. "Is ya ready, Bay? Is ya ready, Carrie?"

"We ready!" yelled Bay and Carrie together.

"Ladies, I'll have you know that Big Mama, God rest her soul, left you fifty thousand dollars!" said Sadie in a deep masculine voice.

"She lef' us fifty thousand dollars? Fifty thousand dollars!" yelled the girls as they fell on the bed. "Now we don't have to stay in that house on Cane Street!" cried Bay, looking snobbish. "Sadie, are we *rich*?"

"No, we're not rich, jus' comfortable."

"Now I kin buy all de books I want!" cried Carrie.

"Girls, wait jus' a minute. First, I'm goin' ta buy a house, 'n' de rest of de money is goin' 'n a trust fund," interrupted Bee.

"I don' care if it's 'n a trust, as long as we ain't dirt poor!" said Bay. "All ma friends live 'n nice, putty houses. I'm ashamed ta invite dem ta our house. I like bein' comfortable much more dan bein' poor. It jus' don' feel right. I don' b'lieve nobody wuz put here ta live dat way."

"I agree," responded Sadie. "Anough of all dis excitement, let's go into de kitchen ta get somethin' ta eat." As they left the room, they were holding hands.

On the day of Big Mama's funeral. Bee rose early to help everyone get ready. She went into Sadie's room and found the girl in tears. She went over and put her arms around her daughter.

"Mama, I'm goin' ta miss Big Mama so, so much. She wuz jus' like a real mother. Yer more like a big sister. I love her! I love her!" cried Sadie, pressing her head into Bee's bosom.

Bee could still hear Sadie's words: "Yer more like a big sister." *How I wish wit' all my heart I had been dere fur ma girls. Ev'n ma religion kin't erase de past,* she thought with sadness.

At last, everyone had gotten dressed. The funeral director and his staff arrived to drive the family to the church. As they stepped into the big white limousine, Bay noticed a long line of cars behind them. "Where did all dose folks come frum?" she asked.

"Dey're s'posed ta be relatives," replied Bee.

The driver drove away and shortly arrived at the church, where there were more people standing in line. The funeral director had to clear the way so Big Mama's family could enter the church first. Bee and the girls walked into the sanctuary, following the pastor as the congregation looked on as they walked in. Bay loved all the attention. After everyone was seated, the choir sang one of Big Mama's favorite songs, "Leaning on His Everlasting Arms."

Suddenly, Bee and the girls heard a woman crying. "Sadie, who's dat?" whispered Bee.

"Don' know. I've never seen her before." When the emotional woman took her seat, Rev. Albertson prayed. Bee was somewhat surprised and quite pleased to see him. *He and the pastor must be very close. I didn't expect him to be here,* thought Bee. She knew that most colored pastors shared their pulpits with pastor friends to assist them at funerals.

Eventually, the funeral was over. Bee and the girls were ushered out of the church, into the limousine, and on to the cemetery for the burial. After the burial, they returned to the church for dinner with Big Mama's so-called relatives and friends. About an hour later, while Bee and the girls were eating, she looked up and saw Rev. Albertson walking toward their table. She almost choked.

"Mama, what's wrong?" questioned Sadie.

"She on fire 'cause Rev. Albertson is comin' over!" said Bay, chuckling.

"He likes Mama. Dey met on de train!" said Carrie, smiling.

"Y'all be quiet!" said Bee softly.

"Mama, it's all right. He won' bite ya unless ya let him!" The girls roared with laughter.

The reverend finally reached their table. "Mrs. McQueen, it's so nice to see you and the girls again," he said, looking at Sadie. "I don't believe I've met this daughter. She's as pretty as a rose."

Sadie smiled. "Thank you," replied Sadie.

Now looking into Bee's eyes, he had one question. "Mrs. McQueen, when are you leaving?"

"Tomorrow morning. The girls have to be back in school Tuesday."

"I was hoping you'd stay longer and visit my church," he said.

"No, I have to get back home," responded Bee, looking down shyly.

"Guess you're anxious to get back home to your husband," said Albertson.

The girls looked at each other. "Well . . . well . . . ah . . . ah . . . yes," stuttered Bee. The girls could tell that their mother was very uncomfortable. They knew their parents didn't have a real marriage.

Sadie, noticing the wedding band on the reverend's finger, decided to rescue her mother. "How's *your* wife, Reverend?" she asked.

He looked rather stunned. "She's at home."

"Do you have any children?" interrupted Bay.

"Yes, one son and two daughters."

Bee smiled. She was so grateful to her girls for rescuing her. "The next time I'm in Astoria, I'd like very much to meet your wife," said Bee.

"Of course, of course," responded Rev. Albertson, rising from his chair. "I've enjoyed your company. If I can ever be of assistance to you, don't fail to call," he continued, handing Bee a business card. Then he walked away.

"He is a pastor wit' a family 'n' a church. He's still not happy," said Sadie.

"Guess he thinks Mama kin make him happy," responded Carrie.

"Girls, let's go. I'm tired!" said Bee. The truth was that there was something about Rev. Albertson that ignited every dormant emotion in her, filling her with excitement and fear.

Bee and her daughters returned to Big Mama's house. She immediately went to her room to rest and finish packing. Sadie took her sisters for a ride to see the college campus.

"Sadie, I didn't know ya could drive!" said Bay excitedly.

"Who taught ya how ta drive like a grown woman?" asked Carrie, smiling.

"Mack Martin taught me," said Sadie, laughing.

Sadie slowed down to show them the library. Bay saw a tall handsome guy. "Sadie, who's dat fine-looking sweet-potato?"

"That's Alex Hawkins. He plays basketball, 'n' ev'ry girl on campus is after him."

"I'd be after him too. He sho looks good!"

"Sadie, ya got a sweet-potato?" asked Carrie, smiling.

"Maybe 'n' maybe not!" teased Sadie.

Sadie and her sisters returned home. They sat up most of the night talking about college, boys, clothes, and a secret Sadie'd held for a long time. Sadie knew the time had come to let Bay and Carrie know about it. Looking at her sisters with motherly love, she said, "Girls, I haf a secret ta tell ya." Bay and Carrie immediately moved closer to her.

"What is it?" asked Bay.

"We're waitin'," said Carrie.

"Remember when Mama 'n' Daddy used ta fight ev'ry weekend?" asked Sadie.

"Yes," responded Bay and Carrie.

"Remember de time Big Mama visited us 'cause someone wrote her 'bout de fightin'?"

"I won' ever forget de way Mama 'n' Daddy used ta fight. It made me feel so alone 'n' unhappy," exclaimed Bay.

"Girls, I'm de one who wrote de letter ta Big Mama," said Sadie.

"Really?" said Carrie.

"I'm glad ya did," said Bay happily. "Gee, Sadie, if ya hadn't, we'd still be dirt poor!"

Both girls hugged Sadie. "Big sister, thank ya! We love ya!" they said.

Early Monday morning at six o'clock, Bee, Bay, and Carrie were up, getting ready to return to Salem. Mr.

Martin arrived about nine o'clock to drive them to the train station. Mack loaded his car with their luggage while they said good-bye to Sadie. Everybody was in tears.

"Sadie, I hate ta leave ya. Ya must come home when school is out," said Bee.

"Mama, don' cry. I'm goin' ta be all right."

"Sadie, I don' wanta leave either, but I hafta go ta school tomorrow," said Bay, crying.

"Sadie, kin I come live wit' ya?" asked Carrie.

"What would Bay 'n' Mama do without ya? Ya need ta stay 'round ta keep Bay outa trouble!"

The girls laughed, and Bay and Carrie reluctantly walked over to Mack's car and got inside. As Mack slowly drove off, Bee and the girls waved good-bye to Sadie.

CHAPTER THREE

After living in Big Mama's beautiful home for two days, Bay wasn't too happy about returning to the big gray barn on Cane Street. Although she and her family had enough money to buy a new home, it couldn't happen fast enough for her. She wanted it now! Just thinking about a new house and a telephone made her feel mighty good all over.

The train pulled into Salem about three o'clock in the afternoon. "Sho look diff'rent from Astoria, 'n' don' haf a bit of class," said Bay snobbishly.

"Bay, jus' 'cause ya been 'round a lot of high-falutin' folks don' mean ya forget where ya come frum," responded Bee, smiling.

"Mama, when we goin' ta git a new house?" asked Carrie excitedly.

"As soon as I kin find un," replied Bee.

"Hallelujah! Hallelujah!" both girls shouted.

Suddenly the train slowed down and made a complete stop. As soon as Bee stepped off the train with the girls, she looked around for a taxi. "Taxi! Taxi! I need a taxi!" yelled Bee.

A taxi driver immediately rushed over and loaded their bags inside his taxi. "Where to, ma'am?" he asked.

"1225 Cane Street," replied Bee.

"Away we go!" said the driver.

As soon as Bee got the girls settled in at home, she went to see Mother Caine to tell her the good news and to call Mr. Harry Nixon, a real-estate agent in the colored community.

However, being back home in familiar surroundings made Bay quite restless. "I'll be so glad when tomorrow comes, so I kin go ta school 'n' see all ma friends," she said.

"Not me. I wish I could live 'n Astoria wit' Sadie furever 'n' ever!" said Carrie.

Bay put her hands on her hips and looked Carrie straight in the eyes. "Carrie McQueen, ya might as well git dat notion outa ya head. I don' know what I'd do wit' you *and* Sadie gone."

"Bay, I'm jus' teasin'. Jus' wanted ta see how ya really feel 'bout me," exclaimed Carrie, smiling.

Bay leaned over and gave Carrie a big kiss on the cheeks. "I love ya! I love ya! A million times, I love ya, li'l sister!"

Bee returned from Mother Caine's house. "It's all set. Mr. Nixon is pickin' me up frum work tomorrow ta look at a house."

"Mama, is we goin' ta git a telephone too?" asked Bay.

"As soon as we move in." She and the girls were so happy. However, for Bee the joy quickly disappeared when LC walked into the kitchen. *Now is de time ta do what I never had de courage ta do,* thought Bee. "Bay, you 'n' Carrie go ta ya room 'n' start gittin' ready fur school tomorrow."

Bay didn't like the expression on her mother's or daddy's face. It brought back old memories. She felt that something unpleasant was about to happen and she couldn't stop it. Bay slowly left the room.

Bee turned and faced LC. "Well, well, how's ya otha family?"

"What otha family ya talkin' 'bout?"

"The woman ya spend all ya time wit' 'n' sleep wit'!" cried Bee.

"I'm here 'cause I want ya ta know how sorry I am 'bout Big Mama," interrupted LC.

"How mighty nice 'n' white of ya. Ya must've heard 'n de streets dat she lef' me 'n' de girls some money!"

"Dis is ma house, 'n' I kin come home whenever I want ta, 'n' ya is ma wife!"

"Not no more!"

"What ya mean?" he said softly.

"I'm divorcin' ya sorry behind. I'm goin' ta see a lawyer first thang tomorrow mornin'. Another thang, ya kin haf dis rented house, 'cause I'm buyin' ma own. Git out 'n' go stay wit' ya woman till we leave," yelled Bee.

"You done got all biggity since ya got money. I don' need ya! I got me a woman who knows how ta make me feel like a real man!" LC said as he turned and walked away.

Suddenly Bee forgot about her religion. "I heard ya ain't de only one she makes feel like a real man. De milkman is gittin' it too!"

Bay and Carrie ran into the room and found their mother on the floor, crying uncontrollably. "Mama, you 'n' Daddy gittin' divorced?" asked Bay.

"Might as well, he ain't never here," answered Bee, wiping tears from her eyes.

"Mama, I would never put up wit' Daddy's ways. He's always at Miss Betty Jean's house!" said Carrie angrily.

"Carrie, never say never. I hear dat when a man git his hooks 'n ya, it's hard ta break free," exclaimed Bay with a serious look on her face. The girls didn't know what else to say or do, so they hugged their mother. Then Bay said, "Mama, God will make thangs all right if ya trust Him."

Joy does come in the morning. Mr. Nixon picked Bee up from work and took her to see a pretty three-bedroom brick house in Oak Woods, a nice new subdivision for colored people. All the lawns were neat and well-kept. Most residents were schoolteachers, preachers, and a few doctors. They were considered high-class. When Mr. Nixon pulled into the driveway, Bee was speechless. "How you like it?" he asked.

"It's real beautiful," responded Bee reluctantly.

"What's the matter?"

"I like it a lot, but don't you think it's too expensive for me? I ain't a teacher," exclaimed Bee.

"Teachers don't have any more money than you. They just like to put on airs," replied Mr. Nixon.

"This really is a beautiful house. The hardwood floors are very nice. Bay and Carrie can have their own bedrooms!" said Bee. *A house of ma own, 'n' LC had nothin' ta do wit' it*, she thought. She closed her eyes. "Thank ya, Big Mama," she said softly. She turned and walked over to Mr. Nixon. "I'll take it. I'm just as good as anyone in Oak Woods!"

"Super," shouted Mr. Nixon. "We're going to my office to sign some papers and set a date for the closing." After she signed the papers, Mr. Nixon dropped Bee off at home. She felt mighty good inside.

Bay and Carrie met their mother at the front door. "Mama, didya find a house you liked?" asked Bay.

"Yes, I sho did," answered Bee, smiling.

"Where is it?" asked Carrie.

"It's 'n Oak Woods."

"In Oak Woods!" cried Bay enthusiastically.

"Yes, Oak Woods!"

"That's where de high-class folks live!" said Bay, closing her eyes with a smug look on her face.

"Mama, did ya buy it?" asked Carrie.

"Yes."

"I'm so excited. We're goin' ta be living in Oak Woods!" said Bay. Nervously Bay added, "Mama, we have to watch our speech. We should talk proper."

"Mama talked real proper when we went to Astoria, especially around Rev. Albertson!" said Carrie, laughing.

"Sure wish we could move tomorrow!" asserted Bay.

"When can we see de house?" asked Carrie.

"We can see it tomorrow. Mother Caine is goin' ta drive us over."

The girls came straight home after school and waited for their mother. Finally, Bee arrived. They immediately went over to Mother Caine's house. She was thrilled to drive them to Oak Woods, because she was as anxious to see their new home as they were. Mother Caine talked all the way there and drove twenty-five miles per hour. *I'd've been there 'n' back a hundred times!* thought Bay.

Bee was as tired as the girls from the drive. Eventually, they pulled up in front of the house. "I'm not going to try to drive into the driveway. I might hit something," said Mother Caine, looking around at the other houses. She was a very nice lady, about seventy years old, and could eat anything without getting sick. "Lord, look at all these beautiful homes. Colored folks are sure moving up in this world!"

Bay and Carrie were so anxious to see the house, they left Bee and Mother Caine behind. Carrie looked back at her mother. "Mama, dis is a putty house!"

Bay was shocked. "Is dis our house?" she asked excitedly.

"Yes, it's ours," replied Bee.

"We ain't never got to move no more!" said Bay, standing on the porch with her hands on her hips.

Everybody walked inside the house. Mother Caine and the girls could not believe how beautiful the house was. "Bee, you've moved up in the world. Now you must improve yourself," said Mother Caine.

"What you mean?"

"You don't need to continue working in white folks' houses living here. You need an office job in a school, so you can make money to save and buy a car!" said Mother Caine.

"You're right, Mother."

After seeing the house, Bee, Mother Caine, and the girls returned to Cane Street. Bee and the girls were so tired from the drive with Mother Caine, they quickly ate supper, bathed, and went to bed.

The following morning after getting to school, Bay saw Savannah. They began talking. "Where do you live?" asked Bay.

"Oak Woods. Why?"

"Mama just bought a house there!" said Bay.

"Terrific, we can really become close friends!" They saw Sam approaching. "Sam, hurry, I have something wonderful to tell you!" continued Savannah.

"What's the news?" asked Sam, smiling.

"Bay is moving to Oak Woods!"

"Bay, that's super. I'm glad you're our new neighbor!"

"Gee, I didn't know you lived there too," said Bay.

"I sure do. When y'all moving?" asked Sam.

"I think we're moving next Saturday." The school bell interrupted their conversation. They went in different directions.

Saturday finally arrived. Bee and the girls moved into their new home. They had plenty of assistance. Several of the men from their church helped. Everyone thought the house looked like a mansion. Word had gotten out in the community that Bee had inherited a million dollars. Bay and Carrie were so excited. Bay couldn't believe she would be living in such a beautiful brick house and would finally have her heart's desire: a telephone. Bay and Carrie were standing in the foyer looking at the telephone. "Carrie, is dis real, or are we dreaming?" asked Bay.

"It's really real, my dear," Carrie said, smiling and speaking in a refined Southern accent. Bee walked by carrying boxes.

"Girls, don' stand dere all day looking at dat phone. There's lots of work ta do!" said Bee.

"Okay, Mama," they responded. Soon the moving was over. The rest of the afternoon was spent decorating the house.

Living in Oak Woods was ideal for Bee and the girls. They were exposed to another world. Though their neighbors were better off financially, they were still wounded souls. One day, the doorbell rang. "I'll get it!" cried Bay.

She opened the door and a lady was standing with a lemon pie in her hands. "Hi, honey, is your mother at home?" asked the lady.

"Yes, ma'am," replied Bay politely.

By that time, Bee was at the door. "Come on in!" she said.

"Thank you, my name is Maxine Evans."

"I'm Bee McQueen."

"I just came over to welcome you to the neighborhood. Are you married?" asked Maxine.

"Why?" asked Bee.

"My husband loves light-skinned women. Just want you to be aware of it," she said.

"Look, Maxine, I can't help what color I am, and I don't want your husband. I don't even know him."

Maxine began crying. "Bee, I'm so sorry, but when you're dark like me and your husband is always talking about how he wished he'd married him a red-bone, it hurts so bad. Sometimes I just want to die!" exclaimed Maxine. After she regained her composure, she apologized to Bee, turned, and walked out the door.

Bee felt sorry for the woman. She'd thought the color problem among colored folks was over. After Maxine left, Bee noticed the frightened look on Bay's face. The girl was darker than Maxine. Bee walked over and put her arms around Bay. "Don't let dat bother ya. It ain't what's on de outside. It's what's inside dat matter!"

Bee and the girls looked around in pure amazement. "Our home is as putty as any white person's house 'n dose magazines!" cried Bay. The three of them looked at each other as though they could read each other's minds and said together, "Thank you, Big Mama!"

Rising early the following morning, Bee prepared breakfast while Carrie went outside to get the Sunday paper. On the front page was a picture of Rev. Jack Albertson. Carrie couldn't wait to show it to her mother. She quickly ran into the house. "Mama, Mama, look whose picture is 'n de paper!"

Bee left the food on the stove to look at the newspaper.

"It's Rev. Albertson. He's havin' a revival right here 'n Salem at Gethsemane Baptist Church!" said Carrie.

"That's de biggest church 'n de city," said Bay. "Mama, are ya going?"

"I jus' might."

"You'd better be careful, Mama. He might bite!" said Bay, chuckling and making a biting sound. Bee and Carrie laughed at the funny expression on Bay's face.

"Let's finish our breakfast. We need ta git dressed fur church," said Bee.

"Are we goin' ta our church or Gethsemane?" asked Carrie.

"We're goin' ta our church."

Bay and Carrie looked at each other. They sure didn't feel like sitting through the same boring deacon's devotion and the pastor's dry preaching. "Mama, why don' we go ta Gethsemane ta see Rev. Albertson? I know he will be glad ta see ya," said Bay slyly. "De way he prayed at Big Mama's funeral, I know he will really set our souls on fire!"

"I b'lieve with all ma heart dat he is a true servant of God!" responded Carrie, smiling and looking up at the ceiling.

"Girls, don' try dem tricks on me. I wasn't born yesterday. Anyway, if we decided ta go ta Gethsemane, how would we git dere? We're not walkin'."

"Dey haf a bus ta pick up people!" interrupted Carrie.

"We'll go Friday night. Girls, let's git dressed," said Bee, walking toward her bedroom. "Mother Caine is on her way." An hour later, they heard Mother Caine toot her horn.

Friday morning, Bee called Gethsemane Church and made arrangements to attend the revival. The church's bus driver picked them up at six o'clock that evening. After arriving at the church, they entered the sanctuary and were seated by an usher. Now comfortably sitting on the pew near the back in the middle area, Bay began observing the beautiful huge building and all the finely dressed people. Bee's church was no comparison. *Dere's some fine-looking sweet-potatoes 'n dis church!* thought Bay.

The choir stood up and did an opening selection. Afterward, the ministers walked in and sat on the pulpit. The church was packed, so Rev. Albertson didn't see Bee and the girls. The choir sang another song. Bay and Carrie stood up and began clapping their hands. Before long, almost everybody was standing and rocking. "I like dis church!" said Carrie.

"Me too!" responded Bay.

Finally their mother joined in. "Can't sit while ev'rybody else is praisin' God!" asserted Bee.

By the time Rev. Albertson got up to preach, many folks were asleep from all the exercise. It didn't last long. He was such a great orator, the crowd came alive, especially the women. One woman kept running up and down the aisles, while some were falling out. Bay got a big kick out of the whole thing. "Carrie, let's go down dere 'n front of ev'rybody 'n' shout!" said Bay quietly.

"Not me!" replied Carrie, smiling.

"Mama, why don' ya join me? Rev. Albertson will really git a chance ta see ya 'n action!"

"Bay, hush, before folks hear ya!" replied Bee defensively.

The shouters finally sat down. Rev. Albertson preached a red-hot sermon! You would have thought that he was immune from problems.

When the service ended, everybody walked to the front of the church to shake the preacher's hand. However, Bee and the girls headed out of the church. Suddenly, Rev.

Albertson saw her. He excused himself from the group he was talking with and rushed over to speak to Bee. "Sister McQueen, how are you doing? This is certainly a surprise!" Bay and Carrie looked at each other. "Girls, how's school?" asked Rev. Albertson.

"Fine," they responded, smiling.

"I really enjoyed your preaching," said Carrie.

"I enjoyed it too!" stressed Bay.

"Thank you, dear," he replied.

"Hopefully, I'll get to hear you again," said Bee, rather proper and polite.

"I won't be leaving for Astoria until Sunday. Maybe you and the girls can come over and eat dinner with me tomorrow at the church. They're having a big spread for me," exclaimed Rev. Albertson.

"What time is it?" asked Bee.

"I don't know exactly. Tell you what; give me your phone number. I'll call you to give you the time."

Bay and Carrie were very excited. "Rev. Albertson, thank you so much for inviting us!" said Bay, smiling.

"Girls, we'd better go. Goodnight, Rev. Albertson," said Bee. The reverend was still watching her as she and the girls left the building.

The following morning, Rev. Albertson called Bee to let her know the time of the dinner. After hanging up the phone, Bee looked flushed. Deep within, she felt alive. Bay rushed into her mother's room. "Mama, was that Rev. Albertson?"

"Yes."

"What time do we hafta be at de church?"

"We hafta be dere at one o'clock."

"We'd betta start gittin' dressed. It's already ten-thirty," replied Bay. She rushed out the room to tell Carrie.

About twelve-thirty, the bus from Gethsemane pulled into their driveway, and the three of them got inside. Fifteen minutes later, they were at the church. Everybody exited the bus and entered the huge fellowship hall. *It's decorated so putty!* thought Bee. Green and pale-yellow centerpieces were on each table.

Bay and Carrie could hardly wait to begin feasting on the food. "Dat food really smells good," said Bay.

"If it tastes as good as it smells, I might join dis church," said Carrie, laughing.

An usher came over to greet Bee and the girls. "Mrs. McQueen, Pastor Albertson reserved a table for you near the front. Come with me." They followed him and were seated. Bee beamed. She felt very special.

"Mama, ain't we somethin' special? We're sittin' near de head table," exclaimed Bay excitedly.

"Bay, don't say *ain't*," said Carrie in a soft voice. "We're supposed to talk proper when we're in public around high-class people."

The tables filled quickly. Then all the preachers and their guests came in and took their seats. Albertson looked over at Bee and smiled. She looked beautiful. She was wearing a pretty pale-blue and white dress.

At one point, a young man stood up to do a solo. He couldn't keep his eyes off Bay. "Bay, I think the soloist is wooing you," said Carrie.

"He sure looks mighty good, but he's supposed to be wooing God, not me," replied Bay.

Soon the dinner was over. Rev. Albertson worked his way through the crowd over to Bee.

"Rev. Albertson, thank you so much for the reserved table. This is a beautiful church," said Bee.

"I'm told that it's one of the oldest churches in Salem," responded Rev. Albertson. "Let me give you a tour."

"Girls, are you coming?" asked Bee.

"No, Carrie and I will stay here. I'm not interested in looking at this big church."

"Me either," said Carrie.

Rev. Albertson and Bee walked through double doors and entered the education wing. He showed her the very large classrooms. From there, they walked into the pastor's office. Rev. Albertson introduced Bee to the pastor, who was on his way out. Taking a seat in one of the large, comfortable chairs, Rev. Albertson invited Bee to do the same. "Mrs. McQueen, please have a seat."

"Okay," replied Bee, nervously.

"How are you and your husband doing?"

"We're getting a divorce," she responded.

"If you can't get along, I guess you have no choice," exclaimed Rev. Albertson.

"How long have you been married?" Bee questioned.

"All my life . . . no, about fifteen years," answered Rev. Albertson with a big smile.

Bee began to feel a little uncomfortable. She got up from her seat. "I know the girls are ready to go home. I have to leave now," she said.

"Okay," replied Rev. Albertson.

As they rose to leave, he and Bee found themselves facing each other. They felt as if their bodies were being pulled together by some invisible magnetic force. There was no thought of "Thou shalt not commit adultery." Now they were in each other's arms, kissing passionately. They looked into each others' eyes and remembered that they were in a church. Bee pulled away. "I'm so sorry. I don't know what got into me," she said apologetically.

"I should be the one apologizing. I'm the minister," replied Rev. Albertson sadly. "Why can't I be happy? There's still something missing in my life. I'm supposed to know God, but sometimes I feel so empty, even when I'm preaching," he continued, now putting his hands in his pockets. Bee looked at him with all the compassion in her soul. "Bee, there's something about you that makes me feel happy just being with you," said the reverend.

"Rev. Albertson, it's going to take more than me to heal your soul. It's not just you. I've been searching for happiness all my life," replied Bee.

"It appears to be a universal thing," said Rev. Albertson, opening the door to leave the pastor's office. Finally, Rev. Albertson and Bee reached the fellowship hall.

Bay and Carrie hardly realized their mother had been gone for so long. Bay was involved in a conversation with the soloist, and Carrie had made new friends too. Bee turned to face Rev. Albertson. "Thank you so much. I had a wonderful time," said Bee softly. "Bay, Carrie, it's time to go!" While Bee waited for her daughters, the reverend walked away.

The school year seemed to fly past. Soon it was June of 1961, summer vacation had started, and Bee and the girls were preparing for Sadie's visit.

"I'm so glad Sadie's finally comin' home!" cried Bay excitedly.

"Sadie's a busy young woman. It's a job going ta school 'n' studyin'," replied Bee.

"Mama, where is Sadie goin' ta sleep?" asked Carrie.

"With you or Bay."

"I want her ta sleep wit' me," said Carrie.

"No, she's sleepin' in ma room!" shouted Bay.

"I'll settle de whole thing. Sadie kin sleep wit' me," interrupted Bee. "I hear a car!" she continued excitedly.

Bay and Carrie peeped out the window. "It's a taxi! It's a taxi! It's Sadie!" cried Bay joyfully.

"It's Sadie! It's Sadie!" cried Carrie, jumping up and down. She rushed outside to meet her sister. Bay followed and then Bee.

They ran to Sadie and embraced her. Everybody was so excited, it took them a moment to notice the bundle Sadie was carrying in her arms. Suddenly, Bee asked, "What's dat ya have dere?"

"It's a baby," replied Sadie softly, holding her head down.

"Whose baby is it?" questioned Bee nervously.

"Mine."

"Let's go inside. We need ta do some serious talkin'," said Bee, walking toward the house.

By this time, the taxi driver had unloaded all of Sadie's bags and left. While the girls followed Bee, Bay asked, "Is de baby a boy or a girl?"

"It's a girl. Her name is Sara," Sadie replied. When they reached the living room, Bee asked Bay and Carrie to watch the baby while she and Sadie went into her bedroom.

Sadie followed Bee inside. "Girls don' haf babies without husbands. Sadie, do ya haf a husband?" asked Bee angrily.

"No, Mama."

"Were ya pregnant when we came ta Big Mama's funeral?"

"Yes, Mama," replied Sadie, turning her back.

"Sadie, don' ya turn away frum me. What were ya thinkin'? I wanted ya ta go ta college to make somethin' outa yourself, not ta git pregnant!" shouted Bee. "What am I goin' ta tell folks? These days it's a scandal fur women ta git pregnant without a husband! I tried ma best ta make good, respectable young women out of y'all!"

"Ya through, Mama? You weren't all dat concerned 'bout what folks were sayin' when ya wuz gittin' drunk 'n' walkin' de streets while I looked after Bay 'n' Carrie!" responded Sadie angrily. "I didn't deliberately git pregnant. I did de best I could, so don' judge me. I never judged you, even when you weren't around fur Bay, Carrie, or me. You 'n' Daddy wuz always thinkin' only 'bout yourselves 'n' de crazy world ya lived 'n, but I still loved ya. Now I've made a mistake, 'n' ya act like ya don' know what love is!" continued Sadie, crying hysterically.

After hearing all the noise, Bay opened the door to her mother's room. She gave the baby to Carrie and walked over to embrace Sadie. "Sadie, please stop cryin'. Ev'rythin' is goin' ta be all right."

Though the talk between Bee and Sadie had become calmer, Bee had more questions to ask Sadie, so Bay and Carrie left them in the bedroom.

"Bay, can you b'lieve Sadie has a baby?" asked Carrie.

"I never really thought dat much 'bout it, but wit' all dose good-lookin' sweet-potatoes on campus, Sadie jus' couldn't help herself!" replied Bay, chuckling and kissing Sara.

"Bay, wouldn't ya like ta know who is Sara's father?"

"That is none of our business," snapped Bay. They didn't know that the same discussion was going on between Bee and Sadie.

Bee broke the silence that had grown between her and her daughter. "Sadie, who's de father of ya chile?"

"Mama, it's not important," replied Sadie coldly.

"I'm ya mother. I haf a right ta know."

"Well, I'm not tellin' ya. I'm a grown woman!"

"Whose goin' ta help ya take care of Sara?"

"So dat's what yer worried 'bout? You don' hafta worry. I won' ask ya fur anything. You didn't take care of ya own children!" cried Sadie cruelly.

"Guess ya won' ever let me forget ma past," replied Bee. She walked over to the bed and sat down. "If I could do it all over again, I would. God knows I would!" Bee was hurting so much. Suddenly, she just turned over on the bed, laid her head on the pillow, and cried softly.

Sadie was sorry she and Bee had gotten into it, but she had nothing else to say. Sadie left her mother alone. She found her sisters and Sara in Bay's bedroom. Bee stayed in her room all night. However, Sadie decided she'd be nicer the next day.

Bee rose early to prepare breakfast. When Sadie entered the kitchen, she saw pots and pans on the stove, coffee perking, and bacon and toast sitting on the counter waiting to be placed in the oven. "Mornin', Mama," said Sadie, holding Sara. "Hope ya slept okay. I'm sorry 'bout las' night," she continued, calmly and lovingly.

"Sadie, ya don' hafta tell me 'bout Sara's father till yer ready. I love ya, honey," replied Bee.

Bay walked in just as perky as always. "Good mornin', ev'rybody. Dis food sho smells good. I'm so hungry, I could eat an elephant!"

Bee and Sadie laughed. "Just so ya leave enough fur ev'rybody else," replied Sadie.

"Hello, ma sweet Sara," said Bay joyfully.

"Where's Carrie?" asked Bee.

"Carrie likes ta sleep more dan eat," responded Bay with a smile.

Finally, Carrie came to breakfast. "Good mornin', family. Sadie, I miss ya cookin'. Mama kin cook, but de cats 'n' dogs won' eat Bay's cooking!" teased Carrie.

"I'll remember dose words when ya beg me ta fix flapjacks," replied Bay, chewing on bacon and toast.

It was like old times having Sadie home. But the time passed, and Sadie had to return to Astoria.

That morning, Sadie got up, finished packing, and dressed herself while Bee dressed Sara. "Mama, I really had a good time. I jus' love de house!" said Sadie happily.

Bee's mind was distant. She was thinking about Sadie and Sara going back to Astoria and living alone. *Who will look after Sara while Sadie attends school?* she thought.

"Mama, ya haven't heard a word I said. I like ya house," said Sadie.

"Thank ya, honey," replied Bee. "Sadie, who's keepin' Sara while ya go ta school?"

"There's a nursery on campus. I'm goin' ta let her stay dere three days a week," replied Sadie pleasantly.

"I'm jus' concerned 'bout you 'n' ma grandbaby."

Sadie walked over to her mother. "Mama, don' ya worry 'bout us. Big Mama made sure of dat," she responded. Finally Sadie got all her luggage together, and then she awakened Bay and Carrie to say good-bye while Bee called a taxi. Within an hour, Sadie was on her way to the station to catch the eleven o'clock train to Astoria.

After Sadie left, Bee and the girls missed her. All through Bay's sophomore year in high school, she didn't have much excitement in her life besides talking on the phone or listening to music. She loved to dance and became quite good at it. She was the best dancer at her school. She'd even taught Carrie some of the new dances. While their mother was at home, they didn't play their music loud and dance. Bee called it devil's music.

One day during summer vacation, Bay and Carrie were really into dancing when they heard footsteps on the porch. "Carrie, turn off de record player!" yelled Bay. "Dat might be Mama comin'!"

Carrie ran over to switch off the record player by the window. She peeped outside. "It's not her. It's Savannah!" cried Carrie.

Bay ran and opened the door. "Come on in, Savannah. We're doing the Hurley Girley!" said Bay excitedly.

Carrie turned the music back on. Bay, Carrie, and Savannah were moving and wiggling to the rhythm. Bay began chanting, "Two steps to the right, two to the left, two to the back, two to the front and turn." The music stopped, and everybody laughed with excitement. "We'd better stop. If Mama catches us, we're going to be in serious trouble," said Bay. Her instincts were good. About fifteen minutes later, Bee came through the front door.

After greeting Savannah and her daughters, Bee went to her bedroom. Bay and Savannah went for a walk, while Carrie snuggled up with a book. When the telephone rang, Carrie rushed over to answer it. "Hello, yes, just a minute," she said. "Mama, the telephone is for you."

Bee picked up the phone in her room. "Hello, yes, I'm still interested. Monday and Wednesday nights at seven-thirty will be fine. Thank you!"

The phone call was good news. It was a confirmation for Bee to begin typing classes at night. She was very excited. She had taken the first step to make a better life for herself. That night she sang and cooked the best supper ever. As the fall of 1962 approached, it seemed as if life was leading Bee on a very successful path. But Bay's junior year in high school would make it a little bumpy.

Like most girls her age, Bay's hormones were working overtime, and being a junior didn't make it any easier. Most girls and boys were having sex. The only advice Bee had given her on that subject was to keep her dress down and panties up. Sadie taught her what she knew. Yet that didn't prevent her from being adventurous.

One day, she and Savannah were walking home from school. "Have you ever done it, Vannah?" asked Bay.

"Done what?" replied Savannah, smiling.

"You know what I mean—had sex, that's what! Don't act dumb!" said Bay, laughing.

"Of course I have, but wasn't nothing to it!"

"You weren't scared you'd get pregnant?"

"Sure I was scared, but I did it anyway. You mean Sam hasn't ever asked you?"

"Of course he has. If Mama knew it, she'd have twelve bitties. She's always warned me about getting pregnant," said Bay.

"You're not going to get pregnant if Sam uses a rubber," said Savannah.

By this time they had reached Bay's house. "Vannah, the next time Sam asks me, I'm goin' ta say yes!"

"Maybe you and Sam can go to the drive-in theater with Kirby and me Saturday night."

"I'll ask Mama," said Bay, walking up her driveway.

John Kirby, Savannah's boyfriend, was a pretty nice kid, but he had some problems. He was very possessive and jealous of Savannah because she was light-complexioned. She made him feel important. He was always bragging about dating a red-bone.

Bay went inside the house. Bee was in such a good mood, Bay decided to ask her about going to the movie with Savannah, Sam, and Kirby right then. "Mama, kin I go to de movies wit' Savannah, Sam, 'n' Kirby Saturday night?"

Bee stopped cooking for a minute. "Guess so, you're sixteen now. Just remember, a man only wants one thang, 'n' dat never satisfies him," said Bee.

"Thank you, Mama, I won' forget," said Bay cunningly.

The Wounded Whole

After arriving at the movie, Bay forgot everything her mother said. She and Sam were in the backseat, smooching and going on like they were trying to make up for lost time. Kirby and Savannah were no amateurs. They got right down to business. There was so much heat in the car, you couldn't see out the windows.

That was the night Bay lost her virginity. When she got home, she sneaked into her bedroom and cried from disappointment. Sex wasn't what she thought it was. As the saying goes, she didn't feel no good feeling. How she wished she could talk to Sadie.

From that night on, Bay and Sam became a twosome. In other words, they were going steady. However, Bay became tired of him. All he ever wanted to do was to have sex, which he wasn't good at. She wanted more out of life. Bay decided to tell Sam she didn't want to go with him anymore. They were sitting on the school campus after school. "Sam, if I say something, will you promise you won't be hurt?"

"I can't promise no such thing, if I don't know what it is," responded Sam.

"Well, I guess I just have to tell you like it is," said Bay. "I don't want to go steady anymore."

"I thought we were going to get married after graduation!" exclaimed Sam, surprised.

"Married? I'm not ready to get married. Mama wants me to go to college," she replied.

Sam grabbed Bay and pulled her toward him angrily. "You got somebody else, don't you, Bay?" he yelled.

"No, Sam, turn me loose!" cried Bay. "If you don't, I'm going to tell my daddy."

"Your daddy," said Sam sarcastically, releasing her. "Everybody knows your daddy ain't worth a shit. He don't care nothing about you. Bay, nobody cares about you!"

Bay stood up listening with tears running down her cheeks, and then abruptly turned and walked away. Watching her go, Sam knew he had hurt her. Little did he know he had hurt himself. For the rest of their junior year, Bay didn't accept any phone calls or speak to him at school. He couldn't take it anymore, so he began following her everywhere.

One night after Bay left Savannah's house and was walking home, Sam jumped from behind some very tall bushes and grabbed Bay, putting his hand over her mouth. "Don't try nothing. It's just you and me, and nobody can hear you," said Sam softly. "You been acting mighty biggity. Act biggity now!" Bay couldn't believe Sam was acting so crazy. Then he said, "Bay, you been giving my stuff away, haven't you?"

Suddenly Bay took her right foot and kicked one of his legs as hard as she could, elbowed him in his side, and ran home screaming, "Sam, leave me alone! You done gone slap crazy!" She ran into the house crying, "Mama, Mama, Sam just tried ta hurt me. He wuz choking me! I'm so scared!"

Bee put her arms around Bay. "Honey, it's goin' ta be all right. I'll call ya daddy, 'n' we will have a talk wit' his parents."

"Everywhere I go he follows me, 'cause I don't want to be his girlfriend no more," exclaimed Bay.

Bee continued holding her. "Bay, you 'n' Sam ain't been messin' 'round, haf ya?"

"What do ya mean, messin' 'round?"

"Havin' sex is what I mean," replied Bee.

"If we did, he shouldn't act like dat."

"Some men kin't handle sex. What on earth do ya think 'bout a boy? After de thrill, dey think a woman's body 'n' soul belong ta dem. Most of 'em git real possessive 'n' crazy. It ain't 'cause dey 'n love. Somethin' is wrong 'n dey heads," exclaimed Bee.

Bay raised her head and looked her mother in the eyes. "Mama, please tell Daddy ta talk ta Sam. If he keeps on botherin' me, I'll stop him wit' a gun!"

"No, Bay, dat's not de way!" cried Bee.

Bay stood up. "If you 'n' Daddy won' look out fur me, I will. I know exactly where ta git a gun!" asserted Bay. She walked out of the room, leaving Bee standing helplessly.

Bee decided not to wait until tomorrow to call LC. She walked over and picked up the telephone. "Hello, Betty Jean, this is Bee. Can I speak with LC?"

"Just a minute," Betty Jean replied.

"Bee, dis is LC."

"Bay needs our help. Sam tried ta hurt her tonight. She says she's goin' ta kill him if he don' leave her alone and we don' look out fur her. Can you talk ta his parents? You comin' now?"

"I'll be dere in 'bout twenty minutes!"

LC arrived at Bee's house. As he walked up on the porch, he couldn't help but admire her beautiful home. *Bee 'n' de girls is livin' as good as or betta dan mos' white folks*, he thought. He knocked on the door.

Bee opened it and asked, "What did Sam's parents haf ta say?"

"I haven't been ta talk ta them. You need ta go too."

"Okay, let me slip on another dress," she responded as LC continued standing at the door. "I almost forgot ma manners. Please come 'n 'n' haf a seat. I'll be back 'n a few moments," said Bee, walking out of the room.

Carrie came out of the kitchen eating a peanut-butter sandwich. "Daddy, would ya like a sandwich?" she asked, smiling.

"No thanks, baby," he responded, hugging Carrie.

"Where are you 'n' Mama going?"

"We goin' over ta Sam's house ta talk ta his parents 'bout how he treated Bay tonight."

"Bay told me 'bout what happened. Wait till I see dat ol' crazy Sam!" said Carrie angrily.

Just then, Bee came out of her bedroom looking more presentable. She and LC left, and Carrie's eyes followed them from the window. *Sure would be nice if Mama 'n' Daddy would git back together,* she thought.

After returning from Sam's house, Bee and LC stood outside her house and talked. "Bee, I don't know whether talkin' ta Sam's parents did any good. They act like it's all Bay's fault," said LC.

"I know. I don' know what else ta do!"

"Maybe I scared him when I told him ta stay away frum Bay or he's goin' ta have ta deal wit' me," replied LC.

"I sho hope so. I don' want Bay ta get in any trouble 'cause of Sam."

"It's goin' ta be all right," said LC reassuringly. They looked at each other, seemingly wishing things had been different between them. "Well, Bee, I'm goin' ta say goodnight. I got ta go ta work 'n de morning."

"Me too. Thanks, LC," she said as she walked toward the door. Seems as if their being apart had made LC more hospitable.

The following afternoon, something happened that would shake the small colored community of Salem. About six o'clock, the police drove into Oak Woods with Savannah in the car. Carrie and her friends were outside talking. They wondered why Savannah was in the police car. It was very rare to see a police car in this part of town. Carrie ran inside to get Bay. Immediately they returned. Bay wanted to go to Savannah's house, but she knew she'd be turned around. By this time, lots of people were standing in their yards and beside the road.

Bay saw one of the football players walking home from summer practice and called him. "Hey, Pee Wee, you know what happened to Savannah? Carrie just saw her pass by in a police car!"

"I heard Kirby shot himself and tried to kill Savannah. She got out of the car and ran! She tried to break up wit' him. He said if he couldn't have her, nobody could!" exclaimed Pee Wee. "You know, Kirby had this color thing real bad. He was always bragging 'bout his red-bone. I'll tell you this much, ain't gonna kill myself over no red-bone, green-bone, white-bone, or black-bone!" continued Pee Wee, laughing.

Bay didn't think it was so funny. She felt real sad inside. She knew Savannah must be hysterical and scared. She wanted to be with her, but she knew she had to wait until the right time to see her.

That time came the very next day when Bee went to Savannah's house to take food to the family. Bee rang the doorbell as Carrie and Bay stood beside her. Mrs. Pierce, Savannah's mother, opened the door. She was very fair, like Savannah. "Mrs. Pierce, I'm Bee, Bay's mother."

"Come in, Mrs. McQueen. Girls, please come in. Bay, Savannah really wants to see you. She's in her bedroom," said Mrs. Pierce.

Bay walked down a long, wide hallway to Savannah's room and knocked on the door. "Savannah, it's Bay. Can I come in?"

"Yes, come on in."

When Bay opened the door and saw Savannah lying in her bed on her stomach, she wanted to cry. "Vannah, I'm so sorry about what happened," said Bay.

Savannah sat up with tears running down her cheeks. Her skin was almost beet red. Bay sat beside her. "Oh, Bay, it was awful, just awful. Kirby wanted to kill me too, but I jumped out of the car and ran to a house for help!" cried Savannah. Now looking into Bay's eyes in horror, she continued, "Bay, I was so scared. I didn't know what else to do. While I was running, I didn't look back. I just ran. Then I heard a shot!"

Tears filled Bay's eyes. Now Bay was holding Savannah in her arms. "Vannah, I'm so sorry. Wish I could make the pain go away!" asserted Bay.

Savannah got out of bed and walked over to the window. She turned and said loudly, "Why can't I be loved for me? Kirby is dead because he loved my color. He didn't really love me. I was just a trophy. All he wanted was a yella gal! The boys want me 'cause I'm the closest thing to a white girl! I *ain't* white! Don't want to be nothing but who I am down on the inside! Some folks my color take pride in being near white. Bay, that is not me. I'd rather have genuine love than skin color!" cried Savannah, sobbing loudly.

"Vannah, it's going to be all right. You'll see. We will be seniors next year."

"Bay, things aren't going to change. They're even worse for you. At least I can go a long ways because of my color. Bay, it's not fair. You're the most beautiful person on the inside and outside," said Savannah compassionately.

"It's the sixties, things will get better!" replied Bay enthusiastically.

"Sorry, Bay, but I'm not waiting around to find out."

"What do you mean?"

"I'm leaving Salem. I'm going to live with my aunt in California to finish school," said Savannah.

"Oh, no, Vannah, colored folks are color-struck no matter where you go!"

"After what happened to Kirby, I can't stay here. It's too painful." Now hugging Bay, Savannah continued, "I'm going to miss you so much. I'll be back to visit you the summer after graduation."

Bay began to cry. "I understand," she said sadly. "Just seems like everybody I love leaves me right here in Salem. Sadie left, now you."

"You're leaving Salem one day too. You just wait and see."

There was a knock at the door. "Bay, it's time to go," said Carrie.

"I'm coming," replied Bay. "Vannah, when are you leaving?"

"I'm leaving in two weeks."

"I'll see you tomorrow," said Bay. She walked out of Savannah's room and closed the door behind her.

When Bee and the girls returned home, they talked about Savannah moving to California. "I think it's a great idea fur her ta move away after what happened," said Bee.

"Don' mean ta talk bad about de dead, but Kirby sho had it bad 'bout color," exclaimed Carrie.

"Kirby ain't the only one. This whole country is messed up. Carrie, ya ain't as dark as me, so you'll be treated better by mos' folks, 'specially by dose who think dey're high class," exclaimed Bay.

"Bay, don' talk like dat," said Bee.

"Mama, de truth is de truth. Just 'cause yer light, ya won' haf a problem gittin' another man," said Bay. "I know a girl at school who kin't spell *cat*, but the boys is crazy 'bout her 'cause she's light!" Carrie hollered with laughter. "Tell ya one thang, I might be as black as a blackberry, but ain't nothin' goin' ta stand in ma way," said Bay confidently.

Savannah moved to California. Bay began her senior year and was determined to accomplish something positive in her life. Being young, she didn't realize that old traditions die hard—not just among white folks, but colored ones as well. Many of Bay's classmates encouraged her to run for Homecoming Queen. She became very excited and agreed to do it. It didn't seem to bother her that one of the contestants would be Joan Hudson, a very light-complexioned girl whose father was a prominent colored doctor in Salem. Bee bought Bay the most beautiful gown, and she looked simply gorgeous in it. Surely the judges had to feel the same way.

The night of the pageant, the auditorium was packed. When every contestant had finished performing, it was time to select the Homecoming Queen. The master of ceremonies called the third runner-up, who was an eleventh-grader; the second runner-up, a tenth-grader; and the first runner-up, a senior. Now the audience quietly awaited the name of the new Homecoming Queen. The emcee opened the envelope. "The 1963 Homecoming Queen is none other than the beautiful Joan Hudson."

When Bay heard those words, her heart sank. Her dream of doing something positive ended. *Vannah wuz right, ain't no hope fur a darkie like me!* she thought. Then Bay did something quite extraordinary and rebellious. When the queen began taking her walk, Bay walked ahead of her with all the poise and class she could muster. Some shouted, "Sit down!" Most were shouting, "Do it! Do it! Git it on!" After completing her walk, Bay left the stage, and Joan Hudson, in tears.

Immediately, Bay ran out of the auditorium. Bee and Carrie jumped up and ran after her. Then some of her classmates followed. They reached the outside and saw her cross the campus, walking toward the woods.

"Bay, wait! Bay, wait!" shouted Bee. Bay kept walking, and then she began running.

"Mrs. McQueen, it's mighty dark back there, and there's also the Winding River back there," said a boy from Bay's class.

"Oh, no, call the police! Carrie, call your daddy!" cried Bee. Bee and the students ran faster. By the time they reached the river, Bay was standing real close to the edge, getting ready to jump. "Bay, I come ta take ya home, so we kin talk 'bout how putty ya looked tonight 'n' how good ya did," said Bee, softly and gently. "I'm so proud of ya."

"Ain't nobody proud of me!" shouted Bay. Suddenly, she looked up at the sky. "Mama, nobody loves me! I mean, *nobody* loves me, not even God!" LC and Carrie appeared.

Carrie began crying and walking toward Bay. "Bay, I love ya wit' all dat's 'n me. Sadie loves you too. If ya jump, Sadie won't ever git over it," she said calmly.

"Please, Carrie, don' come no closer!" responded Bay with tears running down her cheeks. "I ain't yella! I ain't white! I'm just as black as de night, but when I jump in dis river, ev'rythin' will be all right!" yelled Bay as loud as she could.

While Bay was talking, her classmates were crying and so was Bee. In the meantime, LC was trying to sneak up on her from behind. Finally, he walked up behind Bay and grabbed her.

"Leave me alone!" cried Bay. "Turn me loose!"

"Baby, baby, it's Daddy!" said LC, holding her.

"Oh, Daddy, I jus' want ta die! I'm too black! The world don' want me here!"

"Bay, I want you. Dere are a lot of folks jus' waitin' fur you, but more dan anything, ya got ta want yourself. Ta me, yer de prettiest 'n' sweetest girl 'n de world. It don' matter 'bout ya bein' black as a blackberry!" exclaimed LC as he kissed Bay, picked her up, and carried her in his arms. That night was the first time she ever felt loved by her father. As they left Winding River, Bay realized that when life seems too hard to go on, good is always there.

CHAPTER FOUR

In June of 1964, nine months after Bay's attempted suicide, she graduated from high school and continued to live at home, with no job or educational goals. Bee had just received her certificate in secretarial science, and she was on her way to an interview at Carver High.

While Bay lay on the sofa looking at soap operas, Bee walked in. "Bay McQueen, ya mus' think you some rich white woman. You need ta git yourself outa here tomorrow mornin' 'n' look fur a job. I ain't 'bout ta take care of ya de rest of ya life! Carrie is 'n school. I'm tryin' ta do betta, but ya ain't tryin' ta do nothing! Ya could even babysit fur white folks."

Bay sat up on the sofa and looked at Bee. "Mama, I ain't workin' 'n no white folks' houses, cleaning up behind dem 'n' dere young'uns'!"

"Well, ya hafta do somethin'. I haf de number of de employment office," said Bee, reaching into her purse, taking out a business card, and giving it to Bay. "When I git back, ya betta haf an appointment fur tomorrow mornin'!" Bee looked at her watch. "Ya 'bout ta make me late fur ma interview!" she said and rushed out the door.

Bay got up off the sofa and went to her room. She fell on her bed and cried. She didn't know what to do with her life. Savannah hadn't returned to Salem as she had promised. She was in college, majoring in business. Sadie was teaching school, and Carrie would be going off to college in two years. Bay pulled herself off the bed, walked over, and looked in the mirror like she used to do when she was a little girl. "Bay McQueen, ya got ta do somethin' wit' ya life. Ya ain't got no desire ta go ta school, but yer meant ta be somethin', else ya wouldn't be here," she said, wiping tears from her eyes and pulling the employment agency's card from her pocket. She walked over and picked up the telephone nervously. She didn't know exactly what she should say, but she assumed she should use correct English, or "talk proper" as colored folks would say.

After she dialed the number, a white woman answered. "Salem's Employment Agency. May I help you?" the woman asked in a very dignified voice.

"My name is Bay McQueen. I would like to make an appointment for tomorrow morning to discuss employment."

"What about ten o'clock?" the woman asked.

"Fine, I'll be there."

Bay could have been an actress—she sounded so professional and natural, the lady on the phone thought she was white. Bay watched so much television, she could mimic anybody she wanted to, and she often used that ability in different social settings and situations.

After Bay hung up the phone, Carrie walked in from school. "Hi, Bay, what did ya do all day besides watch de soaps?"

Bay turned around in a circle and looked at Carrie with a smile. "Miss Carrie McQueen, my dear, I'll have you know that I have an appointment at the employment agency tomorrow morning."

"Gee, Bay, dat's terrific. Maybe you'll git a real good job!" replied Carrie excitedly as she headed to the kitchen to get a snack.

Bay followed her. "What's happenin' at Carver dese days?"

"Not much. I'll be so glad when I finish." Suddenly Carrie remembered something she had heard. "Bay, guess what I heard today?"

"What wuz it?"

"Sam, ya old flame, has gone into de Air Force. Wit' so many colored guys bein' drafted 'n de Army 'n' gittin' killed, he knew he couldn't escape, 'cause he ain't blind, deaf, mentally ill, or dumb—so he signed up fur de Air Force!" said Carrie, laughing.

"I don' blame him. I know a lot of guys who died over dere," responded Bay sadly.

The girls heard Bee close the door. "Bay, Carrie, I'm home!"

The girls came out of the kitchen to greet her. "Hey, Mama, how did de interview go?" asked Carrie.

"I got de job! No more workin' 'n white folks' houses. I'll be workin' 'n de principal's office at Carver Elementary School."

"I'm sho glad it's not de high school. I would never be at peace," responded Carrie, laughing.

"Mama, I'm so happy fur ya!" said Bay.

"Did ya call de number I gave ya dis mornin'?" asked Bee.

"Yes, Mama, I sho did. I haf an appointment fur tomorrow mornin' at ten o'clock."

"Honey, gittin' a job will help ya feel good 'bout yourself. When ya go fur ya appointment, look ya best 'n' talk right."

"I know, Mama." Little did Bee know that being in the right place at the right time would give Bay just what she needed.

The next morning, Bay got out of bed at eight-thirty. Bee and Carrie had already left. It was April, and she hated getting up. However, she knew she had to keep her appointment. She took a hot bath and pulled a pretty, conservative black skirt and jacket out of the closet. *Dese clothes should help me git a job*, she thought. Then she pulled out her favorite black two-inch pumps. After laying everything on the bed, including the pearl necklace and earrings Sadie gave her for Christmas, she began getting dressed. When she finished, she looked in the mirror, combed her hair, and thought, *Bay McQueen, ya sho look mighty high-falutin'*. She looked at her clock. It was nine-fifteen, and she hadn't called a taxi. Bee had left her money for it. Immediately, she went into the foyer and made the call. About nine-forty, the taxi driver pulled up in front of the house and blew his horn. Bay rushed outside. Ten minutes later, she walked into the agency.

Bay walked up to the counter. A young white woman about twenty years of age asked, "How may I help you?"

"I'm Bay McQueen. I have an appointment to discuss employment."

"Have a seat. Someone will be with you shortly," said the young woman. *Never would have guessed she was colored*, she thought.

Bay sat down and waited about thirty minutes. She was beginning to get very impatient when a young white man about twenty-three walked over to her. "Hello, I'm Bill Durkston."

"I'm Bay McQueen."

"We'll go to my office so we can look at some jobs and decide what's suitable for you," said Bill cheerfully, thinking, *What a beauty!* Bay followed him to his office and sat in a chair in front of his desk as he began looking at her through his brilliant blue eyes. "Don't think I'm trying to act inappropriately, but have you ever been told how beautiful you are?" asked Bill.

"Course . . . ah . . . *of course* I have," stuttered Bay.

"Well, you are."

"Mr. Durkston, what about jobs?" asked Bay, changing the subject.

"You can call me Bill."

Bay smiled. *I like him. He's rather handsome!* she thought. Bill Durkston was about six feet tall, weighed 165 pounds, and had blond hair. *Salem ain't ready fur no mixin' of de races*, she thought.

"Bay, I have the right job for you. You're not the type to work in a factory. How about a job at the bank?"

"The bank? Only white folks work there."

"Times are changing. Colored preachers and consumers are threatening to boycott the bank if more colored people aren't hired," exclaimed Bill.

Bay couldn't believe what she was hearing. "I don't have any experience working in a bank."

"Don't worry. Management will be more than happy to provide training. White people don't like to lose money," said Bill, laughing. "Fill out this application, take it over to the bank, ask to see Mr. Jim Durkston, and give it to him."

After completing the application, Bay stood up. "Thank you, Mr. Durkston. I mean, *Bill*," said Bay, smiling and shaking his hand.

By this time, Bill was standing. "Bay, may I call you sometime, just to talk?"

"I don't know . . . No, I don't think so. You're a very nice person, but we're living in Salem."

"I know," he replied sadly.

"It was nice meeting you."

"Don't worry, I'll be checking on you over at the bank," said Bill.

"Bill, I'll always be grateful for your help!" replied Bay as she walked toward the door. She turned around and asked, "Is Mr. Jim Durkston related to you?"

"Yeah, that's my dad," responded Bill, smiling.

Bay forgot her professionalism. "Great smokin' Joe!" she responded. Bill laughed. He really liked her. She closed the door behind her and went across the street to the bank.

When Bee and Carrie heard the good news about Bay's new job, they were so happy and couldn't believe she would be the only colored person working at the bank. The following morning, Bay became a working woman. Her days of leisure were over. The people at the bank were nice and didn't waste any time in training Bay. She really liked the pay, but most of the time she felt out of place. There were no other colored tellers. She didn't have anybody to socialize with.

After she'd been working at the bank for three months, Bay's job became more exciting. A young white woman, about twenty, began working there. Usually Bay would take her break alone, but one morning, the young white woman walked in with a brown paper bag. "Hi, my name is Charlotte Wells!" she said, taking a seat across from Bay.

"I'm Bay McQueen." They didn't say much to each other.

Finally, Charlotte asked, "How long have you worked here?"

"I've worked here about three months."

"Do you like it here?"

"It's all right," said Bay, eating crackers with peanut butter. *Charlotte seems ta be nice, but ain't nothin' like bein' with ya own kind*, thought Bay.

"Bay, don't you think things are getting better between the races?"

"Guess it is, or I wouldn't be here, would I?" said Bay sharply.

"Bay, I know it's boring here, so why don't you join me for a movie Friday night?"

"Charlotte, you must have forgotten where we're living. This is Salem, Georgia, not California!" exclaimed Bay, rising from her seat.

"Nobody is going to tell me how to live my life. It's July 1965. Colored and white can sit together at the movies!" asserted Charlotte.

Time had come for them to return to work. "If you're willing to take a chance, I will too. Both of us might end up in jail!" said Bay, laughing, as Charlotte followed her out the door.

Charlotte picked Bay up at seven o'clock. "Hi, Bay, we're going to have a good time!" said Charlotte, smiling. They sped off in her pretty blue convertible.

"This is some car! How do you pay for this pretty thing?" asked Bay, looking around excitedly.

"My parents help me."

They arrived at the movie, bought their tickets, and entered the theater, where a lot of people were watching the movie, colored and white. They noticed Bay and Charlotte walking in. Young men began whistling and yelling, "Blackberry and vanilla!" Some shouted, "I'll take the vanilla," while others screamed, "Gimme gimme some a dat blackberry!" The whole theater rocked with laughter.

After leaving the theater, Bay and Charlotte went to the Hamburger Stand, a regular hangout for young people. While they were ordering their burgers, French fries, and milkshakes, all eyes were on them. Both of them were very pretty and shapely, with long black hair. Bay and Charlotte sat down, ate heartily, and talked about the men at the movies. When they were ready to leave, they saw a group of white guys standing very close to Charlotte's car. Bay became a little nervous. "Charlotte, why are those guys standing next to your car?"

"Oh, they're just checking it out!" replied Charlotte, smiling. When Bay and Charlotte reached her car, a tall blond guy opened the door for Charlotte. The other one was about five feet ten inches with thick black hair. He opened the door for Bay, closed it, stuck his head through the window, and said, "I do love chocolate ice cream!"

"That's mighty white of you," replied Bay, smiling. Everybody laughed. Bay and Charlotte drove off, looking through the mirror and laughing.

"Bay, that was so much fun. We had a great time. We'll have to do it again!"

Charlotte dropped Bay off at her house about ten o'clock. Bee and Carrie were still awake. They were in the kitchen waiting for her. They were curious about how things went. Bay walked into the living room and noticed Bee and Carrie in the kitchen, eating a snack.

"Bay, how did thangs go at de movies?" asked Bee.

"Charlotte 'n' I had a dynamite time!"

"That sho wuz a beautiful car Charlotte wuz driving," interrupted Carrie.

"It's all hers!"

"Do Charlotte's parents know she has a colored friend?" asked Bee.

"I really don' know, Mama," answered Bay.

"Bay, you done got ta be real high-class," said Carrie, raising her head in the air. "By de way, some guy called by de name of Durkston. He sounded mighty, mighty white ta me."

"Yes, he is white, wit' blond hair too," responded Bay sarcastically. "He's de one responsible fur gittin' me de job at de bank."

"Now he wants ta collect!" said Bee firmly.

"No, Mama, Bill 'n' I are jus' friends."

"So it's *Bill* now," teased Carrie, getting up from the table.

"Bay McQueen, watch yourself. You don' want a bad name 'n de colored community fur goin' wit' white men," said Bee sternly.

"Okay, Mama, I'm goin' ta watch it as hard as ya watch yourself 'round Mr. Singleton, the principal where ya work," said Bay, chuckling.

"Ain't a thang goin' on between me 'n' dat man," replied Bee defensively. "Bay, git outa here wit' dat trash!"

Bay ran into her bedroom laughing.

"Ev'rybody knows Mr. Singleton's reputation. De sayin' is, if it's ta be gotten, he will sho git it!" said Carrie, laughing.

"Whatcha talkin' 'bout?" asked Bee, embarrassed.

"Whatever dey call dat between a woman's legs," replied Carrie, chuckling.

Bee left the kitchen and went to her room. Carrie ran into Bay's room laughing. Finally, they went to bed.

The next morning, Bee was out of bed before nine o'clock. She was expecting Mother Caine. After getting dressed, she went into the kitchen to begin breakfast and examine the house to make sure it was presentable. Mother Caine was known for walking over the house to inspect it.

While half asleep, Bay smelled bacon, coffee, and toast. She rolled over, sprang out of bed, and went into the kitchen. "Mornin', Mama. I might be high-falutin' through de week, but ain't nothin' like ma mama's cookin'!" she said.

Bee had known Bay would show up as soon as she smelled food. "Bay, ya need ta git a bath 'n' git dressed. Mother Caine is comin' over in 'bout thirty minutes," said Bee, smiling.

"Mama, are ya serious?"

"Yes, as serious as ya are 'bout dis food."

"I really don' feel like hearin' Mother Caine's same old tune, 'Lordy have mercy on my soul, Bay, what are you doing with your life? When you going off to college like Sadie?'" said Bay, sounding just like the woman. "I'd betta go git Carrie up. Mother Caine will say, 'Bee, you mean you let Carrie stay in bed all day like that? In my day, child, we had to get up with the chickens.'" Bay left the kitchen and opened Carrie's door. "Carrie, wake up! We're havin' a visitor 'n 'bout thirty minutes. Guess who it is."

Carrie peeped out from under the covers. "Who?"

"Mother Caine is comin'!" shouted Bay as loud as she could.

Carrie jumped out of bed. "I don' feel like hearin' Mother Caine's old worn-out words, 'Carrie, you're getting a little plump.' I kin be as skinny as a straw. 'Carrie, you looking mighty plump,'" said Carrie, talking to herself.

Bay and Carrie finished dressing, went into the kitchen, and sat at the table.

"Girls, we hafta wait on Mother Caine before we eat," cautioned Bee.

At last, there was a knock at the door. Bee rushed into the living room to open it. "Hi, Mother Caine, I'm so happy ta see ya!" she said happily, giving the woman a big hug.

"I'm so glad to see you too, baby. Lord, Bee, everything looks so nice," she continued, walking over to Bee's bedroom and opening the door. "Still as nice as the first day I saw it," she said, walking into the kitchen. "There are my girls," said Mother Caine. Both got up from the table, went over, and gave her a big kiss on the cheeks. "Bay, I hear you're finally doin' something right with your life, the only colored teller at the bank. That's good! When are you going to college? You can't ever tell about white folks. They like you one minute and will chew you slap up before you know it!"

Bay didn't say a word. It wouldn't have done any good. Mother Caine always did the talking and had the last word. In the meantime, everybody sat at the table.

"Bee, this food sure looks good and smells good too. Child, you know how I just love your biscuits!" said Mother Caine, putting one in her mouth, "Um, um, this biscuit is delicious! It tastes just like the one folks used to make years ago." Bay and Carrie looked at each other, smiling. "Bee, don't you think it's about time for you to get a car?" asked Mother Caine.

"Yes, I do. I'm savin' fur un."

Bay and Carrie couldn't believe their ears. "Dat's super!" asserted both girls at the same time.

"Bay, don't you start thinking about driving your mama's car. You have a job. Buy your own car!" responded

Mother Caine sternly. "Bay, by the way, when are you going to get your own house? Child, when I was your age, I was saving money to buy me a house!" Bay and Carrie got up from the table and began removing the dishes while Mother Caine continued to talk.

Bay was tired of Mother Caine's chatter and wondered how to get the woman to close her mouth. Remembering that she liked to keep up with who died and who was sick. Bay decided to force her to change the subject. "Mama, did ya hear 'bout Mr. Sam dyin'?" asked Bay. "He's de man dat delivers wood ta white folks' houses."

"Lord, child, folks are leaving this world!" replied Mother Caine. "When it's your time, you've got to go, you've got to go! Bee, did you hear about Bertha Warren passing two weeks ago?"

"No, I didn't."

"She was eighty years old and looked just like a white woman! The folks tell me that no colored man ever looked down in her face. All of her children from white men. Well, she's gone now," exclaimed Mother. "Well, Bee, I guess I'd better be going. It takes me a while to drive to the house." She slowly got up from the table. "Before I go, I'm going to look around a little more," said Mother, heading in the direction of Bay's and Carrie's rooms. Bay and Carrie stayed behind in the kitchen, washing dishes.

"Lord, colored folks sho leavin' dis world!" said Bay, laughing. The girls laughed so hard Bay bent over on the table and tears filled Carrie's eyes. Suddenly, they heard Mother Caine and Bee coming back to the kitchen.

"Girls, Mother has to go. Come give me a hug!" She hugged and kissed both of them and then walked toward the door. "Bay, don't forget what I said. White folks are something else! Have they invited you to eat with them? Invited you to go to church with them?" asked Mother.

"Sorry to disappoint you, Mother, but Charlotte and I have eaten at the Hamburger Stand and enjoyed a movie!" said Bay, smiling.

"You what? Went where?" uttered Mother in disbelief. "Bay McQueen, you sure this girl is pure white?"

"She is very, very white!" responded Bay, laughing.

"Well, don't think you're special. Bee, honey, come walk Mother to the car," said Mother Caine.

"Yes, ma'am, I'll be glad to," responded Bee lovingly. Mother Caine was just like a mother to Bee. She had helped Bee in so many ways.

Once Mother Caine was safely inside her car, she began backing out slowly. She rolled out into the road and almost backed into the neighbors' yard across the street. Bee was standing in the yard watching in horror, but Mother hit the breaks, pulled back into the road, and took off, blowing her horn.

Bay and Carrie laughed so hard tears filled their eyes. They talked about Mother Caine and her driving for a long time.

Monday, the following morning, Bay, Bee, and Carrie left the house and went their separate ways. As always, Bay took a taxi to work. Bee got a ride from one of her coworkers, and Carrie walked to school. It was only three blocks from their house. When Bay entered the bank through the employee's entrance, she ran into Bill. "Hi, beautiful, I called you Friday night," he said.

"I heard. Charlotte and I went to see a movie. I wasn't about to call your house," she replied.

"We could go out sometime, and nobody would have to know."

"Has a brick fallen on top of your head? I'm not going to hide and sneak around with you. This town ain't ready for no race mixing!" asserted Bay. "Bill, I appreciate everything you've done for me, but we can't go out together."

"There's something beautiful and wonderful about you, and I won't give up," said Bill.

A month later, Durkston came into the bank. He wrote Bay a note and gave it to her. "Bay, I'm leaving Salem. I'm moving to Nevada. Come with me. I'll arrive at your house about eight-thirty tonight."

At eight-thirty that evening, a beautiful black car pulled into Bay's driveway. Bill got out of his car, walked onto the porch, and knocked on the door. Carrie peeped out the window. "Mama, dere's a white man knockin' at de door." Bee opened it.

"Good evening, ma'am, I'm Bill Durkston. May I speak with Bay, please?"

Who could refuse such a nice, charming young man? thought Bee. "I'm Bay's mother. Please come in."

"Nice to meet you, Mrs. McQueen."

"Carrie, go get your sister."

Shortly thereafter, Bay gracefully walked across the room. "Hi, Bill, I was very surprised about the note," she said.

"Bay, may I talk with you for a few minutes?"

"Okay, let's go outside on the porch."

After they walked on the porch, Carrie began watching them from the window. "Carrie, git yourself away frum dat window," said Bee. "Ya wouldn't want nobody tendin' ta ya business, now would ya?"

"Guess I wouldn't, Mama," responded Carrie, moving away from the window. "Boys don't like me anyway. Dey call me brain 'n' bookworm," she continued sadly.

"Dat's all right, most of dem ain't de kind ta take an interest in, no way!" said Bee, walking over to put her arms around Carrie. "Ya goin' ta be somebody, Carrie McQueen. Ya goin' off ta college ta be a big-time lawyer!" continued Bee proudly. Carrie smiled and went to her room to study. Bee went into the kitchen to fix her lunch for the next day.

Meanwhile, Bill and Bay were standing on the porch in the dark. She didn't want the neighbors to see her talking to a white man. Bill looked into Bay's light brown eyes. "Bay, come with me to Nevada. We can get married. It will be better for us out there. I love you, Bay. The first time I laid eyes on you, I wanted to get to know you," he said, moving closer to her.

She rested her head on his chest. "I like you a lot, Bill. You're the nicest guy I've ever known, but it just won't work between us. I don't want to cause no trouble. When white folks' children marry colored, they take them out of their wills and treat them like outsiders," exclaimed Bay.

"I don't care!"

"That's what you say now, but being poor doesn't feel good. I couldn't live with myself, knowing that I caused you to lose your inheritance. Bill, look at my color. There is no way I can pass for white. Most of my own people treat me like an outcast, and yours would be no different. You would be treated as if you were insane for loving and marrying a darkie."

"Guess what, Bay? I don't give a tinker's damn!" he replied sternly.

Bay looked at him with tears in her eyes. "No, Bill, I can't go. I wish I could. I wish things were different. One day you will be glad that I made this decision," said Bay softly.

"Bay, no matter what you say, I will always love you." Suddenly, they were passionately kissing. "Bay, I don't want to let you go, but I've got to get on the road," he said, releasing her reluctantly and walking toward his car. After Bill got inside his car, he waved good-bye to Bay, backed out of the driveway, and headed west. Their paths didn't cross again for many years.

Bay turned and walked inside the house slowly. Bee came out of the kitchen and noticed tears falling from Bay's eyes. "What's wrong, honey?"

"Bill has gone out west ta Nevada. He wanted me ta go wit' him," said Bay, crying in her mother's arms.

"You did de right thang. Mixed couples haf it hard. Dey end up wit' nobody but each otha, 'cause de white family don't want nothin' ta do wit' dem. Some colored folks only pretend, except dose who feel dat race-mixing give dem a certain social status."

"Oh, Mama, I wanted ta go wit' him. I b'lieve I love him. He tol' me he loved me. Mama, ain't nobody ever been so nice ta me. Bill didn't care 'bout me bein' as black as a blackberry."

"Remember what ya told me when ya daddy 'n' I had a fight before de divorce? Ya said, 'Mama, God will make thangs all right if ya trust Him.' Bay, one day ya goin' ta meet a nice colored man who's goin' ta love ya wit' ev'rything dat's 'n him."

"Mama, do ya really think so?" asked Bay, wiping her tears.

"I surely do. How could any man resist a beauty like you?"

Bay continued to work at the bank. She and Charlotte continued their friendship, but Charlotte was tired of working. She began dating Lance Coombs, the son of a very rich man in Salem. One morning in the break room, Charlotte asserted, "Bay, close your eyes real tight. I have something to show you." She pulled her hand from behind her back. "Now you can open them!"

Bay opened her eyes and cried, "Charlotte, you're engaged! When are you getting married?"

"June of next year!" replied Charlotte happily. Then she moved closer to Bay to whisper in her ear. "I won't ever have to work again." Bay knew their friendship would end when she became Mrs. Lance Coombs. Charlotte stood up. "Bay, I want you to be in my wedding. Will you be my maid of honor?"

Bay couldn't believe her ears. "Charlotte, I always have to remind you that we're living in Salem, Georgia."

"Nobody is going to tell me how to run my business. You're going to be in my wedding!" asserted Charlotte stubbornly.

"How will your parents and Lance's parents feel about it?"

Charlotte turned to check the door to make sure that nobody was coming in. "I hear that old man Coombs had a colored mistress until she died. He paid for all three of their children's college expenses, and my parents don't care. So don't you worry," exclaimed Charlotte, bursting into laughter.

June 1966 was a very busy month for Bay. She had to attend both Carrie's graduation and Charlotte's wedding.

THE WOUNDED WHOLE

The graduation was Sunday, June 10, and Charlotte was getting married in two weeks. Of course, Carrie was valedictorian, which was no surprise to anybody. Sadie and her daughter were coming home for the ceremony. They had not visited Salem in five years. Bay was so excited. She kept looking out the window. Finally, she went into the kitchen where Bee was baking sweet-potato pies. "Mama, where's Carrie?"

"She went ta de midget's shop ta buy a dress fur Sara."

"Mama, ya know sweet-potato pie 'n' I kin't live under de same roof!" said Bay, walking over to the counter with a knife.

"Bay, don' ya dare cut dat pie till Sadie gets here!"

"Sadie ain't no company!" cried Bay, running out of the kitchen with a slice of pie in her mouth.

She heard a knock at the door. "Who is it?" asked Bay. Nobody answered. She opened it and walked on the porch with her hands on her hips. "Carrie McQueen, ya might as well come inside 'n' stop playin'!" said Bay firmly. Still, nobody responded. As Bay turned to go inside, she heard a loud whistle.

Before she realized it, Sadie, Sara, and Carrie were all over her. "Bay, we fooled ya. I wish ya could haf seen yourself tryin' ta be so grown, like ya own de world!" said Carrie, laughing.

"I am a full-grown woman with the world in my hands!" responded Bay, laughing.

By now, Bee was on the porch hugging and kissing Sara and Sadie. "Sadie, I'm so glad ta see ya. Ya look so putty! Now, jus' look at ma little lady," said Bee, looking at Sara, who was now five. Taking Sara's hand, Bee walked with her into the kitchen as Bay, Carrie, and Sadie followed.

"I can't believe our baby sister is goin' off ta college. We've come a long way," said Sadie with a smile.

"Sadie, I'm so glad you could come out two weeks early for the big party we're giving Carrie!" said Bay.

"Didn't come home just to sit around, drink lemonade, and talk about old times. Our sister is valedictorian, and that calls for a celebration!" cried Sadie.

The party was held the Saturday after Sadie's arrival at Oak Woods Community Center. Everybody had such a great time.

Carrie's graduation was such a colorful event. She was adorned in the beautiful blue and gold colors. The entire family, including Mother Caine, looked on with joy and excitement as Carrie walked across the stage to receive her diploma. The principal handed her the microphone to give a talk. When Carrie finished, just about everybody stood up and started clapping.

Two weeks later, on a beautiful Sunday afternoon, Bay was standing next to Charlotte as her maid of honor, looking more beautiful than ever. The entire audience was in awe over Bay's beauty. Evidently, they didn't believe anyone as dark as Bay could be so beautiful. Well, the wedding ended as quickly as it began, and Charlotte and Lance went off to Niagara Falls for their honeymoon. Three days later, Sadie and Sara returned to Astoria.

After the couple returned to Salem, Charlotte and Bay kept in touch. One night, Charlotte called Bay to say she would be moving to Galveston, Florida, a large city thirty-five miles away. "Bay, I don't want to go!" said Charlotte, crying.

"You've got to go. You're a married woman now, and what your husband says goes," replied Bay. "Listen, Charlotte, Galveston is only thirty-five miles away from here. We can still call each other and visit sometimes."

"I know, but I feel like a bird in a cage."

"Lord, Charlotte, y'all only been married three months!" said Bay, laughing.

"Bay, I can't talk anymore. Lance is coming. I've got to go!"

Bay had never heard Charlotte sound so fearful. Suddenly, Bay had a strong feeling that Charlotte was in trouble. *I hope Charlotte is all right*, thought Bay.

In September of 1966, Bay began receiving letters from her old boyfriend, Sam Ellis. Usually, Carrie would get the mail out of the box, but she had gone off to college. Bay really missed her and began getting really restless living at home. She reached into the mailbox and pulled out a letter from Sam. *Why on earth is he writin' me?* she thought. She walked back inside the house, opened the letter, and sat down on the sofa to read it.

It started, "Hi, Bay, bet you're surprised to hear from me. I never apologized for the way I acted." Bay didn't get any further than that. She closed the letter and went to her room, threw it into the trash basket, and lay on her bed. She felt really tired and disgusted. She'd been at the bank for almost two years. *Ev'rybody I've ever loved or cared fur has lef' me 'n dis one-horse, do-nothin' town. Why kin't I move on!* she thought, getting off the bed. She walked over and pulled Sam's letter out of the trash.

Three weeks later, another letter arrived. Bay began writing him back. Soon they were writing each other every week. Six weeks later, Bay received the surprise of her life. After picking up the mail, she noticed a large envelope from Sam. She opened it and began reading it. "Bay, I have never stopped loving you. Will you marry me? I will be home in four weeks." Bay couldn't believe what she was reading. She could hardly wait for her mother to get home, she was so excited. Finally, Bee walked through the front door. "Mama, I'm so glad yer home! Guess what? Sam wants ta marry me!" cried Bay excitedly.

"I don' think he's de right one fur ya. Haf ya forgotten how bad he treated ya?"

"He has changed!" replied Bay happily. "If I marry him, I kin leave Salem 'n' begin a new life!"

"Bay, ya kin't depend on nobody else ta live ya life," replied Bee.

"Mama, kin't ya see, dis is ma chance ta haf a real life! I hate ta disappoint ya, but I'm goin' ta marry Sam!"

"Whatever ya decide," responded Bee reluctantly. She really didn't feel good about it.

Sam's time in the military ended. He returned home and married Bay. They rented a small white house in Salem. Bay loved being in her own home, although it was not as elegant as her family's house. She still worked at the bank, but Sam couldn't ever find a suitable job. He wasn't about to settle for just anything. Bay didn't know what to do. *Hopefully things will work out*, she thought.

One night, about three months later, Bay decided it was time for them to talk. Sam was in the kitchen. Bay walked in. "Sam, can we talk?"

"Don't you start nagging me," he replied.

"When are you going to get a job? I'm the only one working."

He stood up and shouted, "I told you not to nag me, and I mean it!" He walked out of the room.

"I wish to hell I'd never married!" cried Bay angrily.

Five months passed, and nothing got better. It was August 1967, and Bay was still the only one working. If that wasn't bad enough, she discovered she was pregnant. She became distraught. *What am I goin' ta do about money ta take care of a baby?* she thought. Bay didn't want to discuss her marital problems with her parents. Both were not pleased with her decision to marry. However, after agonizing over the situation, she decided to talk to her mother.

Bee greeted Bay at the door. Bay started crying. "Oh, Mama, I wish I had never married Sam. I'm so unhappy. He won't work. No job is ever good enough fur him. I cook, feed, 'n' give him a place to live. Now I'm goin' ta haf a baby. What am I goin' ta do wit' a baby?"

"Love it," responded Bee.

"Oh, Mama, what's wrong wit' me? Why can't my life be like Sadie's 'n' Carrie's lives? I'm still in Salem, wit' a baby on de way, a dead-end job, 'n' a sorry, no-good nigger called a husband!"

"Calm down, chile. Dis doesn't help de situation none. Let me remind ya of what Big Mama tol' me when ya daddy 'n' I wuz fightin' ev'ry weekend. If I want betta, I must *be* betta," said Bee.

"Guess Big Mama wuz right. It's really up ta me. I need ta change. Now it's time ta think 'bout de baby. I should've listened ta ya. How could two confused folks make a happy marriage?"

Bay walked over to the door to leave. "There's somethin' I'm s'posed ta be doin'. I'm really not livin' de life I desire. If I were, I'd be happy. Mayb' I should've jumped into Winding River."

"Don' ya ever let me hear ya say dat ya should've committed suicide; ev'rything yer goin' through is gittin' ya ready!" said Bee sternly.

"Goodnight, Mama," said Bay as she walked out, closing the door behind her.

When Bay arrived home, Sam wasn't there. She prepared dinner and thought about being a mother. *If Sadie did it, I kin too*, thought Bay. Just then the phone rang, and as if the thought had conjured her up, Sadie was at the other end. "Sadie, I'm so glad ta hear ya voice," said Bay, tears running down her cheeks. "Sadie, I'm goin' ta have a baby. Sam 'n' I ain't doin' good at all. Mama tol' ya de whole story?"

Sadie told her things would be fine and invited her to come to Astoria for a visit.

"Sadie, thanks so much fur inviting me ta visit. Sister, I love ya," said Bay. Then she said good-bye and hung up the phone. She finished cooking and looked at the clock, which read eight o'clock. *Usually Sam is home by now*, thought Bay. Finally she sat down and ate supper alone. Afterward she washed the dishes, took her bath, and went to bed. The following morning, she had to be at the bank an hour early for a meeting.

Upon rising, Bay noticed that Sam had not been home. She became concerned and called his parents to find out if he stayed with them. "Hello, Mrs. Ellis, is Sam there?"

"Ah . . . ah . . . he was, but he's not here now," she replied hesitantly.

Bay could tell she was lying. "Well, Mrs. Ellis, I tell you what, when you see Sam, tell him not to ever come back to my house ever again! Furthermore, tell him to come pick up all of his junk off my front porch, and I will be seeing a lawyer tomorrow to divorce him. Can you remember to give your baby boy this message?" continued Bay, angrily slamming the receiver down on the phone.

The next day, Bay did exactly as she'd said. She put all of Sam's belongings on the porch and made an appointment to see a lawyer to file for a divorce. Four weeks later, the marriage was over. Of course, it was really over before it began.

I'm glad ta be a free woman again. I don' need Sam or anyone else ta help me take care of ma baby, and no man will ever enslave me again! thought Bay.

Saturday morning about ten o'clock, Bee called Bay and told her to get dressed; she'd be over to visit to show her a wonderful surprise.

Wonder what de surprise is, thought Bay. She rolled out of bed and began getting herself together. Soon it was ten o'clock. She heard a knock on the door and anxiously opened it. "Mama, come on in. Where's de surprise?" asked Bay excitedly.

"It's outside," replied Bee, smiling.

Bay looked out the window and saw a beautiful red-and-white Chevy. "Great smokin' Joe!" shouted Bay. "Mama, is dat ya car?"

"All mine," replied Bee proudly.

"Mama, can we go fur a ride?" asked Bay happily. After getting into the car, Bay forgot her problems. Over the years, Bay and her mother had grown closer.

In May of 1968, Bay gave birth to a healthy eight-pound boy. She named him Zachary. She was out of work for six weeks. The bank administrators were so nice to her. They gave her six weeks of maternity leave with pay, which helped her to remain in her little cottage.

While sitting on the couch nursing Zachary, Bay heard a knock at the door. She walked over and opened it. Sam's mother was standing there with a big watermelon smile. Bay started to slam the door in her face and push her off the porch, but she wouldn't allow her dark side to take over. "Hello, Mrs. Ellis," said Bay hesitantly.

"Bay, I would like to see my grandson. May I come in for just a few minutes?"

"Yes."

"May I hold him? He looks just like Sam when he was a baby."

"I hope he won' be nothing like him!" said Bay sharply.

Mrs. Ellis began to cry. "Bay, I'm so sorry about everything that has happened. My husband and I did the best we could to raise him right," she said sorrowfully.

"I'm sure you did, but I can't understand why y'all are always protecting him, even when he's wrong!"

"I know we spoiled him, but I'm damn tired of him now!"

Bay was surprised to hear her cuss. *Sometimes it takes folks gittin' mad enough ta make a change,* thought Bay.

"Bay, don't hold the past against me. Please let me come over to see my grandson sometimes," she pleaded.

"I will," Bay responded compassionately. She took Zachary out of Mrs. Ellis's arms. "Sorry, but it's time for his nap."

"All right, I'll see you next week," responded Mrs. Ellis, and she walked out the door. Bay didn't want to prevent her from spending time with Zachary, but she sure didn't want her to ruin him like she did Sam.

When Bay had to go back to work, Bee was on vacation for two weeks, so she took care of Zachary. After Bee returned to work, Mother Caine would become his babysitter. One afternoon while Bee was feeding Zachary, the doorbell rang. She walked over to open it. There stood a man with a beard.

"Miss McQueen?" asked the man.

"Yes, I'm Bee McQueen."

"Guess you don't remember me without my suit, and now I have a beard."

"My goodness, Rev. Albertson, how on earth are you doing? It's been about eight years!" said Bee excitedly. "Please come in."

"Whose little bundle of joy?" asked Jack, smiling.

"My daughter Bay's."

Jack took a seat at Bee's request. Suddenly they began staring into each other's eyes.

"Bee, I've never forgotten you. I can't explain it. Have you remarried?" asked Jack.

"No, I haven't. I haven't thought much about it. Are you in a revival in Salem?"

"No, I'm just visiting. I live over in Galveston," said Jack.

"Really, what church are you pastoring now?"

"I'm no longer pastoring. I'm no longer married. I'm divorced. It should've happened years ago," he said. "Living a lie takes a lot of energy. I had gotten to the place I had none. Now I'm happy. I teach at Galveston Community College. I had to come to Salem, so I decided to find you. I looked up your address in the phone book. Here I am! How about going out to dinner with me next Saturday night?" he asked.

"I hope not here in Salem," replied Bee.

"No, no, I know a very nice place in Galveston."

"Can colored people eat there?"

"Sure, colored people own it."

"Okay, I'll go. What time do you want me to be ready?" she asked, watching her grammar.

"Will six o'clock be all right?"

"It will be just fine!"

With that, he stood up, and Bee followed him as he walked to the door. "I'll see you next Saturday," said Jack, walking out the door.

After he left, Bee stood at the window and watched him as he got inside his car. *Am I dreamin', or is dis really real?* she thought.

Two hours later, Bay walked through the front door. "Hi, Mama, how was ya day?"

Bee walked into the living room from the kitchen. "Bay, ya wouldn't believe what happened ta me today."

"Hello, Mama's little Zack-Zack," said Bay, taking the baby out of Bee's arms and kissing him.

"Bay, yer not listenin' ta me," Bee said.

"I am listenin'," replied Bay, now looking her mother straight in the eyes.

"Guess who came by ta see me today?"

"Who?" Bay loved surprises.

"Rev. Albertson!" said Bee, beaming.

"Wow, that was a real shocker!"

"He's coming over Saturday night to take me out for dinner in Galveston," said Bee happily.

"Mama, have ya forgotten, Rev. Albertson is a married man?"

"He used ta be married. He's divorced," said Bee happily.

"If dat's de case, I think ya should. Ya wuz always attracted ta him."

The phone rang. Bee walked over and picked it up. "Hello," she said.

"Mama, what are you doing?" asked the voice on the other end.

"Carrie, honey, how are ya?" asked Bee. "Bay 'n' Zack are fine . . . You are? When? . . . Next Friday? Okay, we'll pick ya up at de train station," said Bee, and she hung up the phone. "Bay, Carrie is coming home ta see Zack."

"Dat is super. I kin hardly wait ta see Little Sister," said Bay happily. Carrie had not been home in two years. Whether Bay and Bee were prepared or not, Little Sister had changed.

CHAPTER FIVE

It was August of 1968. Bay and Bee arrive at the train station early to pick up Carrie. They were quite excited. Suddenly the train pulled in and stopped. They quickly walked outside, anxiously waiting for Carrie. The conductor opened the door and placed steps for the passengers to come down on. As the conductor cautioned the line of passengers to watch their step, Carrie appeared. Bee and Bay were amazed and shocked at her appearance. Suddenly, Carrie saw them and yelled, "Mama! Mama! Bay! Bay! I'm so glad to see you!" Looking at Zachary in Bay's arms, Carrie said, "Li'l Zack, how ya doin', baby boy? You are too cute!" and gave him a big kiss. Then she gave Bee and Bay a big hug and kiss. Finally, she noticed that both her mother and sister looked very stunned. "Mama, you and Bay act like y'all just seen a ghost. It's me, Little Sister, remember? I just look different," said Carrie defensively.

"I'll say you do," uttered Bay, smiling.

"Why ya wearing ya hair bushy like that? Lord haf mercy, jus' look at dem clothes," said Bee.

"Mama, it's the style. Everybody is wearing afros."

"What de world comin' ta? Ya done gone off ta college 'n' come home lookin' like a African," said Bee sorrowfully.

"Carrie, you have made Mama forget how to talk proper," said Bay, laughing. "Anyway, Mama, it don't look that bad. I kinda like it," exclaimed Bay cheerfully.

"What's wrong with looking like an African? That's where we came from. Blacks in America have an identity problem. Maybe I should have stayed in California," said Carrie.

"Let's not air our dirty laundry here at the train station. Wait until we get home and continue this conversation over some food. I'm hungry," said Bay, carrying Zachary toward the car.

The McQueen women and little Zack reached the house. While Carrie unpacked, Bee prepared supper, and they sat down to try to enjoy their meal together.

"I don' mean ta act hoggish, but dere's nothin' like good old home-cooked food. I haven't had food dat taste dis good since leavin' home," said Carrie.

Looking at Carrie's hair, Bee said, "Honey, I'm sorry I keep lookin' at ya hair, but I jus' got ta git used ta it."

"It's okay, Mama. Ya mus' learn ta look beyond clothes, hair, 'n' all dat. Like mos' colored folks, ya concept of beauty has been influenced by de slave master."

"I like it. How can I git ma hair like that?" asked Bay excitedly.

"Wait jus' a minute," said Bee. "You don' wanta mess around 'n' lose ya job 'cause of hair. If white folks see ya walk through dose bank doors wit' ya hair like dat, ya will be history."

"It's not 'bout Bay's job. You work at a black school, but yer still lettin' de slave master define fur ya what beauty is," said Carrie. Suddenly, Carrie saw Zack lying on the sofa; she got up from the table singing, "I'm proud ta be black." She went over and put Zack on her lap, singing louder and clapping, "I'm proud ta be black, ain't dat right. I'm proud ta be black, ain't dat right."

Bay joined in, turning around and clapping, "I'm proud ta be black, hey, ain't dat right, ain't dat right." Bee shook her head, removing the dishes from the table. The telephone rang. Bay ran over and grabbed it. "Hello," she shouted. "One moment. Mama, it's Mr. Albertson."

"Hi, Jack . . . Six-thirty will be fine." She hung up the phone.

"Mama, are you 'n' Mr. Albertson still goin' out tomorrow night?" asked Bay.

"Yes, we are," said Bee, beaming.

Carrie jumped up, put her hands on her hips, closed her eyes, and said jokingly, "I kin't believe it. You mean you're dating at your age!" Bay laughed hysterically. "Who is dis Mr. Albertson?" continued Carrie.

"It's Rev. Albertson, remember? De man Mama met on de train when we went ta Big Mama's funeral?" interrupted Bay.

"Before ya ask, he's not married, nor is he a reverend either," responded Bee.

As she walked into the kitchen, Carrie laughed and said, "Mama, remember—keep ya dress down 'n' panties up."

"Lord, Carrie, ya ain't got a bit of sense. Don't ya worry 'bout me 'n' Jack; we're grown 'n' know how ta carry ourselves," replied Bee.

Suddenly there was a knock at the door. "Who's dere?" cried Bay, walking over to the door. She turned on the porch light and peeped through the window but didn't see a thing. Carrie got up off the sofa carrying Zack, walked over, and opened the door. She didn't see a thing. "Guess we're hearin' thangs," said Bay, closing the door. As they turned to walk away, they heard another knock at the door and another one, only louder.

By this time, Bee had come out of the kitchen. "What's goin' on in here?"

"Somebody keeps knockin', but when we open de door, nobody's dere," said Carrie.

"Bet it's de Willis's bad youngun'," responded Bee, walking toward the door and opening it. When she did, there stood Sadie, Sara, and Mack Martin, Big Mama's neighbor, who had picked them up at the station for her funeral.

"Sadie, Sadie, Sadie, Sara, Sara!" shouted Bee, Bay, and Carrie.

"What a surprise!" cried Bay.

"Oh, look at li'l Zachary," said Sadie excitedly. "He is so handsome, and de first boy in the family." Sadie grabbed Carrie and gave her a big hug, "You look wonderful wit' ya afro."

"Aunt Carrie, can I get my hair like yours?" said Sara, smiling.

"Sadie, what a surprise! When we talked, ya said ya couldn't come home," exclaimed Bee.

"Mama, don' always believe what I say. Ya know I wouldn't miss seein' Carrie."

They were so overwhelmed and surprised about seeing Sadie, they forgot about Mack Martin. He made himself comfortable, observing the McQueens.

Suddenly, Bee realized a guest was present. Looking at the man who was now seated, Bee extended her hand and asked, "We've met before, haven't we?"

Now standing, Mack said, "We certainly have. I picked you up at the train station for Big Mama's funeral."

"I remember. You're Mr. Martin, with the red Thunderbird," said Bee.

Sara walked over and stood beside him. "Daddy, may I have some ice cream tomorrow?"

"Sure, honey."

"Daddy?" Bee said softly, looking confused. "Mr. Martin, aren't you married?"

"I'm divorced."

Sadie walked over quickly. "Mama, don't give Mack the third degree. I'll explain everything later. For now, let's just enjoy each other."

"I agree," said Bay, smiling. "Anyway, Mama got ta git herself together fur tomorrow night. She's goin' on a date wit' Rev. Albertson."

"What your church goin' ta say 'bout you datin'? Wait till Mother Caine finds out," said Sadie, laughing.

"Can't we invite her over before I leave Sunday?" asked Carrie excitedly.

"Lord, Carrie, I kin't wait till she lays her eyes on ya hair," said Bay, smiling.

Before going to bed, Bee called Mother Caine and invited her over for Sunday dinner.

Saturday night, Bee and Jack kept their date as planned. She enjoyed the drive to Galveston. They talked a lot about everything except sex. Finally, they arrived at the restaurant. A waiter led them to their table. Bee couldn't believe she and Jack were having dinner together, and at a colored restaurant. *Seems as if we're moving up in de world, as Mother Caine would say*, thought Bee.

"Sir, are you ready to order?" asked the waiter.

"Yes."

After ordering, they just sat and looked into each other's eyes. Suddenly, Bee felt him touch her hand and then hold it. "Jack, don't let go," she said softly.

"I won't," he said, and he leaned over and kissed her on the cheeks and then the lips.

Then they heard the waiter. "Sir, your order is ready."

Two hours later, Jack and Bee left the restaurant. When they reached the car, he opened the door for her and said warmly, "Bee, I'd like to show you my home before we head back to Salem."

"I . . . I guess so."

"You're not afraid, are you, babe?" asked Jack, smiling.

"Of course not. I just don't want nothing to happen we both will regret."

"It won't, I promise. Anyway, I'm no longer a preacher, so the devil won't bother me as much." Both laughed as they drove off.

Finally, they reached Jack's house. He lived near his job at the college. "Jack, this is a nice neighborhood," said Bee.

"I really like it. Just wish you were here with me."

"Jack, it's mighty nice of you to say that. You're a sweetheart."

Before she realized it, Jack was pulling into his driveway and then his garage. It was a beautiful, elegant brick house with a very pretty lawn and lots of beautiful flowers. "Do you take care of your own lawn? It's so nice."

"Sure do," responded Jack proudly.

Now inside the house, Jack invited Bee to sit down. "May I get you some dessert? I have cake, pie, and ice cream," said Jack.

"No, no, no, I am about to pop," said Bee, smiling.

"Well, what about a kiss?" said Jack, sitting next to her.

Before she could say anything, she felt his lips touching hers. Without hesitation, they were kissing passionately. She wanted him as much as he wanted her, but she remembered Carrie's words: *Keep your dress down and panties up*. "No, Jack, please, I can't."

"Why, baby, why?"

Looking at him and smiling, Bee explained, "I promised the girls I'd keep my dress down and panties up."

All Jack could do was laugh. "Okay, okay, well, will you marry me?"

"Marry you! When, where—wait, let me think about it, no—I mean yes. Jack, I love you."

"I love you too. I've never forgotten you. Let me take you home. I can't wait to see the McQueen women's faces when they hear the news."

"We can't tell them tonight," exclaimed Bee. "Let's break the news at Sunday dinner. Everybody will be there, even Mother Caine." Jack put his arms around her, and they left his place.

Jack dropped Bee off at one-thirty a.m. He walked her to the door and kissed her goodnight. When Bee unlocked the door and walked inside, Bay, Carrie, and Sadie were sitting on the couch, looking at her. "I had de best time of ma life," said Bee, smiling and turning around like a girl.

"What were y'all doin' all dis time?" said Sadie, smiling and looking at her watch.

Opening the Bible, Carrie asked, laughing, "Y'all didn't do no fornicatin', did ya, Mama?"

Bay, looking straight in Bee's eyes, said, "You did remember to keep ya dress down 'n' ya panties up, didn't ya?" Everybody just roared with laughter.

"For a while, it got so hot I almost pulled off all ma clothes!" shouted Bee, laughing while walking into her bedroom. The three sisters fell on the couch screaming with laughter.

The McQueens were so happy to be together again. The following morning, Bee got up early to prepare Sunday's big dinner. It was huge. Bay, Sadie, and Carrie helped her. Bee was planning to have so much good food: sweet-potato pie, banana pudding, greens, ham, turkey, homemade rolls, lemonade, green beans, and macaroni and cheese.

"Mama, I hope Mother Caine don' make herself sick eating too much sweet-potato pie and greens," said Bay, laughing.

"You know she has a healthy appetite and is always talkin' 'bout how I've gained weight," interrupted Carrie, laughing.

"Jus' leave Mother alone. She's not here ta defend herself," responded Bee, smiling.

Sadie was sitting at the table, cutting celery, and Bay said, "Sadie, you might as well git ready, she's goin' ta question ya 'bout Mr. Martin."

"She's not de only one who wants ta question me 'bout Mack, isn't dat right, Mama?" asked Sadie, smiling.

Sunday, about one-thirty, Mother Caine rang the doorbell, and Sadie answered it. "Mother Caine, it's so good ta see you," said Sadie, reaching over and giving her a big hug and a kiss.

"Lord, child, you sure are as pretty as a picture. Looking more like your mama every day," said Mother Caine, walking beside Sadie and holding her hand. Suddenly, she noticed Mr. Martin sitting on the couch holding Sara. "How do you do?" said Mother Caine.

"Mack Martin," interrupted Sadie.

"How are you, Mr. Martin?" asked Mother.

"Fine, Mother Caine," said Mack.

"Lord, even *you* know me. I know they been talkin' 'bout me," said Mother, smiling and walking away from Mack, still holding Sadie's hand and moving toward the kitchen. She whispered in Sadie's ear, "He's a fine-looking man."

Finally, Sadie and Mother reached the kitchen. "Bee, it's so nice of you to invite Mother to dinner. Help me sit down. Ain't as young as I used to be." Bee made room for her at the table. "Bee, how was your date last night? You didn't forget your manners, did you?" Mother asked, laughing.

"No, ma'am, I didn't."

"Where is that Carrie? I sure want to see that child going to law school, and so smart. One day she's gonna make Salem proud. Bee, did you know Carrie will be the first colored lawyer from Salem?" exclaimed Mother Caine.

"No, I didn't," said Bee, preparing the food with Sadie's help.

"Bee, where is Carrie? Carrie! Carrie! Come in this kitchen," yelled Mother Caine, looking around. Suddenly, Bay and Carrie appeared. "Lord, Carrie, you got one of them new afros. Can't turn on the TV unless I see afros. Never thought I'd see a colored person with hair looking like that! Bee, when children go off to college, ain't no tellin' what they goin' to look like when they come home," said Mother sadly.

Bay could hardly contain herself. She was about to burst into laughter.

"I plan to let it grow longer and thicker," said Carrie jokingly.

"Lord, Bee, what you got to say 'bout Carrie's hair?" asked Mother.

"I was shocked, but I decided ta try ta look beyond hair 'n' clothes 'n' see de heart," said Bee.

Changing the subject, Mother said, "Bee, everything looks so nice. I smell some good collard greens and sweet-potato pie. Lord, child, you know exactly what Mother likes to eat."

While Mother Caine and the McQueens were in the kitchen, the doorbell rang, "That must be Jack," said Bee, and she walked quickly to the door. "Jack, sweetheart, come in," she said, embracing him. Immediately, she introduced him to Mack Martin and took him into the kitchen to meet Mother Caine and greet Sadie and her sisters. "Mother, this is Jack Albertson," said Bee.

"Hello, Mr. Albertson, sure is nice meeting you. You and Bee had a nice time last night? I hear she's been smiling ever since," said Mother Caine, laughing.

"Jack, you remember Sadie and Carrie, don't you?" asked Bee.

"Of course, no one could ever forget the McQueen women," replied Jack, smiling. The girls smiled back.

"Okay, let's go into the dining room for dinner. I'll help Mother Caine," said Bee.

"No, Bee, let Mr. Albertson help me," said Mother Caine, smiling. Bay and Carrie looked at each other and grinned.

They all reached the dining room and took their seats. Jack seated Mother Caine next to him. Bee smiled and sat at the head of the table. "Jack, would you please bless the food?" she asked.

After the blessing, as usual Mother took center stage. "Lord, Bee, the food looks so good and smells good too." She opened her mouth and put a big scoop of potato salad in it. "If this salad tasted any better, I don't think I could stand it! God sure loves us to give us such good food."

"I'm so glad you're enjoying the salad," said Bee.

"Mama, pass the rolls," said Bay.

"Mr. Martin, I thought I heard Sara call you Daddy, so you're the one Sadie's been keeping a secret?" questioned Mother Caine.

Before Mr. Martin could answer, Bay interrupted. "Guess what I heard at the bank the other day? Mr. Sutton's daughter committed suicide!"

"What?" shouted Bee.

"Some think she didn't really kill herself. They believe her husband did it," continued Bay.

"Do they have any proof?" asked Carrie.

"Sort of. They found her hanging on the inside of the closet door, but there was no chair or stool. Folks at the bank said he was having an affair and had recently bought a big insurance policy."

"Sounds like a great case for somebody," said Sadie.

"Lord, ain't no tellin' what happened," said Mother Caine. "Poor child. I been tellin' y'all, white folks will do anything to get rid of you, and that includes killing you off!"

"Mother, all white folks don't do harm to people," exclaimed Bay.

"Lord, Bay, just 'cause you work with 'em don't mean they love you enough not to eat you slap up!" responded Mother Caine jokingly.

"It's time to change the subject to more pleasant conversation. I have a very important announcement to make," said Bee, smiling. The girls looked at each other. "Jack, would you like to do it?" continued Bee.

Jack stood up. "To the McQueen women, Mother Caine, Mr. Martin. I've asked Bee to marry me, and I hope that you will wish us well. I've been in love with her for a long time. As a matter of fact, I fell in love with her the first time I laid eyes on her." He sat down.

Mother Caine struggled to her feet and began clapping. "Bee, this is a blessing. This is a real man! Lord, if I were twenty years younger, I'd marry you, Mr. Albertson!" Mother leaned over to give him a kiss.

"Mama, I'm so happy for you," said Sadie and Carrie.

Bay looked rather shocked. "Oh, my goodness, this means I'll be left here in Salem," she said sadly.

"We haven't set a date yet," said Bee.

"Bay, nobody is leaving you here. You *choose* to stay," said Sadie.

"Be happy for Mama. Now maybe you'll discover the real Bay," said Carrie lovingly.

Suddenly, Bay tried to act more mature. She walked over to Bee and Jack. "Mr. Albertson, I'm really happy for you and Mama. She deserves to be happy."

"Bay, I think you're finally growing up. You're not the only one God is concerned about," said Bee lovingly.

While everyone was standing except Mack and Sara, Jack reached into his pocket, pulled out a small box, and took Bee's hand. "Bee, will you please marry me?"

"Oh, Jack, it's so beautiful!"

"I'm glad you like it."

Everybody clapped. Clapping and smiling, Mother Caine said, "Lord, never thought I'd live to see Bee get married again. You had a hard life, trying to do right and raise your girls with LC." Mother Caine pulled a handkerchief out of her pocket and began wiping the tears from her eyes.

"Don't cry, Mother. You're goin' to make me cry," said Sadie, wiping her eyes. Then Carrie began wiping hers.

Bay, mimicking Mother Caine, said, "Lordy, y'all, ain't God good? Never thought I'd see this day!"

"Bay McQueen, I know you imitating me!" said Mother Caine, laughing. She hit Bay on the fanny.

An hour later, Mother Caine had to leave. "I ain't had such a good time in a long time, but now it's time for Mother to go. Girls, y'all come walk Mother to the car." Looking over at Mack and Sara, still seated at the table, she said, "Mr. Martin, hope you visit Salem again real soon. Sadie, he's got a lot of class." Then she whispered in Sadie's ear, "Class can't pay the bills. He got any money?"

Sadie smiled. Mother continued, "Lord, that youngun looks just like him. Come on, girls, walk with me." Bay, Sadie, and Carrie began following Mother. Mother Caine stopped to give Bee and Jack a big kiss. She pulled Bee off to herself and whispered, "Do everything Mother would like to do," and left laughing. "Come on, girls, before I fall on the floor."

Mother Caine and the McQueen women reached her car. Bay opened the door. "Lord, Bay, you're getting prettier and prettier every time I see you. Don't matter, 'cause you're black as a blackberry," said Mother Caine, kissing her on the cheek. "Carrie, hold my purse. Can't do too many things at one time," said Mother, smiling.

"You can't prove that by me. The way you were looking at Mack and flirting with Mr. Albertson," said Carrie, laughing.

"Girls, you quit that foolishness," said Mother Caine, laughing heartily.

By this time, Mother was seated in her car.

"Now, Mother Caine, don't you go driving ninety miles an hour down the road. I don't wanta have to get you out of jail," said Sadie, laughing.

Finally, Bay closed the door and Carrie handed Mother her purse. "Mother, you drive carefully. I better not come over there and find no man in your bed either," said Bay jokingly. Mother laughed, cranked up her car, and backed out of the driveway and across the road, almost hitting the curb in front of the neighbor's house. She pulled it back in the road and drove off, honking her horn. The McQueen sisters smiled and waved good-bye.

Before Sadie returned to Astoria, she decided to tell her family about her affair. Everyone had gone except the McQueens. Mack and Sara were at Mrs. Lizzie's Boarding House. Colored folks did not stay in hotels. While Bee and her daughters were cleaning the kitchen and putting food away, Sadie said, "Mama, I need ta tell y'all something." Everybody stopped, looked at each other, and sat at the table. "I know y'all are real curious 'bout Mack 'n' me."

"Yes, I am," said Bee. Bay and Carrie just sat quietly.

"When Big Mama became ill, he was always dere ta help do whatever we needed done. When I moved in wit' her, I didn't know how ta drive, so she used ta take me where I needed ta go, or I'd catch de bus. When she got sick, she wasn't able ta drive me 'round anymore. Mack used ta take me places, 'n' he taught me ta drive."

"Didn't ya know he wuz married?" asked Bee.

"Yes, Mama, 'n' I never intended ta fall 'n love wit' him. It jus' happened. Den I got pregnant. I was so scared 'n' felt very guilty."

Bee put her arms around her daughter. "Honey, we all make mistakes."

"Sadie, don' feel bad. Nobody kin judge you. I don' know what I would haf done in de same situation," said Carrie.

"Seems like Mack really loves you. At least ya didn't git mixed up wit' somebody like ma ex-husband," said Bay reassuringly.

"Are ya gittin' married?" asked Bee.

"No, I'm not ready," responded Sadie.

"What ya mean, ya not ready? Y'all just goin' ta live together?" said Bee, somewhat agitated.

"Yes," said Sadie confidently, folding her arms.

"Mama, in case ya forgot, Sadie is grown, 'n' me too! What 'bout ya, Carrie McQueen?" said Bay with a big watermelon smile.

"Bay McQueen, if you don' hush ya smart mouth, I'm goin' ta knock ya all de way ta New York City," yelled Bee.

Bay and Carrie laughed and moved out of Bee's way. "Calm down, Mama!" said Sadie. "I am grown, 'n' ya ain't goin' ta live ma life. If I remember correctly, you had a hard time livin' yours. I love ya, Mama, but ya gotta let me be me!" said Sadie firmly.

"Okay, Sadie," said Bee.

Noticing that Bee had calmed down, Bay and Carrie moved closer. "If somebody ask me ta marry, I'm not interested. I am definitely not interested 'n bein' somebody's property," said Carrie.

"I can't b'lieve what I'm hearing," responded Bee.

"Mama, if you wanta get married, you haf our blessings. We jus' don' wanta be some man's yo-yo," said Bay.

"Amen," asserted Carrie.

Six o'clock the next morning, Bay, Bee, and Carrie said good-bye to Sadie, Sara, and Mack. "Miss McQueen, I certainly enjoyed my visit, and the food was wonderful," said Mack.

"Bay, you 'n' Carrie stay out of trouble," said Sadie, smiling, as she got into the car.

"Sister, I believe yer talking ta Carrie. Ain't no danger of me gittin' into any trouble in Salem," said Bay loudly. Mack cranked up his red Thunderbird and drove away, with Sara waving from the back window.

After Sadie left, Bay and Bee drove Carrie to the train station. About three o'clock, they were back home. As soon as they walked inside the house, the telephone rang about three times. Finally, Bee answered. "Hello . . . just a minute, please. Bay, it's for you."

Bay, looking rather surprised, picked up the phone. "Hello," the voice on the other end said. "Bay, how on earth are you? This is Savannah!"

"Savannah? Well, I'll be doggone! Are you in Salem?"

"Yes, I'll be here for a couple of days. If it's okay, I'll drop by tomorrow. Can't wait to see your new baby, of course."

"Okay," said Bay, and she hung up the phone smiling. She went into the kitchen where Bee was feeding Zachary. "Mama, guess what? Savannah's home. I haven't seen her in about six years. She's coming by tomorrow."

After Bee finished feeding Zachary, Bay and her son went home. While Sadie and Carrie were visiting, she had stayed at Bee's house with her sisters. Now she was eager to get back to her little white cottage.

When Bay got off from work the next day, she picked Zachary up from Mother Caine's house and headed to Bee's to meet Savannah. While riding there in the taxi, she began to feel terrible about herself. Savannah was now at some big company in California as a marketing executive. *What haf I accomplished? I'm workin' at a small bank 'n a small, dead country town*, thought Bay.

"Bay, you must be in another world. We here at yo mama's house," said Mr. Floyd, the driver.

"Sho am—thanks, Mr. Floyd," said Bay, giving him the money for her fare.

"Bay, is dat you?" shouted Bee as she heard the door open.

"Yes, Mama."

Bee walked from her room into the living room and saw the gloomy expression on Bay's face. "What's wrong, honey?"

"I kinda hate ta see Savannah. She's so successful, and I'm a nobody. I'm still here. Sadie, Carrie, Savannah, 'n' Charlotte are gone. Soon you'll be gone too. Why, Mama? Why, Mama?" shouted Bay, throwing her purse on the sofa.

"Only you kin answer dat," responded Bee. They heard someone walk up on the porch, and then the doorbell rang, "Bay, ya need ta go git yourself together. I believe dat's Savannah." Bay walked hurriedly to her old bedroom.

When Bee opened the door, there stood Savannah. "Miss McQueen, I'm so happy to see you," she said, leaning over and giving Bee a hug.

She is jus' as cute as ever, thought Bee. "Savannah, how ya been?"

"Doin' okay, I guess. Haven't married and don't have any children," exclaimed Savannah.

There is something quite sad about her, thought Bee.

"Savannah!" shouted Bay from across the room, making her grand entrance. They swiftly walked toward each other and embraced.

"It's been a long time," said Savannah. Now tears were rolling down her cheeks. "Bay, you still look the same, and more beautiful than ever." Bee quietly left the room so the girls could talk.

Bay and Savannah took a seat on the sofa. "Savannah, you look great too! How's life out there in California? Bet you have all kinds of men chasing you."

"Not really," said Savannah somberly.

"Tell the truth."

"When I moved to California to attend college, the color thing followed me there too. I was always selected for positions over the darker students. I knew it wasn't right, but I didn't know what to do. That's just the way things are. We're still color-struck, no matter how much education we get or money we make."

"Don't blame yourself. You never been color-struck," said Bay.

Savannah stood up and walked over to the window. "Bay, that's why I don't date anymore and haven't married."

"Gee, Vannah, this really got you down."

The Wounded Whole

Now facing Bay with tears in her eyes, Savannah said, "Men don't want me for who I am. They just want me for my damn color, 'cause I look like I'm almost white. They don't care if I don't know how to come in out of the rain. All they want is a red-bone! A yellow-ass body!"

Bay began to cry. She walked over to Savannah, put her arms around her friend, and said, "Oh, Vannah, I'm so sorry. I suffer 'cause of my dark skin, and you're in pain 'cause of your light skin. You're what most men desire and some women envy. What kinda world we living in? How we goin' to get all this shit out our minds? Maybe someday we'll find peace."

"Bay, there's not a day passes that I don't think about Kirby. I hate that he killed himself over me," said Savannah, still crying in Bay's arms.

"I know, Vannah. Listen, it's not your fault. I'm no mind doctor, but it must've had somethin' to do with somethin' already in him." Bay sat Savannah on the sofa. "Let me git you somethin' cool to drink." She went into the kitchen to get some of Mama's homemade lemonade.

I'm glad to be home to spend some time with Bay, thought Savannah.

"Vannah, here's the best lemonade in the whole world," said Bay jokingly.

Savannah tasted it. "Bay, girl, you are sho tellin' the truth! It's really good!"

"Vannah, things are goin' to be all right! Can I make a suggestion?"

"Sure, Bay, I feel so much better talking to you."

"Since you live out there in California, why don't you go talk to one of those . . . ah . . . ah . . . mind doctors?"

"I thought about it, but I was trying to handle things myself."

"It helps to talk to a professional. Sometimes I wish I could talk to someone too. I'd like to know why I can't get my ass outa Salem."

"You will when you're ready."

"I don't know of any mind doctors in Salem. Vannah, can you imagine a colored person goin' to a mind doctor here? Everybody would know their business. Throughout the history of Salem, folks would remember them as Looney Coo-Coo."

They both laughed. After they regained their composure, Savannah said, "I'd better go spend some time with my mother. We'll get together again before I leave for California." Bay walked her friend to the front door and said good-bye.

Two weeks later, Savannah returned to California. She and Bay had spent lots of time together talking, laughing, and crying. Consequently, Bay became more restless and impatient living in Salem. Deep within, she knew something needed to happen to force her out of town. *I'm tired of dis dead-end bank job 'n' not havin' no kinda social life. If I had a car, I could git around town more 'n' meet more people*, she thought.

For the past year, Bay had been saving money to buy her own car. She needed somebody besides Bee to assist her. Bay wanted to surprise her. After work, she called her father, LC. "Hello, Betty Jean, how are you? Let me speak with Daddy," said Bay.

"Heard your mama's gettin' married," responded Betty Jean.

"Oh yes, she is."

"Hold on, honey, I'll get him," said Betty Jean.

"Hey, my girl, what's goin' on?"

"Daddy, I've saved enough money ta buy me a car! Can ya help me look for one?"

"Sure. Baby, you done really grown up—buying your own car. How's my grandson? Is he growing up to be as good-looking as his grandpa?"

"He's fine. Yes, I do believe he's goin' ta be as handsome as you," said Bay, chuckling.

"Where and when do you want me to meet ya, Bay?"

"Can ya meet me at the Oldsmobile place Friday at four-thirty?"

"Sho will."

"See you den, Daddy," said Bay, and she hung up the phone.

The doorbell rang, startling Bay. Nobody ever visited her except Bee and her ex-husband's mother. Bee was still at work, and Mrs. Ellis was out of town. *Who could it be?* thought Bay. She walked to the door and asked, "Who is it?"

"Roberta Fields," the woman responded.

Bay opened the door. There stood a nice-looking, shapely brown woman, about thirty, with a skirt so tight that coughing would be a serious mistake.

"Sorry to bother you, but do you happen to have a cup a sugar I can borrow?" asked Roberta.

We used ta do dis when we wuz livin' on Cane Street, thought Bay. "Come on in," she said, walking toward the kitchen. She returned with the sugar, put her hand on her hip, and said, "Tell me why you don't have no sugar."

"Cause I ain't got no job, no man, no nothing!" exclaimed Roberta.

"Where ya live?" asked Bay.

"With my aunt across the street."

"You mean Miss Mildred's your aunt?"

"Afraid so," said Roberta, now seated at the kitchen table. "I'm from New York. Can't you tell by the way I talk? Aunt Mildred wants me to work in white folks' houses. I will never stoop that low," she said, standing up with both hands on her hips.

Bay could see herself in this woman. She liked Roberta right off. "You gotta find somethin' to do," said Bay.

"I know. Guess I'll go back to New York. Wasn't my idea to come to Salem, Georgia, anyway!"

"Whose was it?"

"My mother's—she got tired of me living off her. Hell, I don't like living off nobody!"

"Have you ever worked in a bank?" asked Bay.

"No, haven't ever worked anywhere."

"Lord, Roberta," said Bay, slumping down in her chair. "You like children?"

"Yeah, they're okay."

"Why don't you ask Miss Mildred to take you to Carver Elementary, where my mama works, to fill out an application?" suggested Bay. "How much education you got?"

"Chile, I have a degree in education and library science. Nobody wants to pay me what I'm worth," said Roberta, smiling and raising her head in the air.

"Now, what price would that be, Miss High and Mighty?" asked Bay, laughing.

"About fifty thousand a year."

"You're joking, right?"

Laughing, Roberta said, "It's just an excuse. I really don't want to work for anybody but me, me, me! Anyway, what's your name?"

"I'm the one and only Bay McQueen."

"Nice to meet you, Bay. I like you. Guess I'd better be going before Aunt Mildred thinks I've been kidnapped with all these fine hips."

Bay laughed. "You are a mess and a half." Bay walked Roberta to the door. "Bye, Roberta. Maybe I'll see you tomorrow."

The next day, Friday afternoon, LC met Bay at the Oldsmobile dealership to look for a car. She and LC were walking around, looking at cars, when a young white man approached them. "How y'all doin'?" he said with a real Southern drawl.

"Fine," Bay responded, almost as Southern as the salesman.

"We're looking for a nice sturdy car for my daughter."

"How much you willing to pay? Excuse me, what's y'alls' names?" the salesman asked.

"I'm LC McQueen, and this is my daughter Bay."

"Ain't tellin' you how much money I got. You might wanta get it all," said Bay. She folded both arms, closed her eyes, and said, "Let's negotiate."

"Okay, ma'am. Come with me. I have just the car for you," the salesman said, walking down the middle of the car lot. Finally he showed them a pretty blue Plymouth.

Bay opened the door. "Great smokin' Joe. Daddy, it's so beautiful!"

"It sho is, Mr. . . . ah . . . ah . . . what's your name?"

"Jim Clayborn."

"How much is this car?" asked LC.

"Twenty-five hundred."

"Bay, you got that much?" asked LC.

"You never know 'bout a woman," said Bay slyly. "Can we drive it? Ain't buyin' nothin' without tryin' it out."

"Okay," said Clayborn, reaching in his pocket for the keys. They hopped in the car and headed down the road.

"Bay, I didn't know you could drive," said LC, sitting next to her.

"Sure can. Mama taught me. I really like this car. Kinda want a red one like Mama's and Mack's. Yet there's somethin' real classy 'bout dis sky blue," said Bay, smiling.

They returned to the dealership and got out of the car. "Mr. Clayborn, you said twenty-five hundred, didn't you?" asked Bay.

"Yeah, sure did."

"Sorry, I only have two thousand cash," said Bay shrewdly.

"Wait a minute, let me go inside to talk to my boss," said Clayborn. He quickly returned. "Y'all come on inside my office to fill out the papers. It's a done deal," he said excitedly.

"Wonderful! Wonderful! Wonderful! Now I have my own car!" exclaimed Bay. She signed all the paperwork and closed the deal.

"Daddy, ain't I first-class? Drivin' ma own car. Wait till Mama sees it. She's goin' ta flip!"

Before Bay realized it, she had reached LC's house. She leaned over and kissed him. "Thanks, Daddy, fur comin' wit' me."

"Bay, you know I'll do anything for you. How much money did you really have?"

"Twenty-five hundred," replied Bay, smiling.

"You are too much. You've come a long way. You didn't need me to go with you," said LC, chuckling.

"Yes, I did. I love ya, Daddy." She reached in her purse, pulled out a hundred dollars, and gave it to him.

"No, baby, ain't taking yo money," said LC.

"What's mine is yours. Git yourself outa ma car. I got things ta do 'n' places ta go," shouted Bay as she pushed him out of the car, laughed, tooted her horn, and sped away.

While driving to Mother Caine's house to pick up Zachary, Bay was thinking about how shocked Mother was going to be about her new car. She arrived, went on the porch, and knocked on the door. Bay heard Mother Caine saying, "Come on, Zack, let's open the door for yo mama."

"Mommy, Mommy," said Zack.

Finally, Mother opened the door, holding Zachary in her arms. "Lord, Bay, I'm so glad you're here. This boy's been a handful today." Bay took Zachary from Mother's arms and gave him a big kiss. Suddenly, Mother noticed the car. "Who brought you over here in that fine-looking blue car?" she questioned, smiling.

"Nobody. It's all mine."

"Yours?" shouted Mother Caine. "Lord, child, let me get my good shoes and my eyeglasses so I can look real good!"

Bay could hardly contain herself. Mother didn't walk too slow then. She got energy from somewhere. She reached the car and opened the front door. "Lordy, Bay, what a beautiful car! This is the prettiest car I ever seen."

She told Mama de same thing about her car, thought Bay, smiling.

"I know Bee is proud of you," said Mother.

"She doesn't know yet," said Bay.

"What?"

"Don't ya dare tell her, either."

"I won't, honey," Mother responded sheepishly.

Bay couldn't let Mother spoil it. "Why don' ya ride over ta Mama's house wit' me ta witness the surprise? I'll bring you back home."

"Child, I wouldn't want to miss that for anything in the world. Go lock my door. I got my keys in my pocket," said Mother Caine, holding Zachary in her arms.

Fifteen minutes later, Bay drove into Bee's driveway and parked behind the red car. She left Mother Caine and Zack in the car, went on the porch, and rang the bell.

"Who is it?" yelled Bee.

"I got somethin' real putty ta show you," Bay responded.

Finally, Bee opened the door. "Who's dat in dat blue car?"

"Zack 'n' Mother Caine," Bay said.

"Whose car?" Bee asked, looking more puzzled.

"It's mine, it's mine!" shouted Bay excitedly.

"Wait, Bay, let me grab ma shoes so I kin go outside ta git a good look," said Bee, laughing. She put the shoes on and hurried outside. "Bay, it's beautiful! I didn't know ya were plannin' ta buy a car."

"Bee, our Bay is moving up in the world," said Mother Caine, beaming.

"I'm so proud of you. How much did it cost?" Bee asked.

"Two thousand," replied Bay. "Daddy went wit' me."

"That's good!" Bee walked over to the side of the car where Mother Caine was sitting and kissed Zachary. "Hey, MiMi's baby!" said Bee.

"Bay, we'd better be goin' before it gets dark. We don't wanta get in no trouble with no menfolk," said Mother Caine, laughing. Bay got inside the car, laughing, and left.

Bay took Mother Caine home, helped her inside, and hurried home to show Roberta her new car.

Roberta was sitting on her aunt's porch when she saw Bay drive into the yard. Although she was curious, she didn't make a move. She continued to watch the strange car. Suddenly, she saw Bay get out of the car and go to the other side to get Zachary. Roberta hopped up out of the chair and walked as fast as she could over to Bay's house. "Bay! Bay! What you doing with that car!" she cried excitedly.

"I bought it," replied Bay proudly, with a smile.

"How'd you manage to get enough money to buy a car?"

"Save! Save! Save!" said Bay.

"Girl, when are you taking me for a ride? Let's go over to the Night Spot in Galveston."

"What's that?"

"Mean to tell me you never heard of the Night Spot? Girl, you are real green! It's a club, and all the fine things go there. You need to get out sometime. How you going to meet the right man? Please, please, please!" pleaded Roberta.

"It would be nice. I haven't been out dancing since I slipped to Mr. Jakes in high school. Okay, you got yourself a date. What about next Friday night?"

When Bay told Bee about her plans to go to the Night Spot, Bee wasn't too happy. She knew Bay had a wild side. She didn't want her to start clubbing, as folks called it. Of course, Bee couldn't babysit Zachary because she and Jack had a date, so Bay asked Mother Caine to look after him.

Friday night about eight-thirty, Bay and Roberta knocked on Mother Caine's door. Roberta was holding Zachary, who had fallen asleep. Sometimes Mother couldn't hear because of her television. Bay had to knock several times.

Finally, Mother Caine opened the door. "Come on in, girls, put Zack in my room on the bed. Bay, come on back in the sitting room. I need to talk to you before you go clubbing in Galveston. Tell the other girl to come on back too."

"Her name is Roberta," interrupted Bay.

By this time, Roberta was walking into the room. "Roberta, you come on in and sit down. Mother needs to talk to you and Bay," she said seriously. Mother was seated on her big old-fashioned rocker with two cushions on it. Bay and Roberta sat next to each other on the love seat. "Let me tell you girls somethin.' Don't y'all go over there to that Hot Spot or Damn Spot, whatever you call it, and get y'all selves into trouble," said Mother. Bay and Roberta nudged each other in the sides with their elbows. "Men ain't after but one thing. Do I have to spell it out?" she asked.

"No, ma'am," said Bay, smiling.

"When I was a young woman 'bout twenty-six, I used to slip to the Palace. This old, ugly guy with a tooth missing in the front came over and asked me to dance. He was so ugly, my eyes began to hurt and run water." Bay and Roberta were about to burst with laughter. "If that wasn't bad enough, he grabbed my behind and then ran off. If I had got my hands on that ugly scoundrel I'd've wrapped a rope around his neck." Bay and Roberta couldn't contain themselves any longer. They laughed so hard, Bay bent over on the floor with tears rolling down her face. Roberta was laid out on the love seat, laughing loudly. Now Mother Caine was shaking with laughter.

After the comic relief, Bay told Mother they had to leave. Bay and Roberta left and headed to Galveston.

CHAPTER SIX

Bay and Roberta pulled into the parking lot of the Night Spot. They were amazed at the huge brown building that resembled a warehouse. They could hear the music a hundred feet away.

"Girl, look at all dese cars. Dat place is packed!" said Bay excitedly. As they got closer, they began feeling and moving with the music. "I feel good. I could dance all night!" continued Bay, stopping and moving her hips.

"Watch yourself!" responded Roberta, laughing, turning around, and shaking all over.

Finally Bay and Roberta reached the door, opened it, and walked into a huge foyer. People were standing and sitting at a long bar, while others were seated at tables laughing and talking. Suddenly, all eyes were on Bay and Roberta.

A group of men were seated together at a table. One got up, walked over to them, and invited them to sit with his group. "Well, well, the Lord sho answers prayers. Believe y'all came right down from heaven with y'all pretty fine selves. My name is Arthur Taylor. Everybody calls me Tadpole."

"I'm Bay McQueen."

"I'm the one and only Roberta."

"Y'all come on over and sit with me and my homeboys," said Tadpole.

"Maybe some other time. We just want to dance. By the way, where's the dance floor?" asked Bay.

"Over there where the guy is standing by the door next to the table."

They walked over to the man, paid for their tickets, and entered the room. Before they could find a vacant table, guys started asking them to dance. Without hesitation, they were on the floor, rocking and rolling.

Bay's partner returned her to the table Roberta had found for them, where Roberta and some guy were acting real cozy. "Roberta, I'm havin' a very good time!" said Bay, smiling.

Roberta awakened from fantasyland. "Oh, Bay, this is Alan Long. Alan, this is my friend Bay McQueen."

"Nice to meet you," said Alan.

After Bay sat down and had a chance to catch her breath, a tall, dignified, light-complexioned guy came over. He reached for Bay's hand. "Would you like to dance?" She was quite flattered.

"Sure, why not?" replied Bay.

"My name is Will McCoy," he said as they started dancing. "What's yours?"

"I'm Bay McQueen."

"You're a great dancer."

"I haven't danced in such a long time. I was afraid I wouldn't remember," said Bay, smiling and watching her grammar.

The music ended. Will escorted Bay to her seat. "Thanks, Bay," said Will, and he walked away.

Now Roberta and Bay were seated alone. "I see how you're looking at that fine thang you were dancin' with," teased Roberta.

"Yeah, girl, he is a fine sweet-potato for sure!"

"Don't go getting your heart too set on him. His kind don't usually take to our color," said Roberta.

"Speak for yourself. Can't you see he can't keep his eyes off me?"

Bay got up from the table and walked to the restroom. She had the most elegant walk. All eyes were on her, especially Will's.

While returning to her seat, Bay walked past Will. A slow song began playing. Will delicately grabbed her hand and pulled her close to him on the dance floor. "Bay, you are something else. Can I come over to see you tomorrow night?"

"Sure, why not?" said Bay as she laid her head on his chest. He embraced her with great feeling.

When the song was over, Will walked Bay to her table and sat next to her. Bay introduced him to Roberta and Alan. "Roberta, meet Will McCoy. Will, this is Alan."

"Hey, everybody get up and dance. This is the last song!" shouted the bandleader. Just about everybody found his or her way to the dance floor.

"Bay, Alan and I will walk you and Roberta to your car," said Will.

Finally, they reached the car. "Thanks so much, Will. I really had a great time. I'm so happy we met," said Bay.

She noticed Roberta and Alan kissing passionately. Suddenly, Bay felt Will's hot lips against hers. They kissed as if there was no tomorrow. They looked into each other's eyes and desired more.

"I'll call you tomorrow," said Will.

"Okay," replied Bay slowly. She got inside her car and yelled jokingly, "Let's go, Roberta. You and Alan goin' ta kiss all night?"

Everybody burst into laughter. After getting inside the car, Roberta said, "Girl, ain't you glad we came to the Night Spot tonight? Look at the treasures we found! You think they can do anything?"

"What you mean, do anything?" asked Bay.

"Bay McQueen, don't pretend you don't know what I'm talking about. You Southern belles know more than what you pretend."

Bay laughed. "I know what you mean. You're asking me if I think they know how to stay on course or have some staying power! I sho hope they ain't no jackrabbits!"

"What you mean by jackrabbits?" asked Roberta, looking puzzled.

"I'll explain it to you sometime."

The following morning, about nine-thirty, Bay's telephone rang. She reached for the phone on the table next to her bed. "Hello," she answered.

"Bay, did you have a good time last night?" asked Bee.

"Mama, it was wonderful. I met a very nice guy. We danced, talked, and had a great time!"

"Bay, I have good news!"

"What?" shouted Bay, now sitting up in her bed with Zachary lying next to her fast asleep.

"Jack 'n' I are gittin' married 'n three months," said Bee happily.

"Mama, I hope ya will be very happy," said Bay. Before they said good-bye, Bay told her about Mother Caine's lecture to her and Roberta.

Three months later, Bee and Jack were married at her church in Salem. It was packed, and the other McQueen women all came home for the wedding. Bee was such a beautiful bride, and Jack looked like a distinguished professor. During the entire ceremony, tears rolled down Mother Caine's cheeks. She was so happy for Bee.

After the ceremony, Jack and Bee left for his home in Galveston. The next day, Sadie and Carrie left for Astoria and California. Though Mother Caine, Roberta, and LC were still in Salem, Bay felt awfully alone and afraid. Now she desperately yearned for a relationship with a man. She thought that would make her feel more secure.

Bay had not heard from Will since they met at the Night Spot. Finally, the telephone rang. "Hello," said Bay.

"Bay, this is Will McCoy," said the voice on the other end.

"Will, how are you!" responded Bay cheerfully.

"Fine! Was wondering if I could come over to see you?"

"Sure, what about tomorrow afternoon about two o'clock?"

"Great! See you then."

The next day, Will knocked on Bay's door. After peeping through the peephole, she opened the door, smiling. "Hi, Will, come on in!"

"A nice crib you got here," said Will.

"Have a seat. I need to check on my baby. I just put him in bed for his nap."

"Sure," said Will, somewhat stunned. He didn't know Bay had a child. It didn't matter to him, but it sure would matter to his folks, he thought.

Bay returned to the room. "I haven't heard from you since we met at the Night Spot. What do you do?" asked Bay, curious.

"I'm a student at Stetson University. It's about fifty miles east of Galveston. I'm home for two weeks. Man, I just couldn't get you out my mind." He got up off the sofa, walked over to Bay, pulled her out of the chair, and held her tightly. She could feel the heat from their bodies. Suddenly, they were kissing passionately.

"Bay, I want you so much," said Will.

"I want you too," said Bay, remembering what she had always been told—never do it the first time you're asked. Anything gotten too easy is never appreciated. "Will, I can't. My son might wake up. Anyway, we don't really know each other that well."

"I understand. Can I come over tomorrow night?"

"I'm busy tomorrow. What about Wednesday night about seven o'clock?"

"Okay, sounds good!"

Will did come over as planned. Before Bay and Will could properly greet each other, they found themselves in bed making love, or at least making love according to Will's opinion. Bay was quite disappointed and thought, *Another jackrabbit!* She didn't want to hurt his feelings, so she decided not to tell him that he needed some lessons in lovemaking.

"Bay, that was something else!" said Will, smiling while dressing himself.

"Very nice," said Bay hesitantly. A deep sense of remorse and emptiness welled up in her. She didn't understand it.

"Bay, I got to go. Don't look so sad. I'll call you, and I'll be home next weekend," said Will. He pulled her close, kissed her, and continued, "Don't give my stuff away." He closed the door behind him, smiling.

Ten minutes after Will drove off, Bay heard a knock at the door. She knew exactly who it was. She opened the door. "Guess who!" said Roberta excitedly.

Bay walked into the kitchen with Roberta following her. "Girl, you look real irritated. I thought you and Will were over here having a *real* good time!"

"Another damn jackrabbit!" shouted Bay.

"Please explain to me what a jackrabbit is."

"A man who gits his before I git mine."

"Oh, I get it. He didn't do any foreplay. Where I come from, we call him quick-draw!" said Roberta. Didn't seem as if Bay and Roberta would ever stop laughing.

After that night, Bay and Will became a twosome. They even began talking about marriage. She didn't feel very comfortable discussing marriage because of the problems in her previous relationship with Sam. Yet the more they talked about it, the more comfortable she became—so one Sunday, when Bee and Jack were in Salem, she decided to take Will over to the house to meet them.

"Bay, I don't feel comfortable meeting your parents," said Will.

"If we are serious about marriage, we need to get to know our parents."

Will also wasn't looking forward to Bay meeting *his* parents. *Nobody's ever good enough for me*, he thought. *I know Bay's complexion will be a big problem.*

"A penny for your thoughts," said Bay, smiling, as she turned into Bee's driveway.

The Wounded Whole

"Nothing, babe. This is a nice crib your mama has."

Bay unlocked the door. "Mama! Mama!"

Bee came out of the kitchen. "Bay, I'm so glad to see you. I've missed you and Zachary so much," said Bee, hugging her. She noticed the handsome young man.

"Mama, this is Will McCoy. Remember me telling you about the nice guy I met at the Night Spot?"

"Oh, yes!"

"Will, this is Bee McQueen—no, I mean Bee *Albertson*," said Bay.

"Nice to meet you, Mrs. Albertson."

"Where's Jack?" asked Bay.

"I believe he's in the bedroom reading."

While they were talking, Jack entered the room. "Bay, how are you?" he asked.

"Fine! Jack, this is my friend Will McCoy."

"Nice to meet you," said Will.

"Same here," said Jack, smiling.

Bee walked into the kitchen. "Y'all come have dinner with us. There is plenty for everybody."

Bay and Will enjoyed the meal and the conversation. Will looked at his watch and realized it was time for him to leave. "Mr. and Mrs. Albertson, I have enjoyed your company. I've got to go home to pack. I have to be at Stetson tomorrow morning," said Will, now standing with Bay beside him. "Mrs. Albertson, that sweet-potato pie was outa sight!"

As they turned to walk away, Bay said, "Mama, I'll call you soon. Bye, Jack!"

Bay and Will left holding hands. Bee and Jack stood in the doorway of the kitchen. "Hopefully, Bay has found what she's always been searching for," said Bee.

A year later, in 1970, Zachary was two years old. Bay and Will were still dating. She had visited Stetson, the university he attended. Of course, she had never met his family, and she was beginning to wonder why. *Mayb' he thinks I'm not good enough fur him*, thought Bay. She decided she would ask him when he visited her that weekend.

As usual, about four-thirty Friday afternoon, Will drove into Bay's driveway in his shiny black Pontiac LeMans. She opened the door.

"Hey, girl, couldn't wait to get here so we can make love," said Will, grabbing Bay and pulling her real close to him. Zachary was standing there watching them. They noticed him, and Will walked over to him. "Hey, my man," said Will, as he picked the boy up and kissed him on his fat cheeks.

"Will, I need to talk to you about something," said Bay. From the tone of her voice, Will could tell this was serious. He put Zachary on the floor, and the boy began playing with his toys. Bay and Will walked over and sat on the sofa. "Will, we've been seeing each other for a year. I have never met your family. Why?"

He didn't know what to say. He didn't want to hurt her. "I just haven't done it! My family is strange. They think they're so damn high-class!" cried Will.

"So you're saying they might think you are too good for me?" asked Bay.

"Yeah," responded Will somberly.

"Are they color-struck?"

"They are definitely that!"

Old wounds began to open. Tears rolled down Bay's cheeks.

"Baby, don't cry. If you want to meet them, I'll take you," said Will.

"No, Will, it would be too painful for me."

As Will continued holding Bay in his arms, he reached in his pocket and pulled out a tiny box. "Bay, I have a surprise for you."

She raised her head off his shoulders and saw the box. "Will, it's a ring!" She opened the box. "It's so beautiful!"

"Bay McQueen, will you marry me?"

"Yes! Yes! A thousand times, yes!" shouted Bay, and they kissed passionately. *I haf finally found what I been lookin' fur all my life*, thought Bay.

Bay was officially engaged. Bee, her sisters, Mother Caine, and Roberta were excited for her, but their excitement couldn't create genuine happiness. She began feeling sick and nauseated. Later that morning, she decided to make an appointment with Dr. Clark, their family doctor. He agreed to see her after work.

After the examination, she returned to his office to wait for him. "Bay, I don't know whether this is good or bad news, but you're pregnant, dear," said Dr. Clark. Of course, he didn't tell Bay anything she didn't already know. She could sense things before they happened. Bee had told her to be careful. She had dreamed about fish. That is something colored folks swear by—dreaming about fish is a sure sign somebody is pregnant.

When leaving Dr. Clark's office, Bay was somewhat distraught. *Another baby, no husband, a dead-end job, and a fiancé whose family think dey're high-class 'cause dey're light*, she thought. "Bay McQueen, ya thought ya wuz movin' forward, but ya made a hundred steps backward," she muttered to herself. Suddenly, she felt the need to talk to Sadie or Roberta. She didn't know if she could wait that long.

Bay reached Mother Caine's house to pick up Zachary. Tears began falling from her eyes. She didn't want Mother Caine to see her cry. She reached into her purse and pulled out a tissue and wiped her eyes. Mother was sitting on the porch alone. Zachary was asleep. The closer Bay got to the porch, the more the tears rolled down her cheeks. Finally she reached the porch.

"Lord, child, what's the matter?" cried Mother Caine.

"I went ta see de doctor today. I'm pregnant again. I don' wanta be!"

"Come on in the house. It's some nosy folk round here, especially that Gladys next door," said Mother Caine, looking around. Mother Caine put her arms around Bay's waist, and they went inside. "Honey, all Mother can tell you is God loves you. Everybody done made mistakes, including me. Least you engaged. Now y'all can get married and nobody will never know the difference," said Mother Caine, smiling. Talking to Mother Caine made Bay feel better, but she didn't want to tell Bee. "Bay, there's one thing I want you to promise me you'll do," said Mother. "Call Bee and let her know whatcha goin' through."

"Okay, I will, Mother Caine," replied Bay reluctantly. She awakened Zachary and left for home.

After breaking the news to Sadie, Carrie, Bee, and Roberta, Bay waited for the weekend to tell Will. Bay heard a knock at the door. She opened it. "Hey, babe," said Will.

"Hi," responded Bay.

"Is that all you going to say? Aren't you glad to see me?"

"Yes, Will. I'm always glad to see you, but there's somethin' we need to talk about," said Bay somberly.

"What?" Will said, putting his hands in his pockets with a very puzzled look.

"I'm pregnant."

"Pregnant? I have another year before I finish school. I don't need to feel no pressure."

"Don't worry, Will, I won't pressure you," said Bay, surprised by his response.

After that weekend, Will's weekend visits to see Bay became sporadic. She felt that something was about to happen, but she didn't know what. She'd called Stetson to talk with him, but no one knew his whereabouts. A month later, one Saturday afternoon, Bay was in her house doing her regular chores, and she experienced a strong sense that something traumatic, beyond her control, was happening to her. She began to cry uncontrollably. There was a knock at the door.

"Bay, it's Roberta!"

Bay opened the door and fell into Roberta's arms. "Somethin's happening, Roberta. I don't know what it is!" cried Bay.

"Calm down, Bay. It's all right. Whatever it is, it's going to be all right!" cried Roberta. She couldn't bear to mention that she knew why Bay was crying. Will had married someone else. Roberta's Aunt Mildred heard about it at the beauty shop. Will's wedding was to take place that day at three o'clock, the same time Bay became upset. *That dirty son of a bitch*, thought Roberta.

Finally, Bay stopped crying. "Roberta, there's something going on."

"Bay, I didn't want to tell you, but the sooner you know, the better. Aunt Mildred heard at the beauty shop that Will is getting married today. Aunt Mildred brought the *Stetson News* home with their picture in it," exclaimed Roberta.

"Is she light-complexioned?" asked Bay coldly.

"Yes!" replied Roberta, tears swelling up in her eyes.

"Is she pretty?"

"Hell, no!" shouted Roberta.

"What does she do?" asked Bay sadly.

"She's a teacher."

Bay slowly got up off the couch, "Roberta, take care of Zack fur a while. I'm goin' ta git a gun, and I'm goin' ta kill dat yeller no-good bastard!" screamed Bay.

"No, Bay! No! He's not worth it! What about Zack and the baby you're carrying?"

Suddenly, Bay heard Zack crying, "Mommy, Mommy, please don't go!"

She reached down, picked him up, and held him tightly. "Mommy is not going anywhere. I love ya wit' ev'rything dat's in me."

Bay never saw Will again. Eventually, he began sending her messages by Alan, but she never responded. Bay decided that she would raise her child without any assistance from the McCoys.

CHAPTER SEVEN

Bay continued to work at the bank. Now she was feeling very paranoid. She was afraid that she would lose her job when her supervisor found out about her pregnancy. One day, after Bay finished helping a customer, one of the customer-service clerks came over to Bay's station and whispered into her ear, "Bay, you have a very important phone call. It's an emergency."

Bay became quite concerned. She immediately thought something might be wrong with Zack, Bee, or her sisters. Finally, she reached the telephone. "Hello, Bay McQueen speaking."

"Bay, it's Charlotte Coombs. Please don't tell anybody about our conversation," she said softly.

"Gee, Charlotte, I haven't heard from you since you called right after you and Lance were married. What's the matter?"

"It's been hell. I need your help!" Now breaking down crying, she said, "Bay, please don't say no. I need your help desperately!"

"What is it, Charlotte?"

"Can my daughter, Leslie, and I stay with you for three days until I can get to Utah? Nobody will look for me at your place."

"Most colored folks think white folks don't have problems. They seem to think all y'all do is sip tea, eat fancy food, and keep us down, but things aren't always as they seem. No, friend, I don't mind you staying, but I do need to know what ya running from," said Bay.

"Someone killed Lance, and they think I did it," said Charlotte.

"Did you?"

"No, I didn't. But there were many times I wanted to."

"How are you goin' to get to my house?"

"My mother will bring me. Just give me the directions," said Charlotte.

Bay gave them to her and hung up the phone.

At seven o'clock, Charlotte arrived at Bay's house. Bay heard a knock and opened the door. Charlotte entered quickly. "Thanks so much," she said.

Bay noticed that her friend looked quite pale, had gained about thirty pounds, seemed older, and was no longer footloose and fancy-free. Charlotte had been through a lot.

"Mommy, I'm hungry. I'm sleepy," cried Leslie.

"What about a peanut-butter and jelly sandwich and a glass of milk?" said Bay.

"Yes, ma'am," responded Leslie. After she finished her snack, she was content. She fell asleep. Charlotte put her to bed. Bay knew it wouldn't be long before Roberta would be knocking on the door, so she decided to make some coffee and sandwiches so Charlotte and Roberta could have something to eat. Roberta had a tremendous appetite.

While Bay was preparing the food, Charlotte walked into the kitchen. "Charlotte, I know you're hungry. Sit down and have a ham-and-cheese sandwich and a cup of hot coffee," said Bay, smiling.

"I haven't eaten in days. This is really the first time I've felt a little relaxed."

As Bay expected, there was a knock at the door. Charlotte ran into the bedroom to hide, but Bay knew it was Roberta. She peeped through the peephole to make sure and then opened the door. "Hey, Roberta," said Bay.

"Who were those white folks over here earlier?"

"Anybody ever told you that you're one nosy dame?" said Bay, smiling, with her hands on her hips.

"Yep! Many, many times," responded Roberta, chuckling. "You haven't answered my question. What those white folks doing at your house? When white folks start hanging around, you're asking for trouble. They bring it with them." Before Bay could respond and tell her that a white person was in the other room, Roberta continued on. "An elderly colored lady, Mrs. Lucy Fuller, who lived over in Jackson, Georgia, didn't have nothing to do with nobody but white people. When she died, they stole every piece of her land from her blood relatives. They got away with it because they were roguish lawyers."

By that time, Charlotte had come out of the room. She couldn't take it anymore. "All white people aren't crooks!" shouted Charlotte, walking over to Roberta.

"They might not all be crooks, but y'all have done enough damage to my people that I can't see the difference!" yelled Roberta.

"Shut up, both of you! Sit your asses down and let's eat!" shouted Bay. Everybody sat down. "Listen, Roberta, Charlotte might be white, but she's my friend. I haven't seen her in about four years, but she's still my friend."

"Well, I said what I did because I didn't know that a white person was in your bedroom. Course, I'm not taking nothing back. If you're a friend of Bay's, there's got to be some good in you," said Roberta.

"Same here," responded Charlotte softly.

Roberta thought, *I've seen Charlotte before somewhere.* Then she remembered: *That's the woman on the evening news! She's wanted for the murder of her husband!* "Bay, if the police catch Charlotte here, you're going to jail too!" exclaimed Roberta.

"Roberta, what on earth are you talkin' about?" asked Bay, slyly rising from the table and placing the dirty dishes in the sink. Charlotte sat quietly.

"I just remembered where I'd seen Charlotte before. The police are looking for her for killing her husband. Bay, you're harboring a criminal."

"I am not a criminal. I didn't kill my husband. No, I won't call him my *husband*. I didn't kill that no-good bastard I married. I'm glad *somebody* killed him! I didn't have the guts!" She became hysterical. "What would you do if you were married to a man who kept you locked up in the house while he went to work and would beat you if you disobeyed him? A man who instilled such fear in you until you no longer knew who you were? A man who beat his little girl until she was black and blue with scars all over her little swollen body and refused to take her to the doctor and wouldn't allow you to get help for her? The only thing I knew to do was to pray and treat her myself." She fell to her knees. "When I saw my baby, I died! Bay, I died inside. It hurt so badly and nobody was there to help me. I didn't know what else to do."

Now Bay was on the floor holding her. "Oh, Charlotte, it's goin' ta be all right. It's all right ta cry. Let it out."

"Damn, Charlotte, you've had a rough time," said Roberta compassionately, sitting on the floor next to Bay. "I'm glad the bastard is dead too! Why didn't you stab his ass? David killed Goliath with a slingshot. You should have filled his body with stab wounds and blamed it on an intruder."

"Hush, Roberta, wit' ya crazy self," said Bay, laughing.

Then Charlotte began laughing, "This is the first time in a very long time that I feel relieved and alive. Bay, I'm so glad you're letting me stay with you. Now I know what I must do." Charlotte got up off the floor and said goodnight to Bay and Roberta. Shortly thereafter, Roberta went home.

The next day, Saturday, Bay got up early to prepare breakfast for Leslie and Zachary while they watched cartoons. As she began pouring their cereal into bowls, Charlotte came into the kitchen. "Morning, Bay," she said.

"Slept good?"

"Sure did. I haven't slept like that for a long, long time," responded Charlotte, stretching and yawning.

"You do look more rested and like your old self. Sit down and have some breakfast."

"Bay, you're such a good friend. I'll never forget your kindness," said Charlotte, eating her cereal quite heartily.

"I've had some rough times myself. I know how bad things can get."

Charlotte sat quietly, looking down into the empty cereal bowl. "Bay, I'm tired of running. I didn't kill Lance. I'm going to turn myself in."

"Oh, Charlotte, that's great! You're making the right decision. Your parents can get you a real good lawyer and prove your innocence. With all the stuff that low-down scoundrel did, they can't help but let you go."

"Bay, let me use your phone. I need to call my mother."

While Charlotte walked into the hallway to make her call, Roberta knocked at the door. Bay walked over, unlocked the door, and opened it. "Good morning, Miss

McQueen," said Roberta, smiling. "How did Charlotte sleep last night?"

"Real good. She's turning herself in. She's calling her mother right this minute to come pick her up."

"The system throws the book at women, especially when they're accused of killing a man. Guess they think if one of us gets away with murder, it'll be open season on all men," exclaimed Roberta, now seated at the table, helping herself to breakfast.

"Roberta, I don't know how you come up with your strange thinking. By the way, don't eat all the bacon."

"When I get my big job, I promise to buy you all the bacon you want," replied Roberta, chuckling. "Now, to answer your question about my strange thinking, most educated folks are considered strange. I might not have a job, my dear, but I do have two degrees," continued Roberta with her chest stuck out.

"Girl, you are one serious clown!"

Charlotte came into the kitchen. "Hi, Roberta."

"Hey, girl, you sure look a whole lot better than you did last night. Bay tells me you're turning yourself in. Sure you wanta do that?"

"Yes, I do. I'm tired of running. I have a daughter to raise and a life to live. I want to enjoy life. Lance can't hurt us anymore."

"Lance should have had a lot of insurance. Did he?" questioned Bay.

"I really don't know. He kept me out of our personal and business affairs."

"If he did, you and Leslie won't ever have to beg or borrow from nobody," said Bay.

"If it's true, it's just reaping time for all his dirty deeds against you and your baby!" replied Roberta, smiling.

"Unused degrees can't get *that* for you, can they, Roberta?" asserted Bay, laughing as she walked over to the refrigerator to put something in it.

"Bay McQueen, I'll remember that smart remark," said Roberta.

There was a knock at the door. Bay peeped out the window. "Charlotte, it's your mother." Bay opened the door. "Hi, Mrs. Wells. Please come in."

"Not this time, dear, but I certainly want to thank you for all you've done for Charlotte and Leslie."

Charlotte grabbed her bags and took her daughter's hand. "Bay, I'll talk to you later," said Charlotte, walking out the door with Leslie waving good-bye.

"Good luck," said Roberta as she closed the door behind them.

Two days passed. Bay didn't hear from Charlotte. She hardly ever watched the news, but she really didn't have to—Roberta kept her informed about everything. This time, though, it wasn't Roberta who gave her the update. Tuesday morning during her break at the bank, Jan Sterling, a coworker who thrived on gossip, said, "Bay, remember Charlotte who used to work here at the bank? Y'all were friends, remember? Have you heard?"

"Heard what?" asked Bay. *Lord, Jan acts like she's on a sexual high*, thought Bay. "Heard what?" she prodded impatiently.

"Honey, it's so dreadful," she continued. "Nobody from Salem has ever, I mean *ever*, done anything like that!"

"Like what?" asked Bay, now very frustrated and tired.

"She murdered her husband, Lance Coombs, who was a member of one of the richest and most prestigious families in Salem!"

"I don't believe Charlotte killed her husband any more than I believe you're having an affair with Mr. Whitmore, the bank's attorney," said Bay slyly.

"Who said that?" asked Jan defensively.

"I heard it, but I don't believe a word of it. I have learned you can't always believe what you hear or see."

"If Charlotte didn't kill him, who did? I heard they've arrested her. Her parents have hired a lawyer from over in Alabama," said Jan, getting up from the table.

"It's time for me to get up too," said Bay, feeling triumphant and thinking to herself, *Jan will think a hundred times before she corners me off with her gossip*. They left the break room and returned to their work areas.

After Bay left work, she decided to pay Charlotte a visit at the jail. Charlotte came over and sat behind the partition. "Bay, I'm so glad to see you," she said somberly.

"Charlotte, is there somethin' you ain't tellin?" asked Bay.

"Like what?"

"They must have some pretty strong evidence to keep you locked up like this," said Bay.

"The only evidence they have is circumstantial: a million-dollar insurance policy and no sign of a break-in."

"Sounds pretty darn serious to me. When is your lawyer coming?"

"Tomorrow."

"When will the case go to trial?"

"About four weeks," replied Charlotte. "I've asked myself many times, why is this happening to me? I thought Lance was what I needed to be happy, to fill that emptiness in me," said Charlotte softly.

Bay said, "I thought I was the only one who felt that way. Now I know everybody feels empty sometime or another. They are trying to fill it with things on the outside of them, which makes matters worse."

"So true. When I married Lance, I thought all my problems would be solved, but they only increased. Now I'm in jail for his murder. Bay, I can't believe this is happening to me," uttered Charlotte, now sobbing uncontrollably.

"Oh, Charlotte, I hate seeing you cry. Things are going to work out. You've got to believe it. I believe it, because I believe in you," said Bay, trying to hold back her tears.

A female officer came over and escorted Charlotte back to her cell.

Two weeks passed. John Corbin, the sly lawyer from Alabama, went to question Charlotte. Evidently the DA didn't have quite enough evidence, because the lawyer won her release until the trial. It was the talk on television and everywhere.

At eight o'clock that night, Bay's phone rang. "Hello," said Bay.

"Bay, I'm so glad to be out of jail," said Charlotte on the other end.

"Girl, I'm so happy! Is there still goin' to be a trial?"

"Yeah, but I don't have to live like a bird in a cage. I can't stand it! Why don't you, Roberta, and I go to a movie Friday night?"

"Charlotte, I believe you're back to your old self. You shouldn't be seen goin' to no movie or shopping. You shouldn't look too happy about anything until the trial is over."

"You're right. When this mess is over, we're going to have a big party!" said Charlotte joyfully.

Bay heard a knock at the door. "Charlotte, someone is at the door. We'll talk tomorrow," she said and hung up the phone.

When Bay peeped through the peephole, she couldn't believe who was standing on the porch. She opened the door.

THE WOUNDED WHOLE

"Hey, Bay, I hope you don't mind Mother coming over to spend a little time with you. Since Bee left, I don't have too many places to visit," said Mother Caine.

"Mother, I'm so glad to see you. You know I don't mind. You're my family," replied Bay, hugging her.

"Lord, Bay, everything sure looks nice and clean," said Mother, taking her seat in a comfortable chair.

"Mother, would you like some ice-cold lemonade?"

"Sure sounds good. Where's my baby?"

"Taking a nap," replied Bay.

"Bay, it's been all on the news 'bout the white girl that used to be with you. They say she murdered her husband in cold blood. They seem to think she poisoned him, 'cause they found it in his body. I told you, white folks will get rid of you one way or another," said Mother, smiling.

"They can't prove that Charlotte bought poison to kill him."

Suddenly Roberta walked through the door. "Hi, Mother Caine," she said.

"Hey, honey, you're the girl that came to my house with Bay."

"Yes, ma'am."

"Bay, when you and your fiancé getting married?" asked Mother.

"Never," responded Bay.

"Why, child? Hope you ain't gettin' like these modern women, having babies and don't want to marry," exclaimed Mother Caine.

"Well, in my case, he chose to marry someone else," said Bay sadly.

"Someone else!" shouted Mother, sitting straight up on the edge of the chair. "Don't you dare worry yourself about it. He probably ain't no good, no way. Bet he wasn't a bit a count in the bed. Bet you never got a cherry," said Mother Caine, laughing.

"Mother, you must be a fortuneteller," shouted Roberta, laughing.

"Mother, you don't have a lick of sense," said Bay, smiling and chuckling.

"Child, don't you never fret over no rotten man. Colored men are somethin' else. I take that back. *All* men are somethin' else, making babies and don't even know how to help a woman get a cherry," said Mother, laughing.

Now Bay and Roberta were roaring with laughter. "Mother, you sure know how to liven things up," cried Bay.

Of course, Mother was having just as much fun as Bay and Roberta.

It began to get dark outside, and Mother didn't like to drive at night. "Girls, I had the most fun. Now Mother got to get on to the house before it gets too dark. Y'all walk me to the car."

"Mother, sure you're going home? Don't you turn no corner and pick up a man," said Roberta, chuckling.

"Don't think I can't. Looks can fool you. There's still some hot fire left in my furnace!" said Mother Caine with a big grin on her face.

"Mother, you get yourself in this car before you kill me and Roberta with laughter," said Bay, smiling.

After Bay closed the door on the driver's side, Mother Caine pulled off very fast.

Monday afternoon, Bay arrived home and was settling in when she heard a knock at the door. When she opened it, an officer said, "Bay McQueen, this is a subpoena requesting your presence as a witness for the defense at Charlotte Coombs's trial. *Why would dey call me to be a witness? I didn't live 'round Charlotte 'n Galveston*, thought Bay. As the officer walked off the porch and drove away, Bay saw Roberta sitting on the porch waiting for the officer to disappear from sight. When the coast was clear, Roberta rushed across the street and met Bay in her yard "What's goin' on?" she asked.

"Guess what? I got to go to court to be one of Charlotte's witnesses."

"Outa sight! I do love court movies. Can I go too?" asked Roberta excitedly.

"Girl, this ain't no movie. This is real. I've never been to court to testify," said Bay nervously.

"You can't get out of it. If you refuse to go, they'll send the police after you."

"That doesn't scare me. I don't wanta go. I *am* the police!" said Bay, folding her arms.

"Okay, Miss Police, I don't want to have to call your mama to get you outa jail," said Roberta, smiling. "Wait a minute, I just thought of something. Being a witness doesn't mean you're going to be called. Somebody might confess! When are you supposed to go?"

"Next Monday morning at nine o'clock."

Monday morning arrived. Bay and Roberta walked into the courtroom. It was packed. Bay noticed Charlotte sitting next to her attorney, Mr. Corbin, who looked to be about thirty-eight, with jet-black hair and olive skin. He appeared to be mixed with something else besides white. Bay and Roberta were seated next to two white women, probably in their seventies. One said, "I never thought the Wellses would birth a child who turned out to be a murderer."

"She ain't been convicted yet," said the other lady.

"Might as well. They found her fingerprints on her husband's glass that had the poison wine in it."

"She was his wife, weren't she? She had to wash and handle the dishes," said the other lady, getting a little loud.

Suddenly, everything got quiet. "All rise. The honorable Judge Roy Sullivan is now presiding."

Judge Sullivan took the gavel in his hands. "We're here today to hear the case of the State of Georgia vs. Charlotte Coombs for the murder of her husband, Lance Coombs. Are both sides ready to present their cases?" asked Judge Sullivan. "Mr. Sims, are you ready to call your first witness?"

"Yes, sir, I call Rev. James Tulley, Mr. Coombs's pastor." Rev. Tulley immediately walked to the witness chair and took a seat. Mr. Sims, with his hands behind his back, said, "How long did you know Mr. Coombs?"

"About four years," Rev. Tulley replied.

"Was he a faithful member in his church?"

"I object," said Mr. Corbin. "Mr. Sims is leading the witness. This question is irrelevant!"

"Objection sustained," responded the judge.

"Rev. Tulley, did the Coombses ever receive counseling from you?" asked Mr. Sims.

"Yes."

"Can you tell the court the purpose for the counseling?" asked Mr. Sims.

"I object," responded Mr. Corbin.

"Overruled. Continue, Mr. Sims," said the judge.

"Well, he was having problems because his wife wouldn't be a wife according to the Bible."

"Can you give me an example?"

"The time he asked her to have his dinner ready at five-thirty, she refused. She never wanted to do her bed work, and she nagged him a lot."

"Thank you," said Mr. Sims, and he walked over to his seat.

"Mr. Corbin, would you like to cross-examine the witness?" asked the judge.

"Certainly would," replied Mr. Corbin. Looking rather sly, with his hands in his jacket pockets, he said, "Rev. Tulley, how long have you been a pastor?"

"About twenty years," said Rev. Tulley proudly.

"So you believe that a man's wife is supposed to obey him?" questioned Mr. Corbin.

"I didn't make the rules, God did," responded the pastor sharply.

"I see," continued Mr. Corbin. "What did you suggest that the Coombses do to fix their problem?"

"I object," interrupted Mr. Sims.

"Objection sustained," said the judge.

"What professional advice did you give the Coombses?" asked Mr. Corbin.

"I told them they should pray together, and Mrs. Coombs should try to become more submissive," asserted Rev. Tulley.

"Even at the expense of abuse?" replied Mr. Corbin loudly, looking sternly into the eyes of the pastor. The courtroom became a little noisy. "I have no more questions," said Mr. Corbin, and he walked back to his seat.

The judge hit the desk with his gavel. "This court is in recess until tomorrow morning at nine-thirty."

The Coombs murder trial was the talk of the town. The case went on for several weeks. It seemed as if Charlotte was destined to spend the rest of her life in prison for a crime she swore she didn't commit. Bay could sense when something wasn't quite right. She believed Charlotte wasn't telling the whole truth. The Sunday before the last week of the trial, Bay called Charlotte to meet her at the Hamburger Stand. Bay arrived first and found a seat in front of a large window.

Five minutes later, Charlotte walked in. "Bay, I'm so glad you called. I needed to get out for a while."

"Charlotte, you ain't tellin' it all. Who are you protecting?"

"I'm not protecting anybody," replied Charlotte.

"You wanta spend the rest of your life in jail and miss out on seeing Leslie grow up?"

Charlotte began to cry. "Bay, I don't know what to do. I didn't kill Lance. I swear I didn't!"

"Who did? Were you seeing someone else?"

Charlotte became very quiet and looked into Bay's light brown eyes. Bay knew the answer. She was protecting her lover. "Who is he?" asked Bay.

"He didn't kill Lance!" shouted Charlotte.

"How in the hell do you know?"

"I just know."

"Have you given this information to Mr. Corbin?"

"No, I haven't, and don't you either. If you do, I won't ever speak to you again!"

"Is he that good? Girl, seems like you have forgotten your child and yourself," responded Bay.

Charlotte got up and ran out the door.

Bay immediately called Mr. Corbin and told him what she had found out from Charlotte. Mr. Corbin went to see Charlotte the next day and forced her to give him her lover's name or he would drop her case. The guy's name was Lloyd Crasher, the gardener, who had a reliable alibi. While investigating Crasher, Mr. Corbin discovered two others who possibly had motives: Lance's secretary and his real-estate partner, Tom Gilliam. At the same time, there were only two more days left to decide the Coombs case, and Charlotte was still the only one on trial. It really didn't look good for her. Something drastic had to happen.

The final day of the trial appeared to bear no surprises. The lawyers gave their closing arguments, and the jury members were dismissed to their quarters to determine the verdict. The courtroom was full, and suspense was in the air. Bay and Roberta were seated behind Charlotte, next to her parents. The Coombses, Lance's parents, were seated on the opposite side. They had blood in their eyes. As far as they were concerned, Charlotte was guilty.

Suddenly, the judge announced, "The court is now in recess until tomorrow morning."

"The jury must be having problems," said Bay. "Guess we'll just have to come back tomorrow. Something's gettin' ready to happen, and I wouldn't miss it for nothin'!"

The next morning, Bay and Roberta were seated in the courtroom. It was jam-packed! Bay heard there had been a break in the case. Mr. Corbin had received some very important information regarding who really killed Lance Coombs.

"All rise, the Honorable Judge Sullivan is now presiding."

"We're here to complete the trial of the State vs. Charlotte Coombs," the judge announced. "We've had a twist in the case. Mr. Corbin, please call your witness."

"I call Miss Abigail Sills to the stand."

A tall, beautiful blonde walked up and stood as the officer, holding the Bible, asked, "Do you swear to tell the truth and nothing but the truth, so help you God?"

"I do." She went to sit in the witness box.

"Miss Sills, what connection did you have with Mr. Coombs?" asked Mr. Corbin.

"I was his secretary."

"Did he ever flirt with you?"

"I object, Counsel is leading the witness," shouted Mr. Sims.

"This question pertains to the new evidence I've received," responded Mr. Corbin.

"Objection overruled," said the judge.

"Miss Sills, did Mr. Coombs ever proposition you?"

"Yes."

"Did you ever have a relationship?"

"Yes."

"You were his mistress?"

"Yes."

"Did you ever tell anyone about your relationship with Mr. Coombs?"

"Yes, I told my former lover about him."

"Why did you tell your ex-lover about Coombs?"

"I didn't want him in my life anymore."

"How did he respond?"

"He was furious! Since Lance is dead, he's been calling me saying, 'Coombs is gone; now you're all mine.'"

Suddenly, Rev. Tulley jumped out of his seat and ran toward the door, but the courtroom guards caught him. While he was struggling with them, he yelled, "Yeah, I killed him! He thought 'cause he was rich, he could buy anything he wanted! I showed him! All that money couldn't save his life!"

The courtroom was in an uproar. The judge hit the desk with his gavel and said, "The case against Charlotte Coombs is now dismissed."

Mr. Corbin thanked Miss Sills. Charlotte's family gathered around her to give their congratulations. She went over to hug her attorney and found herself facing Abigail Sills. Looking into her eyes with gratitude, she said, "Abigail, you didn't have to testify on my behalf. Thanks so much."

"It's the least I could do to make up for the harm I did to you," replied Abigail.

"Oh no, you did me a favor! We had nothing. I'm happy that you could find something lovable in him," said

Charlotte, shaking Abigail's hand. Then she said good-bye, walked over, and hugged Bay and Roberta.

"Charlotte, can you believe a pastor committed a murder? Who would have ever thought it!" said Bay.

"Did Abigail attend the same church with y'all?" questioned Roberta.

"Yes, she did. I am glad this is over. Now I can get on with my life," said Charlotte, turning around in the courtroom.

"Guess you can live real well, since you so rich and all," said Bay, laughing while walking out of the courtroom in front of Charlotte and Roberta.

"Bay," said Charlotte, "drop me off at my parents' house. I'm going to take care of some business tomorrow and leave for Galveston on Friday."

"I thought we were going to have a party," said Bay.

"Why you in such a hurry to get back home?" said Roberta, smiling. "I saw that Mr. Crasher on the witness stand. Wasn't too bad for a white guy."

"Roberta, if you only knew the whole truth," said Charlotte, with a big half-moon smile on her face.

"Y'all are two crazy women!" said Bay, laughing.

Finally, they reached Bay's car and hopped in. She drove off. Fifteen minutes later, they were at Charlotte's parents' house. While Charlotte was getting out of the car, Bay said, "Charlotte, don't leave Salem without an official good-bye!"

"I won't do that. I'll call you!" she said and ran inside.

The night before Charlotte returned to Galveston, she called Bay and asked to meet her at the train station. While Bay was entering the station, Charlotte's parents were leaving. When Leslie saw Bay, she ran to her. "Hi, Miss Bay!"

"Hi, sweetie pie," said Bay as she leaned over and gave Leslie a big hug.

"Can you come live with us?" asked Leslie.

"Not this time. I've got to stay here to take care of Zachary and the new baby that's coming," replied Bay affectionately.

"Okay," said Leslie, taking a seat and browsing through a book.

"Bay, I will never forget you," said Charlotte, now embracing her. "You're just like a sister. I love you."

"Gee, Charlotte, you don't have to get all mushy. You're just going to Galveston," said Bay with tears rolling down her cheeks.

Suddenly, the conductor yelled, "All aboard to Galveston!"

Charlotte and Leslie ran outside the train station to get on the train. As it began moving, Bay could see Charlotte and Leslie waving until they were gone.

CHAPTER EIGHT

Bay was sad to see Charlotte leave but very glad the murder trial was over. Three months passed, and Bay's stomach began getting larger and larger. One Saturday, she lay in bed thinking about her job. *I know ma supervisor knows I'm pregnant. What am I goin' ta do? De bank is de only job I've ever had.*

Tears began rolling down her cheeks. Bay hadn't prayed since she was a little girl, when she asked God to stop her parents from drinking and fighting. She got up and sat on the side of her bed, looking out the window. "God, I know I ain't talked ta ya in a mighty long time, 'n' I'm ashamed, but I need help. I don' know nobody ta ask but you. Please help me outa dis mess."

Suddenly, she felt peaceful. She knew everything would be all right. She lay back in bed, pulled Zack close to her, and fell asleep.

The next morning, Monday, she found a note on her desk telling her to meet with her supervisor. Immediately, she went to the woman's office. "Good morning, Mrs. Mays," said Bay.

"Morning, Bay, have a seat. Bay, you're one of our best employees. I hate that I'm the one who has to meet with you regarding this matter. Are you pregnant?"

"Yes, I am."

"Have you gotten married, or do you plan to?"

"No. I was engaged to marry, but my fiancé married someone else," said Bay softly.

"I'm very sorry. It makes it even harder to tell you that we have to let you go. Maybe after the baby comes you can return," said Mrs. Mays compassionately.

"I do understand. You have to do your job."

As Bay got up from her chair and headed toward the door, Mrs. Mays said, "Bay, take care of yourself, and good luck."

Bay went straight home. She decided to pick up Zachary later. She wanted to be alone. As she got out of the car and walked up on the porch, she could hear the telephone ringing. Quickly, she opened the door and grabbed the phone. "Hello."

"Bay, this is Charlotte," said the voice on the other end.

"Hey, girl, what's happening?"

"I have some great news for you. They've built another large hospital in Galveston. They're hiring people for different positions. Why don't you come over to apply?" said Charlotte excitedly.

"I've never worked at a hospital before. I'm not a nurse."

"You don't have to be a nurse. You could work in the business office. Your experience as a bank teller is perfect," said Charlotte.

"Gee, Charlotte, have you forgotten I'm pregnant? My baby is due in two months. Who's going to hire me? Damn, Charlotte, I've gotten myself in a mess. Today, I was dismissed from my job at the bank. Now I can't work anywhere because I'm pregnant!"

"You could come to Galveston and move in with your mother until the baby comes, and I'll help you out financially until you go to work," said Charlotte.

"How do you know I'll get a job after the baby comes?"

"Because, my dear Bay McQueen, I know the folks doing the hiring," said Charlotte with a chuckle.

"I really don't want to intrude on my mother or you, Charlotte."

"Doggone your hide. You're making all kinds of excuses. It's not your mother or me. I think *you're* scared! Do you really and truly desire to leave Salem? Now's your opportunity," said Charlotte.

"Guess you're right. Let me talk to my mother and Jack. I'll call you tomorrow."

"No you won't, Bay McQueen! You call me back tonight!"

"Okay, I'll call you back tonight, Mrs. Coombs," said Bay, laughing. She hung up the phone and then picked it up again and began dialing Bee's number.

"Hello," said Bee.

"Mama, this is Bay. I have something I need to ask you."

Before they realized it, they had talked for about twenty minutes. Bee wasn't the only one Bay needed to talk to. She also had to get Jack's permission. After finishing the conversation with them, she called Charlotte.

"Hello, Coombs residence," said Charlotte.

"Charlotte, this is Bay. I'm moving to Galveston! I'm finally leaving Salem! Mama and Jack agreed to my living with them for twelve months, which will give me plenty time to get a job, with your help of course, and find a place to live. I'm so excited! I need to start packing right away!"

"Get Roberta to help you," said Charlotte.

Bay had forgotten all about Roberta. "Gosh, I'm really going to miss Roberta."

"Maybe she can eventually move here too."

"You never know about Roberta. Charlotte, thanks so much. I'll call you when I get there," said Bay.

"You'd better." They said good-bye and hung up.

After Bay finished her conversation with Charlotte, she walked over to the kitchen cabinet, pulled out a jar of peanut butter, made a peanut-butter-and-jelly sandwich, poured herself a large glass of cold milk, and sat down at the kitchen table in pure amazement. *Am I really leaving Salem, or am I dreamin'?* thought Bay. *All dese years, now I'm movin' away.* "Hallelujah! Hallelujah!" shouted Bay aloud, jumping up from the table and spinning around as fast as she could.

Before she could get control of herself, she heard a loud knock at the door. It didn't sound like Roberta. Bay peeped through the peephole in the door, and indeed it wasn't. It was her ex-husband's mother, Mrs. Ellis. Bay slowly opened the door. "Hello, Mrs. Ellis," she said dryly.

"Hello, Bay. I hope you don't mind if I come in. I dropped by to see Zachary," she said.

"Of course I don't mind, but Zack isn't here. He's still at Mother Caine's house," responded Bay.

"I guess I'll have to see him another time."

"Yes, it would be better."

"He really should get to know his father," said Mrs. Ellis.

"I would certainly agree, but his father ain't interested in knowin' him. You're the one who seems to be interested in checking on Zack every now and then. Anyway, why don't you stop interfering in your son's life and let him take charge of his own business?" said Bay sharply, with her hands on her hips.

At that moment, Roberta walked up behind Mrs. Ellis.

"Hi, Roberta," said Bay. "This is Zack's grandmother, Mrs. Ellis."

"Good-bye, Bay," said Mrs. Ellis, hurriedly walking away.

"Bay, you must have put some fire under her shoes. She wasn't wasting any time getting out of here," said Roberta, smiling.

"I had to tell her the truth about her low-down dirty son. She didn't want to hear it." After Mrs. Ellis left, Bay decided to break the news to Roberta about moving to Galveston. "Roberta, I have the most wonderful news to tell you," said Bay, looking quite distinguished with her nose in the air.

"Yes? What?"

"It is so wonderful, I can hardly stand it," said Bay teasingly.

"Bay McQueen, you know I can't stand to be in suspense. What on earth is it?"

"I'm moving to Galveston!" cried Bay with excitement, grabbing both of Roberta's hands. "I'm moving in with Mama for twelve months, and Charlotte is going to help me get a job after the baby comes!"

"What about me?" cried Roberta. "When you leave, life will sure be dull around here."

"Charlotte said you might consider moving too. You could follow me later, when I get my own place."

"Oh, hot dog! What fun we'll have," said Roberta, shaking her hips.

"Roberta, you are so crazy!" said Bay, chuckling. "The only thing I hate about moving is packing, and leaving Daddy and Mother Caine," said Bay sadly.

"Girl, I can help you pack, but I wouldn't want to have to tell Mother Caine about your leaving. She's such a sweetheart! Does she have a family?" asked Roberta.

"No, we're her family," said Bay somberly. Now tears filled her eyes.

"It's not like you're moving to Russia. You and your mom can drive over to visit her and take her back to Galveston for weekends," said Roberta, sitting next to Bay on the sofa.

"I'll break the news to Mother when I pick up Zack. Daddy will be all right. He has Betty Jean."

After breaking the news to Mother Caine about moving to Galveston, Bay began packing, with Roberta's help. A week later, a large moving van backed up to Bay's little cottage, packed it, and headed off to Galveston.

"Bay, where on earth are you going to keep all your stuff until you get your own place?" asked Roberta.

"In Mama's storage house."

"I forgot to ask: how did Mother Caine take your leaving Salem?" asked Roberta.

"She pretended to be so sad, but it was all an act," said Bay, smiling. "While I was walking off the porch going to my car, a very nice-looking elderly gentleman passed me, headed for Mother's porch. I happened to look back. He had taken a seat next to Mother Caine. Chile, she was smilin' and grinnin' from ear to ear," continued Bay, laughing.

"Girl, Mother is doing better than both of us in the man department."

Holding Zachary's hand as they stood beside her parked car, Bay was anxious to get on the road to

Galveston. "Roberta, guess I'd better get going so I can begin my new life in Galveston!"

"Don't forget to call me when you get there," said Roberta, trying to hold back the tears.

"Roberta, are you crying?" said Bay, hugging her.

"I've gotten so used to you and Zack and all your good food," said Roberta, laughing.

"I'm gonna miss you too. As soon as I get my own place, you can come live with me until you get your place," said Bay, smiling and getting in her car. Deep within, she felt nervous about leaving the familiar in Salem; she knew what she was leaving behind but not what awaited her. Nevertheless, something was compelling her toward the unknown.

Forty-five minutes later, Bay arrived in Galveston. She was so amazed at the tall, beautiful buildings and the feeling of renewal and zest for life she felt swelling up within her. She could hardly wait to see her mother and Jack. Finally, Bay pulled into their driveway. While Bay was gathering her purse and Zachary, Bee came running outside to meet them.

"Bay, I am so glad ta see ya. Chile, ya sho are gittin' as big as a watermelon," said Bee, laughing and reaching for Zack. "Hey, Granny's li'l sugar daddy. Zack is de handsomest thang 'n de world."

"Haf de movers gotten here yet?" asked Bay.

"Yeah, dey unloaded ya stuff 'n' left 'bout ten minutes ago."

Suddenly, Bay noticed the beautiful brick home she would live in until after her baby was born. "Mama, what a big, beautiful house. You 'n' Jack are really livin' like white folks."

"Honey, white folks aren't de only ones who live 'n nice homes. Most colored folks jus' think so. Don' forget, we lived in a nice house 'n Salem," said Bee, walking toward the entrance.

After they reached the inside, Bay said excitedly, "Our house was nice fur Salem, but nothin' like dis! As Mother Caine would say, 'Bee, child, you sure have really moved up in the world, and you done got all proper and refined too,'" said Bay, smiling.

"Bay, come let me show ya your room," said Bee, laughing.

Finally, Bay settled in. She thought about calling Charlotte, but she was too tired, so she and Zack went to bed.

Two months later, in April of 1971, Bay gave birth to a beautiful girl. The baby was very light-skinned with good hair, meaning she was similar to white folks' babies or not 100 percent Negro, in which all glory, honor, and envy is echoed throughout the community. Bay named her daughter Hannah McQueen. When the nurse brought Hannah into the hospital room, Bay was surprised by how light-complexioned she was. Memories began to surface about Winding River, Kirby's suicide, and Savannah. She didn't want Hannah to live in this cold world of labels that she had no control over. "Hannah McQueen, you're a beautiful li'l girl. You have no control over how the world is set up, but you can choose how you see it. Hopefully, you will find your own way through the clutter," said Bay, holding Hannah in her arms.

While Bay was still engrossed in her thoughts, Bee entered the room, walked over to the bed smiling, and kissed Hannah on the forehead, "Bay, she's a livin' doll! Ya might not want ta hear it, but she looks jus' like Will."

"I know, Mama. I hate dat Hannah won' git a chance ta know her father."

"Bay, I didn't bring dis up ta make ya feel guilty."

"I know, Mama. Whether ya did or didn't, it's jus' de way I feel."

Charlotte walked in, carrying a large vase of beautiful yellow, pink, and white daisies. Bee took the flowers and placed them on the table beside the bed as Charlotte greeted Bay with a big hug. "Bay, you doing all right? You gettin' everything you need?" asked Charlotte, examining the baby. She leaned over, smiling, and whispered something in Bay's ear.

"No," replied Bay, smiling as Bee stood there watching curiously.

"Bay, what's the baby's name?" asked Charlotte.

"Hannah."

"I like it. Hannah is very pretty. Mrs. Albertson, I know you're happy Bay is here in Galveston."

"I sure am."

Suddenly, the nurse walked into the room. "Miss McQueen, it's time to take your little bundle of joy back to the baby ward," she said, smiling.

The phone rang. Bee answered, "Hello, Bee speaking."

"Hi, Mrs. Albertson. I'm Bay's friend Roberta, from Salem," the caller said.

"Just a minute, Roberta, let me give the phone to Bay."

Before Bay took the phone, Charlotte said, "Bay, Mrs. Albertson, I have several errands to take care of. Bay, I'll call you when you get home. Tell Roberta hello." She walked out the door.

Bay excitedly took the phone from Bee. "Hey, girl, you behavin' yourself in the big city of Salem?"

"Chile, that is my life story here in Salem. Since you been gone, it's hell living in this little Georgia clay town. Even my Northern accent is just about gone," exclaimed Roberta, chuckling.

"Roberta, you are so crazy. I've only been in Galveston two months. That's not enough time to lose your accent, but I do understand your boredom," replied Bay, laughing.

"How's the new baby? What's her name?"

Bee interrupted to say, "Honey, I'll see you tomorrow," and she left the room.

Bay waved good-bye to her mother and continued to talk to Roberta. "My little girl's name is Hannah, and she's doin' fine."

"Hannah, Hannah, Hannah . . . that's a pretty name. It has an aristocratic ring to it."

"What does that mean?"

"Old money, influence, and manners," replied Roberta.

"That is wonderful. There is a saying in the Bible, what you believe about yourself is what you experience," said Bay.

"Let's change the subject. I don't know nothing about the Bible, but I do know a lot about other things because I have two degrees," said Roberta, laughing. "Girl, let me get myself off this phone. When Aunt Mildred sees this bill, I won't be able to stay here."

"How did you know I was in the hospital?" asked Bay.

"I called your mother's house, and Mr. Albertson told me. Bay, girl, I enjoyed talking to you. I hear Aunt Mildred coming." Roberta quietly hung up the phone.

After three days, Bay left the hospital. Jack, Bee, and Zachary picked her up. While Jack pushed Bay and the baby in the wheelchair, Bee led Zack by the hand as he walked beside the chair. Bay noticed a sad look in her son's eyes. "Zack, come sit on Mommy's other knee. I missed you so much," said Bay.

"Bay, I think Zack is too heavy ta get in ya lap. He's a big boy who's goin' ta take good care of his li'l sister," said Bee, picking him up and leaning over so Bay could give him a kiss.

"That was some good sugar," said Bay, smiling.

"Mommy, can I hold Hannah?" asked Zack.

"Sure can. Wait till we git home."

Zachary acted very happy. He walked beside Jack, trying to help push the wheelchair and singing, "I'm a big brother, yes I am!"

Jack began to sing along with him. "Zack is a big brother, yes he is!"

Finally, they arrived home. Bay was eager to begin a new life in Galveston. Hopefully, she would find what she'd searched for all her life.

CHAPTER NINE

Six weeks later, Bay began working at Galveston General Hospital as a cashier in the business office. She was thrilled to be getting paid more money than she'd made at the bank. Furthermore, she was grateful that Bee and Jack were allowing her to live with them temporarily.

Four months passed, and Bay had saved up enough money to move into her own place. Charlotte gave Bay the phone number of a real-estate agency to contact. They found the perfect cottage for her. When she saw it, she just loved it. It was pale yellow with a large porch that had an old-fashioned swing and two brown wicker rockers.

"This is the perfect home for my children and me," said Bay to the agent. "I can hardly wait to move in. I'm so excited!"

Bay didn't waste any time. Two days later, she moved in. Some weeks later, while Bay was still in bed relishing the fact that she was in her own place in Galveston, the phone beside her bed rang. "Hello," said Bay.

"Guess who called las' night," said Bee.

"Don' tell me. It wuz Sadie."

"Nope."

"Well, it had ta be Carrie."

"Yes, it wuz Carrie. She's comin' home 'n two weeks," responded Bee.

"Mama, dat's wonderful! Course, you don' sound too excited," said Bay.

"To tell de truth, I'm not. Carrie is bringin' her boyfriend home wit' her," said Bee sadly.

"Great smokin' Joe! Dat's de best news ever! Carrie finally kept her head out of a book long enough ta catch her a man," responded Bay, laughing.

"The way Carrie looked de las' time wit' dat afro, dere's no tellin' how she 'n' her boyfriend are goin' ta look. Dis is Galveston, not Salem," said Bee.

"Mama, I thought you'd moved beyond de hair 'n' de clothes. Ya don' want Carrie ta tell ya off like she did last time. Do ya really love Carrie?"

"Of course I do, she's ma child," replied Bee.

"Love has nothin' ta do wit' hair or clothes. Jus' remember somethin': Carrie loved ya when ya didn't know who ya were. I don' intend ta spell it out! Let's move on!" said Bay seriously. "Mama, I'm goin' ta call Sadie so she kin come too!"

Jack and Zachary were working in the garden when Carrie and her boyfriend, Marvin, drove up. Carrie began blowing the horn. Bay ran to the window. "It's Carrie! It's Carrie! It's Carrie!" yelled Bay, running outside.

Sadie walked swiftly behind her. "Hey, baby sister!" cried Sadie, giving her a big hug.

"Sisters, let me introduce you to my sweetheart," said Carrie, smiling.

Now out of the car, standing, Marvin reached out his hand to Bay. "Marvin Payne's my name."

"Nice to meet you. Bay's mine."

"This is Sadie," interrupted Carrie. Marvin was about six feet five and 185 pounds, with a dark complexion. Bay and Sadie smiled.

What a fine sweet-potato Carrie done caught herself, thought Bay. By this time, Jack, Bee, and the children had appeared. Bee was holding Hannah and was quite pleased that Marvin didn't have an afro, nor did Carrie. She was wearing braids.

"Just look at little Hannah, aren't you adorable? Mama, Jack, this is Marvin Payne," said Carrie proudly.

"It's so nice to meet you. Come, let's go inside," replied Bee.

"Marvin, I'll show you to your room," said Jack, smiling.

"Jack, this is such a beautiful home you have!" said Carrie.

"Thank you, but your mother is the decorator."

"Carrie, you will have to share a room with Sadie," said Bee.

"I know, Mama, I certainly wouldn't want to be responsible for your going to hell for allowing your daughter to have sex in your house without a license," said Carrie, laughing. Bee walked away shaking her head.

Bay and her sisters went in the opposite direction. Finally they reached the bedroom and went inside. "Carrie, how in de world did ya find dat fine thang?" asked Bay, smiling.

"At de Braxton's Library."

"Girl, keepin' ya head in a book really paid off!" cried Bay excitedly.

"Is he as good as he looks?" asked Sadie, smiling.

"Sisters, he is good in ev'ry way."

"Lord, thank ya dat our baby sister ain't mixed up wit' no jackrabbit!" cried Bay with laughter.

An hour later, everybody returned to the dining room for dinner. The table was beautifully set. Carrie walked over and sat next to Marvin, while Bay and Sadie helped Bee place the food on the table. As Bay, Bee, and Sadie took their seats, Jack blessed the food. "Lord, we thank you for allowing Marvin and Carrie to arrive home safely, and we certainly thank you for this meal and the beautiful woman who prepared it. Amen," said Jack, smiling.

"Amen," replied Sara and Zachary, chuckling.

"Marvin, what type of work do you do?" asked Bee.

"I'm a pharmacist. I work in my family's drugstore."

Bay and her sisters looked at each other.

"That is wonderful!" responded Bee joyfully.

"Mama, these greens are delicious!" interrupted Carrie as she changed the subject.

After dinner, Marvin, Carrie, and her sisters went to a movie. She was so happy that Marvin had agreed to visit Galveston to meet her family. Everybody liked him. A week later, Carrie and Marvin returned to California and Sadie went back to Astoria.

For Bay, working in the business office at Galveston General was quite different from the bank in Salem. She shared a very small office with two other women. Both were white and seemed friendly. Sunny was a tall redhead with shoulder-length hair and blue eyes. Marsha was medium height with beautiful, long, thick black hair. The only time Bay had a chance to see other people was during lunch in the cafeteria, which lasted for only thirty minutes. She was used to seeing people come and go all day long. Furthermore, working at the bank, she used to get a lot of attention. *This will take gittin' used ta*, thought Bay.

One day while Bay and her coworkers were walking through the corridor, they saw a tall, handsome colored doctor. "Who's that?" asked Bay.

"That's Dr. Mark Edison," replied Marsha.

"Don't set your eyes on him," warned Sunny. "He only likes blonde white women. That leaves you, Marsha, and me out."

"He's not the only one who feels that way. I've had to deal with color sickness all my life," exclaimed Bay.

As they walked inside their office, the supervisor met them. "Bay, your mother called. She wants you to call her right away. It's very important," said Mrs. Brewster.

Bay immediately walked over to her desk and dialed her mother's phone number.

"Yes, Mama, what's wrong? Are the kids okay?"

"They're fine, but something horrible has happened," said Bee.

"What is it, Mama? Tell me, please!"

"It's Savannah. She's overdosed on sleeping pills."

"You mean she's dead?" said Bay softly, now seated at her desk with tears rolling down her cheeks. "Oh, Mama, I can't believe this. I am so sorry for Vannah."

"Bay, why don' ya come home?" said Bee.

"Okay, Mama, okay. I'll see if I can," said Bay somberly.

"Bay, what's wrong?" asked Sunny as Marsha looked on.

"It's my high-school friend. She's dead."

Mrs. Brewster walked in. "Bay, what on earth is the matter?" she asked compassionately.

"Her best friend is dead," answered Sunny.

"Bay, I'm so sorry. Why don't you take the rest of the day off to pull yourself together?"

"Thank you, Mrs. Brewster," said Bay, and she left the office.

Ten minutes later, Bay walked into her mother's living room. Bee was waiting for her. "Mama, it's so hard ta believe Vannah is gone. What really happened? Did she commit suicide?" asked Bay, walking closer to Bee. "Mama, did she?" Bay yelled.

"Honey, calm down," replied Bee, putting her arms around her daughter. "Yes, she did."

Now Bay was sobbing uncontrollably. "Mama, it's so unfair," she cried, looking in her mother's eyes and pulling away. "I hate dis world wit' its color sickness. If yer too black, yer not good enough! If yer light wit' good hair, yer worshiped! Vannah jus' wanted ta be loved fur herself, not her light skin! Mama, sometimes I wish I'd never been born in a world that despises me because of my color, 'n' that I've been cursed by God!"

"Honey, I know yer very upset, but ya got ta pull yourself together! Savannah is gone. Yer still here. Yer a strong woman. What's ya las' name?" asked Bee, tears rolling down her cheeks.

"McQueen," responded Bay softly.

"Who are ya sisters 'n' mother?"

"Sadie, Carrie, 'n' you."

"We are de McQueen women," asserted Bee, holding Bay tightly.

"Yes, Mama, we are de McQueen women," said Bay softly. Suddenly, Bay realized she needed to call Savannah's mother to find out about the funeral arrangements.

While Bee looked after Zachary and Hannah, Bay took two days off from work and went to Salem for Savannah's funeral. The service was scheduled for Sunday at three o'clock at Shiloh AME Church. Bay arrived in Salem Friday morning. About ten-thirty, she was inside Bee's house in Oak Woods. Bee hadn't sold or rented her house because, during that time, blacks were not permitted to stay in motels and didn't feel safe. After unpacking, Bay called Roberta's aunt. "Hello, Miss Mildred. This is Bay McQueen, your old neighbor."

"Baby, how ya doin'? Sho miss you. You like livin' in dat big city, Galveston?" asked Miss Mildred.

"Yes, ma'am. I sure do. Is Roberta home?"

"Where else she goin' ta be? Don't work. Don't clean up the house and can't cook! But she can eat you outa house and home and talk about dem two degrees," said Miss Mildred, chuckling.

"May I speak with her?" interrupted Bay, laughing.

"Roberta! Roberta! Bay wanta speak witcha."

"Hey, girl, how you doin? You got your own place yet?" asked Roberta.

"I sure do, but I'm here for a friend's funeral. I'm staying at our house in Oak Woods. I'll pick you up in about an hour."

"I'll need more than an hour to pack all my stuff to move to Galveston," responded Roberta.

"I'm not talking about moving. We'll discuss that later. My best friend in high school died. I need you to go with me to visit her mother and attend the funeral," said Bay.

"Chile, I think you're the truest friend I've ever had, but I don't enjoy going to funerals. Folks that aren't even related to the family be crying, hollering, and carrying on," replied Roberta seriously.

"Please, Roberta, don't let me down now!"

"Okay, Bay, for you, only you," responded Roberta hesitantly.

"Thanks, Roberta. Why don't you stay overnight at the house with me? I really don't want to be alone. I can't help thinking about Vannah. You would've really liked her," said Bay softly, with tears swelling in her eyes and a trembling voice.

"Bay, are you crying? Please don't cry, I'll be more than happy to stay overnight with you. I'm so tired of Aunt Mildred, I don't know what to do! Pull yourself together. You can pick me up in about twenty minutes," replied Roberta.

When Bay reached Roberta's Aunt Mildred's house, she couldn't help but glance at the little cottage she once lived in. She thought about the last time she saw Will and the first time she met Roberta. *Don' know what would haf happened if Roberta hadn't been dere fur me when Will walked out on me,* thought Bay, wiping tears from her eyes. Suddenly, she thought about Mother Caine. She had not talked to Mother since she arrived in Salem.

Bay blew her horn. Roberta peeped out the window. A few minutes later, she was off the porch and into the car. "Hey, city girl. It's good to see you," said Roberta, smiling.

"Likewise. Thanks so much for coming through for me again."

"You'd do the same for me. Girl, seems like you're doing all right for yourself! It's time for me to do something with all my degrees. There's got to be more to life than arguing with Aunt Mildred every day."

"When I was a little girl, I remember Big Mama telling Mama, 'If you want better, you got to be better.' Both of us need to consider that. I haven't seen or talked to Mother Caine since I've been in town. Let's stop by to see her before we turn in for the night!" said Bay excitedly.

When Bay parked in front of Mother Caine's house, Mother was sitting on her front porch. She stood up and greeted Bay. "Lord, Bay, it's you! Just look at you, looking so refined and all! Didn't Mother tell you and Bee that y'all would move up in the world?" cried Mother Caine, smiling excitedly.

"Mother, do you remember my friend Roberta?" asked Bay.

"Sure I do. Don't think 'cause my number is more than yours I can't remember nothing!" responded Mother Caine, chuckling. "How's my Zack and Hannah?"

"They're just fine. Hannah's almost a year old."

"Lord, how time flies. Y'all come on in. I know y'all are going to stay with me a little while," said Mother Caine, smiling.

"Not too long, though. I'm here for a funeral," said Bay.

"Who died?" shouted Mother, looking wide-eyed and astonished. Roberta almost burst out laughing but restrained herself painfully. Bay and Roberta followed Mother into her living room and sat on the sofa across from Mother Caine, who was seated on a beautiful antique

Queen Anne high-back chair. "Bay, tell me, who died that you know?" repeated Mother.

"Savannah, my best friend from high school. My ex-husband's cousin," exclaimed Bay.

"No, she didn't! That's the real light-skinned girl that visited you from California and the one the boy killed himself over?" asked Mother.

By this time, Roberta could not take it anymore. "Mother, I need to use your restroom," said Roberta, walking swiftly in that direction.

"Honey, you go right on. You know where it is," replied Mother. "Bay, what happened to the child?"

"She overdosed on sleeping pills," replied Bay sadly, with tears filling her eyes.

"I'm so sorry. I ain't never heard of no colored person killing themselves with sleeping pills or nothing else. Reckon that's the white coming out, poor child. When's the funeral?"

"Sunday afternoon at three o'clock."

"Lord, Bay, you need someone to go with you. This is going to be one of the biggest funerals in Salem! Child, it's going to be real hard on you!"

"That's why I asked Roberta to go with me," said Bay.

"That's good Roberta is going with you, but I need to go. This is the time when you need a praying woman to hold you up in prayer!" replied Mother, smiling with excitement. Now standing, she said, "Bay, you and Roberta go on home. We got a busy day tomorrow. We have to visit the family tomorrow, and I have to find me something pretty to wear," continued Mother Caine, walking them to the door.

When Bay and Roberta reached the car, Bay laughed so hard tears rolled down her cheeks. "Mother Caine is a real cartoon," she cried, trying to calm herself down. "She loves funerals."

"I had to go to the bathroom to get some relief," said Roberta. Bay felt so much better having Roberta with her. Now Mother Caine had volunteered to go along too.

Early Sunday morning about eight-thirty, Bay was awakened by the telephone. *Who on earth is callin' me dis time of de morning? God, I hope nothin' is wrong with ma children*, thought Bay, picking up the receiver. "Hello," said Bay drowsily.

"Bay, just callin' to make sure you're up. We got a big day ahead of us," said Mother Caine on the other end.

"Yes, ma'am. I'm up now."

"Why don't I drive over to your house, so you won't have to come get me?"

"Mother, it's only eight-thirty, and the funeral isn't until three o'clock. Roberta and I are not planning to visit the family until eleven o'clock."

"Eleven o'clock! Lord, y'all young folks don't know how to do nothin' in style," said Mother, upset.

"Mother, tell you what, why don't I pick you up at ten-thirty? That will give us plenty of time to visit the family and get to the church so we can get a good seat," said Bay pleasantly.

"Bay, you're the best child Bee has. I'll be on the porch waiting!"

As Bay was hanging up the receiver, Roberta walked in. She'd heard voices from the next room. "Who was that?" she asked.

"Mother Caine! She acts like we're goin' to the World's Fair or a Marvin Gaye concert," said Bay, smiling. "She wanted to drive over so I wouldn't have to pick her up. I am not about to let Mother drag me out too early. I told her to stay put, and I would pick her up at ten-thirty."

Two hours later, Bay drove up in front of Mother Caine's house. Mother was sitting on the porch all dressed up. Bay had never seen her look so fashionable. Bay and Roberta got out of the car to greet her and help with the food and drinks.

"Gee, Mother, you sure look beautiful. Are you sure you're goin' to the funeral to hold me up in prayer or to look at the preacher?" asked Bay, chuckling.

"I do everything in style. Bay, you and Roberta can learn a lot from Mother," she asserted, laughing as she got inside the car.

"Mother, how nice of you to give all this food to Vannah's family. I'm sure they will appreciate it," said Bay.

Soon they arrived at Savannah's house. Bay knocked on the door nervously. A stranger opened it. "Hello," Bay said. "I'm Bay McQueen. Vannah and I were best friends. These are my friends Roberta and Mother Caine."

"I'm Savannah's Aunt Cora from California. Bay, she spoke often and fondly of you. Please come in, dear."

"Thank you so much for those kind words. We shared so much," said Bay softly, trying to hold back the tears.

"We would like to say a few words to Savannah's mother and leave food," said Mother Caine, holding Bay around the waist.

"Have a seat and I'll get her," said Cora, while Roberta put the food in the kitchen.

Shortly thereafter, Savannah's mother walked into the living room toward Bay, who stood up. The two women embraced. "Bay, thanks so much for coming. I just can't believe that my baby is gone. She never got over Kirby's suicide," said Savannah's mother, trying to hold back the tears.

"I know. I'm so sorry," replied Bay somberly. Mother Caine reached in her purse and handed Bay and Savannah's mother some tissues to wipe away the tears. "Oh, excuse me, this is Mother Caine and Roberta," said Bay.

"Thank you so much for coming. Please excuse me. I need to be alone before the funeral," said Mrs. Pierce.

"Lord, honey, we understand. You go lie down and rest. Bay will show us out," said Mother Caine.

Savannah had a huge funeral. Folks were there who Bay knew and didn't know. The whole church was wailing and yelling. However, the problem with the entire sick affair was that most of them contributed to Savannah's early death because of their own twisted belief system regarding color, which caused her such pain that she committed suicide. Savannah was only aware of her wounds, not her potential for wholeness.

Nothing lasts forever, not even funerals. After the service and burial, Bay drove Mother Caine home. "Mother, who's that man sitting on your porch? He acts like he lives there," said Bay jokingly.

"He does—he's my new boarder," replied Mother, smiling cunningly.

"Your boarder?" interrupted Roberta.

"You see, when you get my number, folks think the fire is out in your furnace, so you just let 'em think what they want to. You just go right along with 'em. But he is much more than a boarder—much, much more," said Mother, laughing and getting out the car.

"Mother, I don't know what we're goin' to do with you," said Bay, laughing.

"Aunt Mildred needs to meet Mother Caine to liven her behind up!" said Roberta, laughing.

"She'd probably liven up if you weren't living with her. She's tired of you," said Bay, chuckling.

"I'm just as damn tired of her!"

"How long do you think it'll take you to pack some of your clothes? We can come back another time to get the rest."

"Thirty minutes!" said Roberta excitedly.

"Let's go do it!"

"Let's do it! Let's do it! Let's do it!" cheered Roberta.

Suddenly, Bay decided she needed to lay down some rules for Roberta. "Wait a minute, friend. I got to let you know exactly what I expect. First, you must have a job in six weeks."

"Six weeks!"

"Yes, ma'am, six weeks. Next, you have to help buy food. Girl, you know your appetite has no boundaries," said Bay, smiling.

"Bay, I promise, I promise to do my part! I just want to get the hell out of Salem!" cried Roberta.

When Bay reached Roberta's Aunt Mildred's house, Roberta jumped out of the car and ran toward the house. After Roberta broke the news to her aunt, Aunt Mildred helped her pack. Finally Bay, Roberta, and Aunt Mildred finished loading the car. Ten minutes later they picked up Bay's luggage from the house in Oak Woods and sped away to Galveston.

CHAPTER TEN

The beauty of Galveston became quite evident during the fall. The trees were so colorful with their beautiful leaves of varied shapes falling to the ground throughout the wooded areas and most neighborhoods. This beauty and cultural environment had a positive impact on Roberta. When Roberta moved in with Bay, she began to get herself together. Bay and Charlotte helped her get a job at the Galveston Public Library as a reference librarian. In May of 1970, Carrie received her undergraduate degree from Braxton and entered law school. The entire family, including Roberta and Mother Caine, went to California for the event.

Three years passed, and it was 1973. Bay was twenty-seven years of age. Zachary was five, and Hannah was two. Bay was still working at the hospital but had started feeling empty. While working at her desk, she thought, *I'm tired of bein' alone. I need a man in ma life.* Bay looked at her watch. *I almost forgot about ma lunch date wit' Charlotte 'n' Roberta!* she thought.

The Wounded Whole

As Bay stood and picked up her purse from under her desk, Marsha said, "Bay, would you like to join Sunny and me for lunch?"

"Thank you so much, but I have a lunch date with two friends."

"Maybe all of us can have lunch together," suggested Sunny.

"I guess. Tell me, why y'all so eager to have lunch with me? You never asked me before," said Bay.

"Well, there's always a first time. Where are we eating?" said Sunny excitedly.

"The Upscale," replied Bay.

"I heard that's the place to be. It's where the high class hangs out. Who you meeting there?" asked Sunny.

"Somebody real high-class," said Bay, lifting her head in the air. "Come to think of it, maybe I shouldn't take you. You might mess things up for me," continued Bay, smiling.

"We promise we won't," said Sunny.

"What about you, Marsha?" asked Bay.

"Of course I won't," replied Marsha slyly.

"Okay, let's go," said Bay.

Bay felt mighty good inside walking into the Upscale, because it was a known fact that colored people were only seen in the kitchen. When Bay, Sunny, and Marsha entered the dining area, it was packed. A hostess greeted them. "Hello, how many are in your party?"

"Five. Two should already be here," said Bay.

"Great! Follow me," said the hostess.

While they were following her, Bay heard Charlotte's voice. "Bay, we're over here," cried Charlotte, as people began to stare. As Bay, followed by Marsha and Sunny, approached them, Charlotte and Roberta looked at each other. They thought it would be just the three of them having lunch together. Bay could sense the disappointment. She needed to break the ice.

"Charlotte, Roberta, how long y'all been here?" she asked.

"About fifteen minutes," responded Roberta.

"Let me introduce my coworkers. This is Sunny and Marsha. I talk so much about y'all, they were just dying to meet you. I told them how pretty and smart y'all are, and that regardless of my faults I could always count on you," said Bay, smiling.

"Bay McQueen, you know you're lying. You're just trying to save your you-know-what!" said Roberta, chuckling.

"Sunny, didn't I say those things?" asked Bay.

"She sure did. Bay's always saying great things about both of you."

"Bay, you should be ashamed of yourself. Now you have Sunny lying," said Charlotte. Everybody laughed.

Meanwhile, the waitress walked over. "I'll move you to a larger table," she said. The women followed her and were seated. "Ladies, are you ready to order?" she asked.

"Yes we are! I am starving," replied Bay.

After everyone had placed an order, they began getting acquainted. Sunny was divorced, Marsha was single and involved with a married man. All of them were enjoying the scenery, especially the fine-looking men spread throughout the restaurant.

"Look, look, look, coming through the door. That is a fine-looking thing!" said Sunny excitedly.

"Please don't pass out. We don't want to have to rush you to the hospital!" said Marsha, laughing.

"He's not bad-looking at all for a white guy, but the thing you need to be concerned about is, does he have anything to work with?" interrupted Roberta, laughing. Everybody roared with laughter.

"I don't know about anybody else, but my honey makes me sing 'The Star-Spangled Banner'!" said Charlotte, laughing.

"Girl, you are so crazy. That is too funny!" said Bay, chuckling. "Roberta has really rubbed off on you! I don't have a man in my life, but I do know how to tell if he's got the equipment he needs to work with," continued Bay, closing her eyes and shaking her head as if she were preaching a sermon.

"How?" asked the group, curious. They huddled their heads together like a football team.

"Well, the first thing you need to do is check out his hands and feet. If he's got little bitty fingers and feet, don't waste your time. He ain't got nothing! Another thing: most of 'em that don't have nothing are jackrabbits. It only takes less than a minute for them to get their thrill and fall asleep. They think 'cause they got theirs, you did too, and walk around with their chest stuck out like they are the greatest lovers in the world," said Bay, laughing.

"Bay, that is funny!" responded Charlotte.

"I bet Sunny and Marsha have not been around such crazy women," said Roberta.

"I love it! I love it! I love it!" replied Sunny.

"Look at him," said Marsha, pointing at a man passing their table.

"Poor thing, he has very small hands and feet. Bet when he finishes making love, he thinks he has really made the earth shake," said Sunny, laughing.

"Girls, we've talked enough about sex today. It's time to get back to work. This has been a blast!" said Bay.

"I really enjoyed this," said Sunny. "Let's do it again real soon!"

"The food and atmosphere were real good, but there's one thing missing," said Roberta.

"What?" asked Charlotte.

"Bay, you know exactly what I'm thinking, don't you?" asked Roberta.

"Yep, we don't see any dark meat in here."

"Find 'em and bring 'em in!" replied Charlotte jokingly, getting up from the table. Bay and the others did the same. They walked out of the restaurant laughing and talking. Roberta and Charlotte went in opposite directions while Bay and her coworkers returned to work at the hospital.

After Bay left work later that afternoon, she drove to her mother's house to pick up her children. Since Bee no longer worked, she had become a full-time babysitter for her grandchildren. As Bay parked her car, she noticed a strange car in the driveway. When she opened the door, she heard Bee yell, "Bay, we're in the kitchen."

Bay walked over and stood in the doorway. To her surprise, there were two handsome guys seated across from Bee, eating. One was holding Zachary and eating like there was no tomorrow. The other one was engrossed in a conversation with Bee. When they saw Bay, both were smitten by her beauty and poise. "Bay, this is Jack's son, Barney." Looking at the other guy, who was holding Zachary, Bee said, "This is Tony Franklin, Barney's friend."

Gosh, he is very handsome 'n' more ma type, thought Bay.

Now totally focused on Bay and feeling a little jittery, Tony asked, "How ya doin'?"

"Great! I'm having a super day!" replied Bay excitedly. "I finally get a chance to meet my stepbrother."

"Stepbrother?" asked Barney.

"Yep, stepbrother!" replied Tony. "Mrs. Albertson, you know you can cook! Zack and I really enjoyed everything. Ain't that right, buddy?" Zachary moved his head up and down. Bay and Bee laughed. Tony got up from the table, walked over to Bay, and stood Zachary beside her. Both smiled and knew that they would get to know each other better.

"Tony, you're in the military?" asked Bay.

"Yeah, I'm a sergeant."

Dat's nice, Bay thought, *but I'm really not interested in another soldier after Sam*. However, something within wouldn't let her resist this experience.

"Say, Bay, why don't you go to the Rocking Chair with me and Tony tomorrow night?" asked Barney.

"Rocking Chair? Is it a club?"

"Yeah, and a jammin' good one too!" exclaimed Tony.

"I don't know. Y'all sure it ain't no hole in the wall?"

Tony and Barney laughed. "Trust us. We would never take you to no hole in the wall," Tony assured her, smiling.

"Tony and I got our papers to go to 'Nam in ninety days. We want to enjoy ourselves," said Barney.

"If mama can look after my kids, I'll go. Can I bring my friend Roberta along?"

"Is she as fine as you?" asked Barney.

"Oh yeah, she's wonderful. Y'all can pick us up at my place about eight-thirty."

Tony took Hannah from Bee and walked Bay to her car.

The following night about seven o'clock, Roberta knocked on Bay's door. "Girl, I can't believe I let you talk me into going on a blind date," she said, walking over and taking a seat on the sofa.

"Stop complaining, you know you want a man," replied Bay, brushing her hair.

"Just look at you. I sure hope when you sit down that dress don't split and show your behind."

"Well, they'll have a lot to see, ain't that right?"

"Bay, how do I look? I'm very nervous."

"You just calm down. You look great."

"He might not like me."

"You might not like him. I can't believe the beautiful, sassy woman with two degrees is scared!" continued Bay. Both laughed. "Roberta, I think I hear a car." They heard footsteps on the porch and then knocking on the door. Bay opened it. There stood Tony and Barney in their uniforms. *They both look quite handsome*, Bay thought. "Hi, Uncle Sam's men, come on in," she said.

"Bay, you lookin' mighty foxy. I can hardly take it!" said Tony, moving closer to her, holding her hand, and placing it on his heart. "Feel the beat of my heart. It's racing for you!"

"Don't pay Tony no mind. He's full of you-know-what," said Barney. Everybody laughed. "Hey, Bay, where's your friend?"

"She's in the bedroom. I'll get her." As Bay turned to leave, Roberta walked in. "Barney, Tony, this is my friend Roberta."

Barney looked quite pleased. "Hello, Roberta, nice to meet you."

"I'm very pleased to meet you too," replied Roberta, glancing at his hands and feet. Bay knew right off that those two would get along just fine by the way they were looking at each other.

"Hey, y'all, we'd better go," interrupted Tony, laughing. "Come on, my livin' prize!" he continued, smiling and grabbing Bay around her waist.

Tony was a handsome, fun-loving guy who loved to joke and play. Underneath that facade, he was afraid to go to Vietnam to fight what he believed was a senseless war that had nothing to do with him. He feared he wouldn't come back.

Finally, they reached the Rocking Chair. They bought their tickets and headed straight to the dance floor. The band was playing a slow song. Tony pulled Bay so close to him, she could feel every part of him. When the music was over, he was still holding her.

"Wake up, Half Pint, the song is over," cried Barney, laughing.

"Half Pint?" interrupted Bay, smiling.

"Yeah, that's my name 'cause I can only drink a half-pint of booze. If I drink more than that, I'll be out of circulation for days."

By about two o'clock, the great fun and conversation were over. The Rocking Chair closed. Barney went home with Roberta and Tony with Bay.

Tony didn't leave Bay's house until five o'clock that morning. They became quite intimate. Tony got the opportunity to share his deep fears about the war. Bay didn't know much about politics, but she did have an opinion about the war. She felt that there was something unfair about it when so many colored boys were being killed and sent home. Just about every other week there was a funeral.

The next morning, Sunday, Bay and Roberta ate breakfast together and compared notes. "Girl, that Barney Albertson is something else," said Roberta, smiling.

"Did you go all the way?"

"What you mean, all the way?"

"Did you give him some cherry pie?"

"Bay McQueen, you're being nasty! I'm tellin' your mama! I really wanted to, but I don't know him well enough. Besides, he's a soldier, and I don't know if I'll ever see him again."

"Roberta, you do like him, don't you? I have never seen this side of you." Bay got up and walked over to her friend.

"What about you? How do you feel about Tony?"

"I really like him. He's a warm, loving, funny guy. I'm scared too. I never intended to get involved with another soldier after Sam. Now I've not only met another soldier, but one who might not return from Vietnam. Know what? I'm not going to let that stop me. I love being with him. I'm goin' ta spend as much time with him as I can before he leaves."

"Bay, you're right. I'll talk to you tomorrow. Barney is coming over for lunch today." Roberta stood up and walked toward the door.

A few minutes later, Bay heard a knock at the door. *It couldn't be Roberta. She jus' lef'*, she thought. "Who is it?" asked Bay.

"It's Tony."

She immediately opened the door, "Hi, Tony, what are you doin' here?"

"Just wanted to make sure no other homeboy is over here tryin' to stack out my territory," he replied, laughing, grabbing, dancing, and swinging Bay around the room.

"Tony, you're so crazy!" yelled Bay, laughing.

"I know it, baby! I know it! I know it! I'm just crazy about you!" They both laughed and fell on the sofa. They looked into each other eyes. "Oh, Bay, I love you. There's something 'bout you that makes me feel real good."

"I love being with you."

"By the way, where are the kids?" asked Tony.

"They're with mama," replied Bay.

Still looking in each other's eyes with their lips touching, Tony said, "Baby, I want you—all of you. You want all of me?"

"Yes, Half Pint, yes, all of you." They kissed passionately and experienced a place of peace and security.

After that day, they spent every day together. A month before he was scheduled to leave for Vietnam, Tony had supper at Bay's house. While Bay was cooking, he played with the children. He had Zachary sitting around his neck on his shoulders. At the same time, Hannah was in his arms. He began turning around in the room. Zachary and Hannah were having a good time. Bay stood in the doorway watching and smiling. "Tony, it's time to eat!" shouted Bay.

"I'm ready!" he said, walking over to the table. Zack sat next to Tony, and Hannah sat on Bay's lap. "Girl, I didn't know you could cook greens like this. No wonder I'm crazy about you!" cried Tony, smiling and winking his eye at Bay.

After supper, he helped Bay do the dishes so she could give the children their baths and put them to bed. Tony had worn them out. Without any prodding from their mother, they fell asleep. Now Tony and Bay had the house all to themselves.

While seated on the sofa, Tony pulled Bay close to him. "Now it's just you and me, my dear," said Tony, kissing Bay around her neck as if he were Count Dracula.

"Oh, please don't hurt me, sir! Please let me live!" yelled Bay, laughing.

"Bay, will you marry me? Baby, I'm not coming back from 'Nam. You and the kids will be taken care of," said Tony somberly.

"Oh no, Half Pint, please don't say that! You are coming back! You have to come back. What on earth will I do without you?" asked Bay, with tears welling up in her eyes.

"I didn't mean to make you cry, but I'm still waiting for an answer. Will you marry me?"

"Sorry, Tony, I can't do that. I do love you, but I will not marry you for money. You can come back from 'Nam, but you have to believe it. It's like you've given up! Please don't give up! I love you with all that is within me," cried Bay, with tears rolling down her cheeks.

"Baby, you're a diamond, you know that? Most women would have jumped at my offer to get paid. I love you, Bay McQueen." He held her so close that her head rested on his chest. "Bay, can I stay with you tonight?"

She hesitated. Bay knew he only had a short time left before leaving for Vietnam. Therefore, she couldn't say no. She hated that he had to fight a crazy, useless war. "Sure, Half Pint."

"I like how you say 'Half Pint.' You will always be a part of me."

Two weeks before Tony and Barney left for Vietnam, they wanted to take Bay and Roberta dancing. They went to the Rocking Chair. While Barney and Roberta were dancing, they noticed a medium-brown-skinned woman about twenty-five walk up to Bay and Tony on the dance floor. She was very angry and loud.

"You low-down dirty bastard. Now I see why you treated me like you do! She ain't no better than me!" yelled the woman, while everybody stopped to watch the show.

"Ruby, this is my cousin!" responded Tony, smiling nervously.

"You mean y'all are cousins?" she asked, looking at Bay.

"Yeah, we're cousins. We're just out having fun before he goes to 'Nam," exclaimed Bay.

"Sorry I acted so foolish. He told me I was the only woman in his life," said Ruby.

"Really? Well, let's get real! Girl, Half Pint is not my cousin! He lied to both of us! I thought I was the only one too! Now, Half Pint, I hope you and Ruby will be very happy." Bay walked over to Roberta and Barney. "Barney, will you and Roberta please take me home?"

"What about Tony?" asked Barney.

"I'm sure he'll catch a ride with Ruby," replied Bay.

"I can't do Tony like that. I'm sure she don't mean nothing to him!" said Barney.

"It's hard to believe Tony is a damn two-timer!" said Roberta angrily.

"Don't be too hard on my homeboy. I'm sure he can explain the situation. I think he was involved with her before he met Bay."

"Don't try to take up for him," replied Roberta harshly.

Tony immediately rushed over to talk to Bay. He knew she was very upset. "Bay, don't leave me like this. Honest to God, I have not been with Ruby since I've been with you."

"Well, why in the hell did you tell me to say we are cousins?"

"To keep her from starting a fight."

"Hey, I don't need you or nobody else to protect me. I'll tear up you and anybody else that'll get in my way!"

"You're not leaving until all of us go," said Tony firmly.

"My name is Bay McQueen. No man can give me orders!" shouted Bay. "Who wants to take me home?" Bay looked over at the male spectators. "Can I get a volunteer?"

"Man, I'll be glad to take you home!" shouted one man, getting up from his chair.

"You'd better keep your ass over there in your seat," yelled Tony.

"You'd better go git Ruby," yelled Bay. "I'm not leavin' dis building wit' no two-timin', fast-talkin', Half Pint dog!"

"Bay is really mad! It's a terrible thing. Homeboy done messed up!" said Barney.

"Listen, baby, I love you. I swear you're the only woman for me. Please stop yelling and showing off! Everybody is looking and wanting my girl. Come on, baby, please forgive me. Come on and dance wit' me. Don't let Ruby come between us." Tony gradually put his arms around Bay's waist like he was trying to tame a wild stallion.

"Half Pint, I'm still mad," said Bay, moving to the music.

"I know, baby, I know." While he and Bay were dancing and laughing, Ruby walked out the door.

Two weeks later, Tony and Barney left for Vietnam. A whole month passed. Bay received only one letter during that time. It was dated two weeks after Tony arrived there:

The Wounded Whole

Dear Bay,

I can't keep you off my mind. I love you very much. Baby, war is a terrible thing! Everything awful you can imagine goes on here. Kiss the kids for me.

Love always,
Half Pint

Three more weeks passed. One night Bay had a dream. She heard shots fired and saw several men lying in blood. All of them were wearing army uniforms. When she awakened and sat up in the bed, she felt that Tony had been killed, but she was hoping she was wrong. Three days later, she received the news. Tony's brother, Hank, telephoned Bay to tell her that Tony had been killed. The following day, the notice was in the newspaper. Bay was so distraught.

Roberta and Charlotte began calling her, but she didn't answer the phone, go to work, eat, or anything. As soon as Bee read the notice in the papers, she rushed over to Bay's house. Bay had told her she wasn't feeling well and asked her mother to keep Zachary and Hannah overnight.

All Bee could think about was Winding River. When Bee reached Bay's house, she pulled the key Bay had given her from her purse. Bee unlocked the door and walked inside. She found Bay in her bedroom, lying on her bed crying. "Honey, I'm so sorry 'bout Tony," said Bee compassionately.

"Oh, Mama, why kin't I be happy? Why did Tony haf ta die like dat? Oh, God! Why? What haf I done ta deserve dis? Tony wuz so good 'n' so funny. Mama, I loved him so. He wuz de best. Mama, tell me, who is God? If dere is really a God, why did he let Tony die like dat 'n' fight a stupid war?"

"Bay, calm down. I don't haf de answers. Right now, I'm jus' concerned 'bout you. Let me git ya some overnight thangs. I'm takin' ya home wit' me."

"Mama, please let me stay here alone."

"No, I will not leave ya 'n dis condition."

Tears continued flowing down Bay's cheeks.

There was a knock at the door. Bee opened it. "Mrs. Albertson, how's Bay?" asked Roberta and Charlotte.

"She's very upset and crying. I'm here to take her home with me, but she doesn't want to go."

"We'll stay with her," said Charlotte.

Roberta and Charlotte followed Bee into the bedroom. For a moment, they stood inside the doorway watching Bay cry. They looked at each other and walked over to her bed, Roberta on one side and Charlotte on the other. "Bay, I'm so sorry about Tony," said Roberta, sitting on the bed.

"Your mother wants you to go home with her," said Charlotte.

"I'm not going!"

The Wounded Whole

"You don't need to stay here all alone," responded Roberta. Bee looked on with her arms folded. She didn't know what to do or what else to say.

Charlotte said, "Bay McQueen, I know you're hurting, but you're not the only one. Your mother, Roberta, and I are hurting too. We don't like seeing you like this." Charlotte touched Bay's hair and rubbed her head.

"Charlotte is right. You're not the only one suffering. If you don't get yourself up and go with your mother, you're going to cause your children to grow up without a mother. Zachary and Hannah need you. Remember, Tony loved them as if they were his own. He wouldn't be happy with the way you're acting," exclaimed Roberta, now standing with her hands on her hips.

Bay sat up. There was one thing that was always successful in getting Bay's attention, and that was anything concerning her children. Their fathers were absent. All they really had was her. "Thank you, Roberta. Thank you, Charlotte. Mama, I'm ready to go."

CHAPTER ELEVEN

After Tony's demise, Bay longed to understand life. Her mind went back to the time when she was five years of age, standing in front of the mirror asking herself, "Who am I?" In October 1974, a year later, while preparing for bed, she found herself asking the same question. "Who am I?" she said sadly, staring into the mirror. "Who are ya behind dose light brown eyes 'n' black skin? Why are ya here, 'n' why kin't ya be happy?" cried Bay, with tears flowing from her eyes. "Oh, God, why did Tony 'n' Savannah die?" She walked over to the nightstand next to her bed and picked up the Bible. Suddenly she became very angry. She threw the book back on the table and backed away. "God, yer just like ev'rybody else. You don' like me 'cause I'm black! Why are ya punishing me? You took Will, my friend Savannah away from me. Now Tony is gone. I'm tired of it! I'm tired of it! I'm tired of it! God, are ya really real, or are ya jus' a worn-out dream?" she continued, now falling to the floor crying, crawling, and finally kneeling beside her bed.

The Wounded Whole

After that night, Bay felt better. She hoped God wasn't too upset with her. Bay decided she needed to move on, and she did. Four weeks later, she and her group—Roberta, Charlotte, Sunny, and Marsha—went shopping and afterward had lunch. This group and their social activities were not the norm. There still existed an enormous barrier between colored and white folks. However, Bay's circle was a different breed.

"Bay, we're so glad you're back. I thought we'd lost you," said Sunny, smiling.

"What do you mean, 'lost me'?"

"Sunny means she thought you had flipped," replied Charlotte.

"In other words, we thought you had gone cuckoo," said Roberta, laughing.

"For a while, I felt like it," replied Bay.

"Bay," said Sunny, leaning over and whispering in her ear, "it must have been real good."

"Sunny, we heard that!" cried the three women, laughing.

"If y'all only knew! You see, if quick-draw is all you're used to and roly-poly comes along, it's hard to let go," replied Bay, squinting her eyes and smiling. Then everybody else picked up a napkin and pretended that they were wiping tears from their eyes.

"It's hard to find a man who knows how to deal a loaded deck," said Marsha.

"Did y'all hear what Marsha said? She said, 'It's hard to find a man who can deal a loaded deck!'" said Roberta, laughing, and the rest joined in.

The manager came over. "Ladies, you're a little too loud. Please quiet down. Other customers are trying to enjoy their dinner."

"We are so sorry," replied Charlotte.

"Sir, do you know how to deal a loaded deck?" asked Bay seriously.

"No, I don't. I have more important things to do than play cards," he replied somberly. While he was walking away, they began giggling like schoolgirls.

Now involved with eating their lunch, they changed the subject. "Roberta, Mama told me that Barney is coming home in three weeks. I know you're happy," said Bay.

"He's not coming to Galveston. He's going straight to Astoria."

"But you're in Galveston, not Astoria."

"I know. There's just too many painful memories here, and there's something seriously wrong with him. The last letter I received from him, he was very paranoid. He thinks he'll never be safe, no matter where he goes. He believes the Vietnamese will find him and kill him. Bay, he's not the Barney I knew."

"War is not pretty," said Charlotte.

"I think he's going to Astoria because he doesn't want me to see him," said Roberta.

"I'm so sorry about Barney. He and Tony were genuine homeboys," said Bay.

"Friends, I have sincerely enjoyed today, but I have to leave," said Charlotte, getting up from the table. They all paid for lunch and left.

Bay hurried over to her mother's house to pick up Zachary and Hannah. When she entered the front door, her children ran to meet her. "Hey, Ma, hey, Ma," they said happily, almost knocking her to the floor.

"Hi, my little precious angels! Have you been good for Granny?"

"Yes, ma'am, we'd better, 'cause Granny Bee has a switch in the closet," replied Zack, smiling.

Zachary was six years old and Hannah was three.

"Bay, how was your day?" asked Bee. "Did you have a good time with your friends?"

"We had a super time! Zack, take your sister into the den to watch cartoons on TV. I need to talk to Granny."

"Cartoons don't come on in the afternoon," replied Zachary defensively.

"Well, y'all look at some of Granny's books."

"Okay," Zack said, taking Hannah by the hand and leaving the room.

Bay followed Bee into the dining room and sat at the table while her mother polished the silver. "Mama, Roberta said somethin' is wrong wit' Barney. He's not de same. He doesn't think he's safe anywhere, and he's not comin' ta Galveston. Mama, what's wrong wit' him?"

"His mind seems ta be gone, 'n' he's addicted ta drugs."

"What kind of drugs?"

"Heroin."

"Oh, no! Mama, why didn't ya tell me? Maybe I could haf written him!"

"You were already grievin' over Tony. I decided not ta burden ya wit' somethin' else."

"How's Jack takin' it?"

"Not good, not good at all. Many nights he doesn't sleep. He cries 'n' prays, cries 'n' prays, askin' God ta heal Barney."

Bay stood up. "Mama, do you think God really hears him? He didn't hear Tony 'n' all de other young men who are prayin' 'n' still dyin' in dat stupid war!"

Bee put down her polishing cloth and walked over to Bay. "I kin't believe you are talkin' like dis! God is good, 'n' He doesn't put no more on us dan we kin bear!"

"Mama, dat is not enough fur me. I need more answers dan dat." Tears welled up in Bay's eyes.

"Honey, why are ya questioning God like dis? You got ta haf faith."

"Mama, I'm sorry, but I kin't haf faith in someone I don' understand!"

"Bay, de problem is ya need ta stop hangin' around dose friends of yours 'n' start goin' ta church."

"Leave my friends outa dis!" replied Bay, storming out of the room. She came back with Zachary and Hannah. "Mama, we're leavin'," she yelled.

"You jus' think 'bout what I said," replied Bee, standing in the foyer.

"Mayb', Mama, mayb'!" shouted Bay, closing the door behind her.

Bay left her mother quite upset. *I really need someone else ta talk ta Bay*, thought Bee. She started to call Sadie but didn't. She realized her eldest daughter wasn't religious, and Carrie was completely out of the question, so she called Mother Caine and told her everything. Being concerned about Bay's lost soul, Mother decided to come to Galveston on the bus to straighten Bay out. She arrived the very next day, at one o'clock in the afternoon. Bee picked her up.

Late that afternoon, when Bay drove over to Bee's house to pick up her children, Mother Caine was sitting in the living room talking to Bee. "Mother, what a pleasant surprise! What are you doing here?" asked Bay.

"Lord, child, Mother got so lonely. I miss y'all so much, so the Lord told me to come on over here to see y'all."

"Did the Lord tell you, or did Mama?" questioned Bay harshly.

"Bay, don't you raise your voice at Mother! Bee, I see what you mean. Honey, I'm sorry about your fella dying in the war and all, but you shouldn't be angry with God, Bee, and Mother. Come sit down next to me."

"Mother, why are we here? Seems as if God doesn't like me," responded Bay.

"Baby, why do you say that? He created you, so he must like you."

"Why does the Bible say I'm cursed 'cause my skin is black? He must not like me," said Bay, now crying.

"Ah, it's not that God doesn't like you. It's how other folks, long ago, thought God felt about dark skin," said Mother. "Lord, child, this is a difficult thing. I don't know any more than you. I've been in the church for forty years and don't know any more than you. Just ask Him to show you and He will." She wiped tears from Bay's eyes. "Bay, now listen to Mother and listen good. I know you got some white friends, but don't listen to them. They'll cause you to lose your mind following behind their mess about God," said Mother, chuckling.

"Mother, my friends aren't like that."

"I know the colored girl, Roberta, ain't," responded Mother.

"We don't use *colored* anymore," interrupted Bay.

"Y'all might not, but I do. I'll always use *colored*, 'cause that's what I know and love!" said Mother proudly.

"That's the name white folks gave us," Bay said, smiling.

"Bay, don't you go getting Mother all excited about being called black. There's nothing wrong with her wanting to remain colored," replied Bee, smiling too.

"Let's just drop the color subject and get back to Bay's problem with God. Honey, promise Mother you'll start going to church somewhere. When you get saved, you become a different person."

"I'll try," Bay said.

"Now, let's go eat some good food Bee prepared," said Mother Caine, walking into the dining room with Bay and Bee.

Everybody enjoyed Mother Caine so much. They tried to convince her to move to Galveston. "Lord, Bee, I had so much fun. I'm going to have to visit more often," said Mother, waiting to get on the bus to Salem. "Bee, these buses are sure slow. I could've been to Salem and back by now."

Everybody knew how slow Mother drove, and now she was criticizing the bus driver. "Why are you in such a hurry to get home?" asked Bee.

"Nothing like your own home," responded Mother sheepishly.

"That's not what I heard," said Bee, laughing. "Bay told me you got a fella."

"He's just a companion. We sit around and talk," replied Mother, smiling.

"Mother, you'd better be careful. He might give you the fever!" said Bee, laughing.

"If there's goin' to be any fever-giving, it's gonna be *me*," cried Mother, laughing with her hands on her hips.

Suddenly the announcer said, "Bus to Salem, Georgia, is now in lane five—load up!"

Bee walked over to the bus with Mother Caine. "Mother, call me when you get home." She waved good-bye until the bus disappeared.

Bay kept her promise to Mother Caine. The following Sunday, she and Roberta went to church with Jack and Bee. The Albertsons were members of Bethel Baptist Church. It was one of the largest black congregations in Galveston. Bee had come a long way from Salem. When Bay and Roberta walked in behind Bee and Jack, everybody turned around in their seats. Bay held Zachary by the hand, while Bee carried Hannah. Finally, they settled in their seats. Roberta and Bay sat behind Jack and Bee. "What a huge church," whispered Bay in Roberta's ear. "This reminds me of Gethsemane in Salem."

"Girl, this ain't nothing but a fashion show. All these big fancy hats and fine suits and outfits. I feel out of place."

Suddenly the choir stood up and began singing. They clapped and shouted. People began standing up all over the church. Bay and Roberta got up from their seats and began clapping their hands. After the choir sat down, a tall, handsome, dark-complexioned guy stood up looking quite dignified and belted out the song "Wade in the Water."

"Lord have mercy, what a fine sweet-potato that is. Girl, I'm 'bout to pass out," said Bay softly to Roberta with a smile on her face.

"He is definitely something fine for sure."

"Make me want to come to church every Sunday and sometimes during the week!" said Bay excitedly. Bay and Roberta enjoyed that part of the service, but everybody else seemed to have been waiting to hear the word. Finally, John J. Burke walked onto the platform. "Yeah, all these women are waiting on the Word all right," said Bay sarcastically. "They are waiting on the opportunity to lust after that fine-looking preacher man. I would get up early every Sunday morning to come to church to get an eyeful of that!"

"Now I see why most of the members are women," responded Roberta.

"We ought to be ashamed of ourselves. We're supposed to be here getting saved," said Bay, still whispering in Roberta's ear.

"Didn't God create a man for a woman to enjoy?" asked Roberta.

Rev. Burke began his sermon. Most everybody was saying *amen, praise the Lord, preach it!* Bay couldn't keep her eyes off of him. She didn't hear any part of the sermon.

When the service was over, Jack and Bee introduced Bay and Roberta to Rev. Burke. A very attractive medium-brown-complexioned woman walked over and stood next to the pastor. "This is my wife, Lee," he said.

"Nice to meet you!" replied Bay and Roberta, feeling somewhat guilty. After officially meeting Rev. Burke and his wife, Bay and Roberta hurried outside, leaving Bee and Jack talking with the Burkes.

Bay and Roberta walked outside and sat on a bench under the beautiful dogwood trees, discussing church. "Girl, I didn't hear nothing about God, I was so busy lusting after the pastor," said Bay.

"You're not the only one. I bet there are one, two, and even three who's done more than lust."

"Stop, Roberta! He's probably very sincere."

"Aren't you sincere?"

"Yeah, I'm sincere, but I was sure lusting after that fine thing," responded Bay, laughing.

"Just because he's a pastor don't mean he walks on water!"

After that Sunday, Bay became a regular at Bethel.

One Sunday morning, to Bee and Jack's surprise, Bay accepted the invitation to dedicate her life to Jesus. She attended Bethel for more than a year, and then she became restless and unhappy with the church's desire to control her as a result of its legalistic ideology. There were complaints about her clothing. Bee disagreed with her regarding dancing and going to parties, so she decided to leave but didn't know exactly how to break the news to her mother.

It was the spring of 1976. Bay knew she had to let Bee know about her decision to leave Bethel. She invited her mother over for breakfast one Saturday morning. After they finished eating, Zachary took Hannah outside on the front porch to push her on the swing. As Bay got up to remove the dirty dishes, she walked over to the kitchen sink and turned around to face her mother. "Mama, I have somethin' very important ta tell ya."

"Yer not pregnant again, are ya?" asked Bee nervously.

"It takes two ta haf a baby. Dere's no man in ma life at de moment."

"Well, what is it?"

"I've decided ta leave Bethel."

"Yer leavin' Bethel! Why? I thought ya wuz happy dere."

"At de beginning, I really enjoyed it, but not any longer."

"Where are ya goin'? Ya need ta be in a church."

"I don't know. I'm jus' sick 'n' tired of all de talk 'bout ma clothes, not dancing, 'n' not going ta parties. I honestly don' think God cares 'bout all dat," said Bay calmly.

"Bethel is a wonderful church wit' lovin' people. You should try ta stay 'n' ask God ta help ya stop findin' fault wit' others," said Bee, with tears welling up in her eyes.

"No, Mama, I kin't stay. I'm tired. Church isn't s'posed ta be full of confusion. Anyway, it's not like I'm leavin' de country. I'm jus' leaving Bethel."

Bee knew when Bay decided to do something there was no stopping her. She left Bethel and never regretted it.

Six weeks later, while Bay was preparing supper, she turned on the television to hear the evening news. The news commentator said, "A very prominent citizen of Salem, Georgia, Mr. William Durkston, president of the Federal Savings, has died." Bay almost forgot about her supper. She had not thought about Bill in years. She began thinking about how kind he had been to her when he helped her get her first job at the bank. She turned the television off, sat at the table, and thought about the last time she saw him. *I wonder what happened ta him through de years. But I'm certainly not goin' ta Salem ta find out,* thought Bay. "Zack, you and Hannah wash your hands and come eat!" yelled Bay.

The next day, Charlotte stopped by the business office at the hospital where Bay worked. Sitting on a chair next to Bay's desk, she asked, "Bay, did you hear about Mr. Durkston?"

"Yes, I heard it last night on the evening news."

"Why don't you go with me to the funeral? We'll get a chance to see everyone we used to work with."

"I don't think so. My reason for leaving wasn't exactly honorable."

"What did you do?" interrupted Sunny, curious.

"If Bay wants us to know, she'll tell us—won't you, Bay?" asked Marsha.

"Marsha, you can't slick me. You're dying to know. I got pregnant without a husband."

"Darn, is that all?" said Sunny, disappointed. "I thought it might have been something like having an affair with the president of the bank or one of those loan officers. Now *that* would be real juicy and scandalous!"

"Bay, what about it? Go to Mr. Durkston's funeral with me," said Charlotte.

"No, I don't think so. I'll probably be the only dark spot there," replied Bay.

"So? You never let that stop you before. Is it because Bill Durkston will be there?"

"Why, no, that's nonsense!"

"Prove it!"

"Okay, Charlotte Coombs, I'll go with you to the funeral."

"Hey, what about me and Marsha? Can we go?" asked Sunny.

"You and Marsha don't know Mr. Durkston," replied Charlotte.

"We don't have to know him to pay our respects," said Sunny in a Southern drawl.

"I thought only black folks went to funerals without knowing the people. I'm learning something every day about y'all. We're more alike than we care to admit!" Bay said.

"Everybody," said Charlotte, "meet me here, Saturday morning, at nine o'clock, in the hospital employee's parking lot. Y'all can ride with me."

As previously arranged, Bay and her friends met at the hospital to ride with Charlotte to the funeral. It was scheduled to begin at ten-thirty. They arrived at Salem Presbyterian Church about ten-fifteen. They entered the sanctuary and sat near the back to the right. The service was over as quickly as it started. *Gosh, dey didn't waste no time*, thought Bay. When the family was walking out of the church, Bay and Bill Durkston's eyes met. He continued walking beside a small, slender brunette. She was holding a small boy's hand. The child seemed to be about six years of age.

When Bill and his family returned to the church from the cemetery, Bay, Charlotte, and their other friends were still waiting at the church to give them their condolences. As Charlotte talked to the Durkstons, Bay, Sunny, and Marsha looked on. Suddenly, Bill walked over to introduce himself. "I'm Bill Durkston," he said to Sunny and Marsha. He looked at Bay and reached for her hand. "Bay, it's been a long time," he said.

"It really has. How've you been? What on earth have you been doing?" asked Bay, smiling nervously.

"I'm a family doctor."

"That's great!"

The same woman with the small boy walked over. "Bill, we've been waiting for you."

"I'm sorry. I was talking with Bay. Laura, let me introduce you. Bay, this is my wife, Laura, and son, Timmy."

"Hi, Laura. Bill helped me land my first job. These are my friends Sunny and Marsha."

"You've already met Charlotte," said Bill.

"Honey, I'm tired. Can't we just go?" asked Laura rudely.

"Sure, Laura. Bay, maybe I'll get a chance to see you and Charlotte real soon," said Bill.

As Bill and Laura walked away, Sunny said, "That Laura seems like a real cold potato."

"She acts very antisocial and stuffy," said Marsha.

"Let's not be too hard on her. We don't know what's cooking in the oven at her house," replied Bay.

"We all have problems, but we don't have to blame the world," said Sunny.

"I'm ready to go too," said Bay.

A large crowd surrounded Charlotte, talking. Bay, Sunny, and Marsha decided to walk outside to get some fresh air and wait for her.

Fifteen minutes later, Charlotte came outside to drive her friends back to Galveston. As she approached them, she could tell Bay was pissed. "Cheer up, girls, have I got a lot of goodies to tell y'all!" cried Charlotte.

"That's why I don't like to ride with folks who don't have any consideration for others," replied Bay sarcastically.

"Bay, don't y'all be mad. I couldn't leave. Everybody wanted to find out what's going on with me since the murder trial," exclaimed Charlotte.

"What murder trial?" interrupted Sunny. "Did you murder someone?"

"Let's get on the road. We'll tell you all about it," replied Bay.

"Gee, this is sounding better and better," said Sunny.

When Charlotte drove off in her silver-and-black Mercedes convertible, Sunny said, "Tell Marsha and me about the murder."

"I was arrested for killing my husband, Lance Coombs, but I was cleared of all charges."

"Oh, yeah, I remember hearing about that murder. I saw it on television. He was real rich," said Marsha.

"Yes, he was rich, but he's long gone," said Bay. "Now Charlotte has his money and she didn't kill him to get it. It's o-v-e-r."

"If we can't talk about the murder, let's talk about you and that handsome Bill Durkston," said Sunny.

"I don't have nothin' to say about that matter," answered Bay.

"You might have nothing to say, but life has a way of helping us face our wounds," said Marsha.

"What are you talking about?"

"Well, in order for us to become mature or whole, we have to face certain things to free ourselves. The more we resist something, the more it persists," Marsha explained.

"Marsha thinks she's a seer," said Charlotte. "Of course, I have to admit that sometimes what she says makes a lot of sense. Marsha, have you freed yourself from the married man yet?"

"That wasn't nice!" interrupted Sunny.

"It's okay," Marsha said.

"I didn't mean to sound mean," Charlotte said. "I just want to know if you have used your own words of wisdom."

"I've learned quite a bit during my life, but this relationship with Adam has me stuck. He says he's not happy in his marriage and intends to get a divorce."

"He's told you that for four years. He's still with his wife," stressed Sunny.

"I don't need my friends to tell me how stupid I am. I already feel bad enough!" said Marsha loudly.

"Y'all leave Marsha alone. It's not easy living in this world. Charlotte, you and Sunny can't judge her. She'll get through it," exclaimed Bay.

"I just don't like to see my best friend being used," responded Sunny.

"She'll wake up one day," replied Bay.

Charlotte drove into the hospital's parking area. Before they separated, they made sure Marsha was feeling better.

CHAPTER TWELVE

Late that night, after Bay had seen Bill Durkston at his father's funeral, she lay in bed thinking about the first time she met him. *Bill 'n' Tony were de only people 'n ma life who made me feel loved. Tony is gone 'n' Bill has come back, but thangs are diff'rent. He's married 'n' his complexion hasn't changed,* she thought. She rolled over on her side and fell asleep.

Little did she know that thirty-five miles away in Salem, Bill was lying next to his wife thinking about how beautiful Bay looked at his father's funeral. *What is it about her that makes me feel this way?* he thought. *I can't help myself. I've tried to forget her, but I can't! Now that I've seen her, my old feelings have resurfaced. What am I going to do?* Since his father's death, he'd decided to remain in Salem to take care of his mother and open his medical practice. Though Salem and Galveston were thirty-five miles apart, Bill knew nothing would keep him away from Bay McQueen.

Six months later, Bill and his family had settled into the quiet small-town life in Salem. Of course, it's vastly different living in a small town if you're rich rather than poor. And Bill Durkston just happened to be the former. He was a member of one of Salem's most prominent blue-blood families. The talk around town was that he didn't have to wait until his mother died to enjoy his inheritance to the fullest. Bill's father fixed it so he could use his part now and receive his mother's portion after she died. That being said, Bill might reside in the small town of Salem, but he was free to travel anywhere and return to his little sanctuary. Yet with all his wealth and social status, he couldn't stop thinking about Bay. *Why?* Bill thought as he drove home from work. *Is it because our relationship is forbidden in society? Now that I've seen her, I want Bay more than ever. Laura is a good mother, but she doesn't really love me. She only cares about spending my money. I want to be loved for me.*

Bill arrived home about five-thirty, just in time for dinner. When he walked inside the foyer, he saw Laura helping Nadine, the housekeeper, set the table. Laura walked over to him. "Honey, how was your day?" she asked as Nadine looked on.

"I can't complain. I'll feel much better after I get some of Nadine's cooking in me."

"I'll have everything ready and on the table in about ten minutes," said Nadine, walking into the kitchen.

Bill and Laura had hired Nadine two weeks after they moved into their new home. They really liked her. Nadine was a light-complexioned colored woman about fifty years of age who took pride in being a mulatto and a member of the first colored garden club in Salem. Her daddy looked just like a white man, so she felt mighty proud. Now that she had become the Durkston's housekeeper, she felt that she was finally living the life she had always desired, to become part of the white world—even if it was in a servant role. Whenever she socialized with other colored folks, she would put on airs and introduce herself as the Durkston's housekeeper.

After Nadine left the room, Timmy, Bill's son, walked in covered with mud. "Wow, you've really been working and having a good time, Timmy, my boy!" cried Bill, laughing.

"Yeah, Pops, I really been busy making stuff! I made me a big castle. You wanta see it?"

"I sure do, son!"

"I have told you about getting yourself so dirty!" interrupted Laura. "We spend a lot of money on your clothes."

"Laura, leave him alone. Let him play and get as dirty as he wants. He's just a growing boy having fun!"

"Pops, you really wanta see it?" asked Timmy excitedly.

"I sure do," replied Bill, grabbing Timmy's hand and walking outside.

"Bill, please don't take Timmy back outside. It's suppertime. Nadine is going to be mighty upset!" yelled Laura, now seated at the table alone.

"Where are Mr. Bill and Timmy?" asked Nadine, carrying a small basket of hot homemade rolls in one hand and a platter of juicy steaks in the other. The enticing aroma from the food could be smelled throughout the house.

"They're outside playing in the damn mud!"

"Stop cursing, Mrs. Laura. It isn't ladylike."

Fifteen minutes later, Bill and Timmy entered the room. Both looked like they had been to a pigsty. "Pops and I had a super time!" said Timmy, laughing.

"Both of you need to clean yourselves up before you sit down at this table for supper," responded Laura firmly.

"We're on our way," said Bill, as Timmy followed him proudly.

A year passed, and Bay was still on Bill's mind. He knew he had to see her again. His medical association had scheduled a meeting in Galveston for three days. He decided to see Bay then. The day before the meeting, he drove to Galveston and checked into his hotel. After he settled in, he opened the city directory to search for Bay's telephone number. His eyes fell on it. "Bay McQueen, 892-4820," he muttered softly, writing it on a small pad. Bill had never been nervous about talking to Bay. Now it was different. *Guess I'm nervous because I'm married. I'm not supposed to be with another woman, especially a black one*, he thought. *If I don't ever see her again, I can't move on.* Suddenly, he picked up the phone and began dialing her number. After the third ring, the voice on the other end said, "Hello."

"Bay . . . ah . . . ah."

"Yes, this is she."

"This is Bill."

"Why, hello, how are you?"

"Just fine."

"I'm so surprised to hear from you."

"I'm here in Galveston for a meeting, so I decided to call you. How about you have dinner with me tomorrow night?"

"Where on earth can you and I go out for dinner together without being noticed by everybody? Bill, you're white, married, and I'm black," stressed Bay.

"We're old friends who only want to have dinner. Is it okay if I pick you up about six o'clock tomorrow?"

Bay gave him directions to her place, and he hung up the phone. Later that night, she began to have second thoughts. *I shouldn't haf agreed ta have dinner wit' Bill. He's married 'n' white. Dis is a very explosive situation fur both of us*, thought Bay. She decided that when Bill arrived to pick her up, she'd not go out with him.

The next night, Dr. Bill Durkston knocked on Bay's door. She nervously opened it and greeted him with a smile. "Hello, Bill," she said. She was wearing a pale blue dress, and the contrast was perfect against her beautiful black skin. "Come in. Please have a seat."

Bill sat down as Bay instructed him. *How beautiful and elegant she looks*, he thought.

Bay was seated on a beautiful white wicker chair next to the couch where Bill was seated. "Bill, I'm so sorry, but I cannot go out to dinner with you."

"I understand. I just want to be with you, to talk. May I stay a while?"

"Sure," answered Bay, standing up.

He stood up too, took her hands, and moved closer to her until they were passionately kissing and embracing. "Bay, I can't forget you."

"Oh, Bill, I really wanted to go with you that night, but I couldn't. Now it's impossible for us to be together because you're married. It's just not right," she said, pulling herself away from him.

"By whose standards? Man's?"

"No, God's."

"All I know is that I love you and want you to be part of my life."

"You mean you want me *and* your wife. That won't work! I don't intend to be your colored mistress!"

"Bay, don't say it like that. I would never do anything to degrade you."

"You can't prove it by me. Bill, it's time for you to go."

"Bay, I'm not giving up. The first time I met you, I knew we were destined to be together."

After closing the door behind Bill, Bay knew she had made the right decision. Though she wanted him as much as he wanted her, she was determined not to surrender. However, deep down in her soul, Bay knew she would eventually give in if she didn't have a support circle. She decided to call Charlotte and Roberta to meet her for supper.

Bay arrived at Charlie's Grill first. She was seated next to a huge window. While she was looking at the scenery outside, Roberta walked over to her. "Hey, girl, what's going on? You don't look too good."

"I have a real problem. I just need to talk and get some advice."

"Let's order. I can counsel better on a full stomach," said Roberta.

"I asked Charlotte to come too. Can we wait a few more minutes for her?"

"There's Charlotte now," answered Roberta.

"Hello y'all. Roberta, I haven't seen you in a while. Have you met Mr. Right yet?" asked Charlotte.

"Nope, still waiting. Anyway, we're not here to talk about me. Bay wants our advice about something that's bothering her."

"Bay, what's wrong?" asked Charlotte.

"Can we place our order now? I'm starving," said Roberta.

After they placed their orders, Bay began talking. "I did something last night that I'm not proud of. I don't know how y'all are going to feel about me."

"We're friends," Roberta said. "There's nothing you can tell us that will end our friendship."

"Bay, we've been friends a long time. Roberta speaks for me too."

"Well, I let a married man come over to my place last night."

"Was it Bill Durkston?" asked Charlotte.

"Yes."

"Who on earth is Bill Durkston?" asked Roberta.

"He's an old friend of Bay's."

"He helped me land my first job at the bank in Salem."

"His father was the president of the bank," Charlotte said.

"Aunt Mildred never told me about a black man being president of the bank."

"Bill isn't black. He's white," responded Charlotte, chuckling.

"No wonder you're feeling guilty, a white man! After all they've done to our people, now you're involved with one," said Roberta.

"Roberta, get off her back! Can't you see she's already feeling bad?"

"Bay, I'm sorry. I don't mean to give you a hard time, but I didn't expect you to be involved with a white man and a married one at that!"

"Look, Roberta, don't judge me. You're no saint!"

"Never claimed to be. I just hate to hear folks talking about you going with a white man."

"You're not concerned about folks talkin' 'bout me. You're just prejudiced," said Bay. "I am not seeing Bill. I made him leave. Anyway, I didn't cause our friendship to happen. Before he left Salem, he asked me to go with him, but I refused because of our racial differences. Now he's back and wants me back in his life."

"What about Laura, his wife?" asked Charlotte.

"Is he going to divorce her and marry you?" asked Roberta.

"I don't know."

"What do you really want?" asked Charlotte.

"I want to be happy."

"Do you think settling for crumbs is happiness?" asked Roberta. "You're my friend, and I don't want nobody using you."

"Bay, Roberta and I can't tell you what to do. It's up to you. I'll love you no matter what," said Charlotte.

"Bay, I'm sorry we got into it, and I tried to place the racial burden on you. Like Charlotte said, it's your decision. Remember this: Grandma used to say, 'If it don't feel right, it ain't.'"

"Thanks for your words of wisdom," said Bay. They finished their dinner and left the Grill.

The following day, while Bay was working in the back, the door to the main entrance of the business office opened, and Bill Durkston walked in.

"Hello, may I help you?" asked Sunny, smiling and thinking, *I've seen this guy before.*

"Yes, I am Bill Durkston. Is Ms. McQueen in?"

"Sure, I mean, yes, I'll get her. Just a minute," she said, hurriedly walking away. "Bay, Bay, there's someone to see you. It's a man!"

"A man?"

"Yeah, he looks familiar. Now I know who he is. He's that friend of yours and Charlotte's. I met him at his father's funeral."

When Bay emerged from the back office walking beside Sunny, she felt tense. As she turned the corner, there stood Bill, looking very handsome and dignified with his thick blond hair and classic blue pinstriped suit. As she approached him, she felt warm all over. She was relieved that no one could hear her heart beating. Their eyes met.

"Bay, I just stopped by to say good-bye before leaving. I'm on my way to Salem."

"It's nice of you to drop by. You drive carefully," said Bay, feeling clumsy with Sunny and Marsha looking on.

"Bay, may I speak with you outside for just a moment?"

"Sure." Bay walked ahead of him as he closed the door behind them.

Now out of the view of Sunny and Marsha, Bay and Bill quietly looked into each other's eyes. Bill broke the silence. "Bay, I'm not going to let you go again," he said calmly.

"Bill, you don't have a choice. You're married with a family and a successful career. It's too late for us. We have to accept it. We were not meant to be together."

"I intend to return to Galveston in two weeks. I'll call you. Bay, you're so beautiful."

"Bill, don't call. It won't do any good."

Bill reached out and held her hand tightly. "I want to kiss you, but we don't want to set the hospital on fire," he said, smiling and walking away.

Bay stood watching him. She didn't know what to do. She felt so powerless.

Two weeks later, Bill did as he had promised. He called Bay and invited her to his cabin in Lamona Springs, about sixty miles east of Galveston. She accepted.

Bay took off from work, and Bill picked her up at seven-thirty Thursday morning. They arrived at Bill's cabin an hour later. It was spread over about thirty acres. "Bill, this is a beautiful place."

"I like to come here. It's so peaceful. I enjoy playing tennis and just getting away." Finally, they reached the house. Bill stopped the car. "Come on inside. Let me show you around." He pulled a key out of his pocket and opened the door.

"Wow, what a beautiful place! I know you and your family really enjoy it." Bay looked around in amazement.

"We don't come here much."

"Why?"

"Laura doesn't think it's high-class enough."

"People have different tastes."

"Guess so," replied Bill, now holding Bay's hand.

The tour of the house ended in a bedroom. Bay knew she could no longer resist. They began kissing passionately. Bill began removing Bay's shirt and then kissed her nipples. Suddenly, all the built-up energy and passion were unleashed. They had finally tasted the forbidden, and their lives would never be the same.

At four o'clock, they packed the car and headed back. Bill had to return to Salem and Bay to Galveston. She felt so empty. She wanted to stay with him. Now he had to go home to his family.

"Bill, I don't like these feelings I'm having. I don't want you to go home," Bay said while they were driving back to Galveston.

"Don't worry, darling, I'm going to take care of you. Bay, I love you. I always will."

Soon afterward, Bill pulled into Bay's driveway and helped her take her bag inside. "Bill, I wish you didn't have to leave." She put her hands around his waist as they walked through the door.

"Honey, I really would like to stay with you forever," he replied, holding Bay in his arms and passionately kissing her. "I'll call you next week," he continued, standing inside the living room. Shortly thereafter, he closed the door behind him and returned to his car.

Now seated on the couch, Bay began thinking about their day together and their first time making love. *The sky didn't crack, but I enjoyed it. I want some more!* she thought. Bill Durkston made Bay feel valued. No one except Tony had ever made her feel that way. Although Bay's skin was black, Bill's opinion of beauty was not based on society's standards. He saw much more. He saw the truth of her being. One day, Bay would see the same thing.

Bay and Bill began seeing each other on a regular basis. However, she was not comfortable with the arrangement. She never dreamed she would be involved with a married man. There was no future in it. She wanted more than just a casual relationship. She promised herself there would be no next time. Bay decided never to see Bill again.

Two weeks passed. Bay had not heard from Bill. She sensed that something was wrong. The next day, while Bay was eating lunch in the hospital's cafeteria, Charlotte came rushing over to her table. "Have you heard the terrible news?"

"What?"

"Bill Durkston was in an accident. He was in his yard working, and a tree fell on him."

"My God, no! Where is he? I need to see him!" She jumped up from the table.

"Bay, wait, you can't do that! Have you forgotten? Bill is a married man!"

"He needs me."

"Are you going to the hospital? His wife is with him. He's going through a lot right now. He doesn't need anything else explosive added to the situation. I understand he's going to survive, but he will never walk again," continued Charlotte somberly, now standing next to Bay.

"This can't be true. Bill is such a kind, gentle person. He's strong. He'll get through this. I know he'll walk again," Bay said as tears filled her eyes.

"Come with me. I'm taking you home."

"What about my car?"

"I'll call Roberta and ask her to drive it to your house. Let's go to your office to clear your leave with your supervisor."

"What excuse am I going to give her?"

"Don't worry. Aren't you feeling bad?"

"Yes."

"I'll fix it up real good."

After Charlotte took Bay home, she called Roberta and told her what happened. Roberta immediately came over to be with them. Later, Charlotte and Roberta went to pick up Bay's car and returned to Bay's house. When they opened the door to her bedroom, Bay was crying.

"Bay," said Roberta, "you've got to get yourself together. Durkston is going to be okay."

"When Roberta and I went to pick up your car," Charlotte said, "I heard that he's being sent to a rehabilitation hospital in Jackson City."

"Why, that's two hours away. It's going to be hard for me to visit him."

Charlotte and Roberta looked at each other. "My dear," said Roberta, "it's really not about you. Have you forgotten something? This man is someone else's husband."

"Guess this is the price I'm having to pay for my sin," said Bay.

"We're not talking about anybody's sin, including our own," said Roberta. "We don't want you to make a gigantic fool of yourself. I just want you to see the situation as it really is, not as you want it to be."

"I know, I know," said Bay.

"Roberta, I believe our friend is going to be okay," said Charlotte, walking toward the door. "Let's go so she can get some rest."

"I'll call you tomorrow," said Roberta, walking behind Charlotte as Bay closed the door behind them.

CHAPTER THIRTEEN

The next morning, a beautiful spring Saturday morning, Bay was awakened by the chirping sounds of birds. Now sitting up in bed, she began thinking about Zack, Hannah, and Bill. The phone rang. "Hello," said Bay.

"Bay?"

"Yes, Mama."

"Jack and I are going to Salem to see Mother Caine. If it's okay, may I take the children with us?"

"I guess so."

"Kiss them for me. I'll pick them up late this afternoon."

"Give Mother Caine my love."

As soon as Bay finished talking to her mother, she pulled herself out of bed and walked inside the bathroom to take a shower. She removed her clothes and stepped behind the shower curtain. *Oh, de water feels so good! If only it could wash away ma troubles*, she thought.

She heard the phone rang. "Who on earth could that be?" she said softly. She grabbed her robe and rushed into the bedroom to answer it. "Hello."

"Hi, Bay."

"Sadie! Sadie! How's Sara?"

"She's doin' great. How 'bout you?" A moment of silence invaded the conversation. "Bay, are ya still dere?"

"Yes, I'm here."

"What's wrong?"

Bay sat down on the bed, "Sadie, I've gotten maself in an awful mess."

"Please don' tell me yer pregnant again."

"No," replied Bay cautiously.

"Bay McQueen, ya need ta come clean. Does Mama know what's going on wit' you?"

"No, Sadie, please don' tell Mama."

"Bay, how kin I tell Mama what I don' know? What is it? If I knew, I wouldn't tell anybody. Once you trusted me wit' ya life. I'm still ya big sister, Sadie, who loves ya wit' all dat's in me," she exclaimed.

"Gee, Sadie, I kin always count on you," replied Bay, now crying.

"Bay, don' be afraid. Tell Big Sister what's bothering ya."

"I'm havin' an affair wit' a white married man."

"How long has dis been goin' on?"

"Almos' a year," Bay said softly.

"Do ya love him?"

"Yes, I do."

"Is he in love wit' you?"

"He says he is."

"Well, is he leavin' his wife ta marry you?"

"No, he can't."

"Bay, I love ya, 'n' I'm certainly not tryin' ta judge, 'cause Mack 'n' I had an affair while he wuz married. But I'm concerned 'bout you. Sounds as if ya lover only wants a mistress. Do ya want that fur yourself 'n' ya children?"

"No, I don'. Of course, he's no longer in a position ta haf a mistress. Yesterday I found out he had a terrible accident. While he wuz workin' in his yard, a tree fell on him."

"Bay, I'm so sorry."

"De doctors say he will never walk again."

"Haf ya seen him?"

"No, I kin't. I'm de outside woman. Sadie, I feel so powerless."

"I know, but you will get through dis. Yer a strong McQueen woman."

"Sister, I feel so much betta. I'm so glad ya called."

"Keep in touch 'n' let me know how . . . ah . . . ah . . . what's his name?"

"Bill Durkston. I call him Bill," answered Bay.

"Well, let me know how Bill is doin'."

They said good-bye and hung up.

Six months passed, and Bay didn't hear a word about Bill's condition. Charlotte hadn't heard anything either. Bay missed him a lot and desperately wanted to hear from him. One day while eating lunch outside the hospital on the beautiful grounds under a large pine tree, Bay thought she heard Bill calling her name: *Bay! Bay! I need you. I need you!*

Now she had to visit him. *I intend ta see Bill right away*, thought Bay, getting up from the bench. *First, I'll call de hospital ta talk wit' a nurse. No, I'll jus' go see him as a friend. Nobody except Roberta and Charlotte knows 'bout our relationship. Tomorrow I'll take off frum work ta visit him. I won't tell nobody.*

The next day, Bay drove to Jackson City to see Bill. *What if his wife is dere wit' him?* she thought. *Surely she wouldn't haf a problem wit' me visitin' Bill. We're old friends. He did help me get ma first job. I hafta remember ta say Mr. Durkston in her presence, even though it doesn't sound right.* Bay turned north down Turner Road where the rehabilitation hospital was located, about five miles down on the right side of the road.

Crescent Rehabilitation Hospital sat far back off the road in the middle of several tall beautiful pine trees and dogwoods that were in full bloom. Bay pulled into a huge parking lot, but Crescent was very small compared to Galveston General. There were not that many cars parked. Bay drove through the parking lot until she saw the sign Patient Information. She parked her car in the space facing the sign. Bay turned the ignition off, took a deep breath, and got out of the car. She stood silent for a moment and looked toward the entrance, not knowing what to expect. Bay walked down the breezeway to the entrance and opened the door. Now inside the spacious, well-decorated visiting area, she approached the receptionist desk. "May I help you, please?" the receptionist asked.

"Yes, I would like to see Mr. Bill Durkston."

"Ah . . . ah . . . yes," answered the woman, wondering why this beautiful Negro woman wanted to see Mr. Durkston. *She sure doesn't look like a maid*, she thought. "Just sign your name and time right here," she said, pulling out a large black book and pointing to the line.

Gee, I didn't know I'd hafta sign ma name ta anything, thought Bay, picking up the pen and signing her name.

"Mr. Durkston is in Room 110B."

"Thank you very much," replied Bay as she turned and walked in the direction of Bill's room.

When she got there, the door was closed. She started to push it open but didn't. A nurse stopped. "Ma'am, may I help you? The colored patients are on the second floor."

"I'm not looking for the colored floor. I'm here to see Bill Durkston."

"This is Mr. Durkston's room," replied the nurse as she continued walking down the hallway.

Quietly Bay opened the door. Bill was sitting in a wheelchair with his back facing the door. He was looking out the window. Bay felt so overwhelmed with emotion. *He doesn't deserve ta be 'n a wheelchair*, she thought. Tears began welling up in her eyes. *I hafta control myself*, she kept thinking. She took a tissue out of her purse and wiped her eyes. "Bill," said Bay softly.

He turned around quickly. "Bay!"

She walked over and hugged him. "I've missed you so much. I'm so sorry about your accident and that I wasn't there with you."

"I know, I know. I feel the same way too." Bill looked into her eyes. "Bay, I'm not the man I used to be. The doctors say I'll never walk again."

"Don't believe them. You will walk again."

"Bay, I wish I were as sure about it as you are."

"You have to believe you will walk again. If you believe you can, you will. If you think you can't, you won't."

"Bay, it's not that simple," said Bill, somewhat agitated.

Bay put her arms around his neck and looked into his eyes. "Bill, please don't be upset with me. I can't help what I believe. There's something inside me that tells me you're going to walk again."

"I love you. If you believe I will walk again, I can too," replied Bill, now holding her in his arms.

They began kissing passionately. "We shouldn't, somebody might come in," said Bay, pulling away.

As soon as they were apart, a male therapist walked in. "Hello, Mr. Durkston. It's time for therapy."

"Well, Bill . . . I mean, Mr. Durkston, it's time for me to go," said Bay. "I'll come back some other time."

"I don't feel like going to therapy. Can't you see I have a visitor?"

"I'm sorry, Mr. Durkston, but I don't make the rules," replied the therapist.

"Mr. Durkston," said Bay, "if you're going to walk again, you need to cooperate with your therapist."

"Bay, when are you coming back?"

"I'll be back next week. I want a very good report," replied Bay, smiling. She turned and walked out of the room.

Bill watched her as she closed the door behind her. He would never forget their first time together. Just those memories gave him the desire to walk again.

Bay continued to visit Bill every week. He began feeling much better. Six weeks later, while Bay played with her kids, the telephone rang. "Hello?"

"Babe."

"Bill, this is a surprise. Are you okay?"

"I'm fine. Just called to let you know that I'm going to be released tomorrow."

"Gee, that's super!" She had forgotten that Bill would eventually be released from the hospital. "Bill, now we won't be seeing each other again."

"You can visit me at the cabin in six months. By then, I'll be walking."

"Bill, it's no use. We might as well stop right now."

"What do you mean? You no longer believe I will walk again?"

"Of course I do, but I'm not going to continue seeing you. Good-bye, Bill," said Bay, and she hung up the phone.

The next day, Bay felt as if part of her had died. She knew she had to find the strength to move forward. She didn't know how it would happen, but there seemed to be something big and powerful carrying her.

CHAPTER FOURTEEN

Several weeks passed. Bay moved on with her life without Bill. However, something mysterious was about to invade her world. Late one night, while Bay was sound asleep, she had a dream. What felt like an electrical current moved through her body. She awoke. The room was filled with light, which disappeared just as quickly. Bay had never experienced anything like it. She never shared that experience with anyone, not even Sadie. She knew it was too sacred to utter.

Bill and Laura were not happy, but everybody thought they were. *Yeah*, thought Bill, while eating breakfast, *people think Laura deserves a medal for putting up with a cripple. They don't know the real reason she's hanging around. She likes my money.*

"Mr. Durkston, would you like another cup of coffee?" asked Nadine, the maid.

"No, thanks."

"I'll drink it!" cried Timmy.

"You can't have coffee. It'll make you black!" said Nadine.

"Nadine, you seem to have something against being black!" replied Durkston sharply.

"No . . . ah . . . ah . . . I don't. I'm not fully colored. I'm a mulatto," Nadine said proudly.

"I don't mean to destroy your illusion, but as far as society is concerned, a mulatto is a Negro."

"Papa, can I be a Negro when I grow up?" interrupted Timmy excitedly.

"Timmy, I'm never prepared for what's going to come out of your mouth. Now you want to be a Negro. Yesterday, you wanted to be a ship," said Laura, entering the dining room and sitting next to Timmy.

"He's just a boy, and a super one too," stressed Bill.

"Thanks, Pop! Can I go outside?"

"Sure, son, you certainly can," said Bill.

"I think it's too early," replied Laura.

"Let the boy go on outside to play. He's not hurting anybody. No son of mine is going to be a domestic pussycat."

"See you later, Dad and Mom," said Timmy, walking out the door smiling.

"Bill Durkston, when it comes to Timmy, you're the biggest pussycat around. I'm always wrong. But who takes care of you every single day?"

"So now you bring it up about me being in a wheelchair. Well, let me tell you something. You can walk! You don't love me. You're in love with my money!"

"You won't let me love you. There's something standing between us. I don't know what it is. I have never been able to get close to you." Laura knelt down beside him.

"I'm sorry for losing my temper. I'm tired of sitting in this house day after day. Sometimes I feel as if I'm about to explode."

"Honey, you must accept the situation as it is. The doctor says you'll never walk again."

"We doctors don't know everything." He could hear Bay's voice: *If you believe you can't, you won't. If you believe you can, you will.* "I will walk again. Tomorrow I will return to work."

"In a wheelchair?"

"Why not? It sure beats sitting around the house like a fat cat."

"How do you intend to get there?" asked Laura, with her hands on her hips.

"Between you and Nadine, I shouldn't have a problem."

"I don't have time to drive you to work. I have to see about Timmy, and Nadine has to help me."

"Listen, if you're too busy to drive me, Nadine will until I hire a chauffeur. Guess you can do without Nadine for about two hours," said Bill, rolling his wheelchair into his study.

Bill's work made him feel useful. Sitting home in his wheelchair was quite different from rolling around in it in his office and the hospital. He didn't consider himself hopelessly handicapped. He knew he would walk again. However, there was still Bay. *There's nothing I can do about how I feel about her*, thought Bill. *She was so angry when she hung up on me. I can't blame her. She never wants to see me again, so I'll respect her wishes.*

The seasons came and went. The saying is that everything in the universe is connected. Every time spring arrived, Mother Caine, now eighty-two, got a stirring on the inside, in her body parts. Most folks think they're washed up sexually at fifty because they think they're too old. It was different with Mother Caine. She believed she was ageless.

One Sunday afternoon, after leaving the church women's circle meeting, she wondered if she was abnormal. She decided to make an appointment with a doctor the following Monday. Of course, she didn't have her own private physician, so she decided to look in the phone book. Guess whose name her finger rested on? Dr. Bill Durkston.

Mother Caine picked up the phone to dial Durkston's office. She heard a voice on the other end. "Willie Mae, you and your half-a-man need to get off the phone. I have an emergency," said Mother Caine.

"All right, Mother."

"Good morning, Dr. Durkston's office," said the receptionist.

"Yes . . . ah . . . my name is Sally Caine. I want to make an appointment to see the doctor," said Mother.

"Have you seen Dr. Durkston before?"

"Honey, you should know if I've seen the doctor or not. No, I haven't. You office workers sure ask a lot of unnecessary questions."

"What about nine o'clock next Tuesday morning?"

"You'd better make that ten. It'll take me a while to get there. I'm a safe driver."

"That'll be fine, Miss Caine," answered the receptionist.

The following Tuesday morning, about eight forty-five, Mother pulled into Dr. Durkston's parking area. "Lord, look at all these pretty cars—yellow, blue, black, and all other kinds. These white folks know they living good!" said Mother Caine joyfully. While trying to park her car, she almost rammed into the beautiful Oldsmobile beside her. "Thank you, Jesus, for not letting me hit that car. I don't have no money to pay for a big expensive car!" said Mother with a big smile on her face. Mother Caine opened the door to the car and struggled to get out. *Lord, I sure hope that doctor don't do no vagina checking, unless he's a good-looking colored man*, thought Mother, laughing to herself. Finally, she reached the desk and rang the bell. "I'm Miss Caine," she said proudly.

"Miss Caine, would you please fill out this form?" asked the lady.

Mother turned and was starting over to sit next to a white woman when the receptionist said, "Excuse me,

Miss Caine, you're supposed to sit in the other room. This area is for whites only."

"Well, before you go any further, I need to get something straight. I was born and raised in Salem. My daddy owned a grocery store right downtown. Furthermore, little lady, I'm going to sit right over there. If that so-called white high-class hussy don't want to sit next to me, she can move her lard you-know-what somewhere else!" exclaimed Mother Caine.

The receptionist left the room quickly. Two nurses peeked from behind a door. The receptionist reappeared, with Dr. Durkston following her in his wheelchair. "Miss Caine, I'm so sorry for your inconvenience. Please follow me. Would you like a cup of coffee?"

"How nice of you!" replied Mother Caine warmly, following him to his office.

"Please come in."

"You have a very nice office."

"Have a seat," said Dr. Durkston, pointing to a chair next to him.

Mother Caine thought, *Dr. Durkston seems to be a very kind man*. But she couldn't understand why his practice didn't reflect his kindness. "Dr. Durkston, you appear to be color-blind, but why do you have separate areas for colored and white?"

"It's just the way society has always been. I certainly don't agree with it, and I haven't had the courage to change my office procedures. From this day forward, I intend to have one lobby for all my patients. I can't promise that it will be successful overnight, but I will give it my best! Let's change the subject. As much as I enjoy your company, I do have other patients to see. Tell me, what type of symptoms are you having?"

Mother began telling Dr. Durkston about her eternal libido compared to other women her age. She felt like an oddball. Dr. Durkston told her that if anybody was abnormal, it was her circle partners. "And many women three times your junior are as frigid as a block of ice," said Bill, smiling while rolling himself out of his office as Mother Caine followed.

"Dr. Durkston, I've enjoyed our talk. You are really a nice man and a good doctor too! I used to always tell Bay that white folks can't be trusted. I have changed my mind."

"Bay? Bay who?" asked Dr. Durkston as he turned his wheelchair quickly to face Mother Caine.

"Bay McQueen. I'm a very close friend of her family. Do you know her?"

"Yes, she used to work at the bank here in Salem. I helped her get her job there."

"So you're the one. That was a great deed you did for Bay. She really learned to take care of herself. Dr. Durkston, I got to be going. I'll see you next time," said Mother Caine, walking out the door.

What a small world, thought Bill as she closed the door.

THE WOUNDED WHOLE

After Mother left Dr. Durkston's office, she couldn't wait to get home to call Bee. Finally inside, she rushed over to the couch, took off her shoes, and dialed Bee's number. "Bee, honey, how ya doin'?"

"Just fine. You sound like you're out of breath."

"I'm just getting back home. I've been to see the doctor about a particular female problem most women would like to have," responded Mother, chuckling. "Course, I didn't call to tell you about my doctor's appointment. Guess what? My new doctor knows Bay. I was plum knocked off my feet!"

"Who is he? Is he colored?"

"No, child, he's white and very nice. He treated me like he been knowing me for years."

"Mother, I'm surprised to hear you say something nice about someone white."

"Lord, I'm just as surprised as you."

"By the way, what's his name?"

"It's Dr. Bill Durkston."

"Bill Durkston . . . I don't think I know him," said Bee slowly.

"He told me he helped Bay get her first job," said Mother.

"Oh, now I remember. Is his hair blond?"

"It sure is."

"He was in love with Bay. At least, that's what he told her," exclaimed Bee.

"What you say? He loved her?"

"Yes, ma'am, he wanted her to go to Nevada with him back in 1965, I believe."

"Well, well, Lordy, Lordy Miss Claude. Never would've thought he and Bay were once involved!" said Mother Caine. "If only times had been different, Bay could've been living the good life!"

"Everything happens for the best," said Bee. "Now changing the subject, Mother, have you decided to move to Galveston?"

"Maybe one day when I'm too old to sit on my porch," Mother replied, laughing.

As soon as Bee hung up the phone, Bay walked in with Hannah and Zachary. "Hi, Mama, today is the first time I met your neighbors in the green house across the street," said Bay.

"You mean the Boxers. They seem to be very nice. I've only met Mr. and Mrs. Boxer. They have one daughter, Emma, but I've never seen her."

"When I drove up, I saw a woman about my age standing in their front yard waving at Zack and Hannah," said Bay.

"Honey, it was probably Mrs. Boxer. She looks really young."

"It was Emma," said Zachary. "She wants to play with us when nobody is around. She really likes Hannah."

"Mama, don't let Hannah and Zack go outside alone. The woman I saw gives me the creeps," said Bay seriously.

"All right, I won't," said Bee. "Guess who called me earlier?"

"Who?"

"Mother Caine, and guess who's her doctor?"

"I have no idea."

"Bill Durkston."

"Really?"

"I didn't know he was back in Salem. You never mention him."

"Why should I? We're from different worlds. After Bill's father died, he and his family moved to Salem."

"Have you seen him?" asked Bee, as she gave Zachary and Hannah a cookie.

"Yum, yum, yum, this is a good cookie," cried Zachary, running out of the room with Hannah following him.

"Yes, Mama, I've seen him. I saw him at his father's funeral. Charlotte, my coworkers, and I went. He's married and has a little boy. Recently, I heard that he had a terrible accident. A tree fell on him. The doctors say he'll never walk again," said Bay, with tears welling up in her eyes.

"Bay, what's wrong? Why are you crying?"

"Mama, I love Bill. He's been so good ta me. I want so much ta be wit' him!" Bay looked at Bee helplessly.

"Bay, you haven't been seein' him, haf you?" asked Bee, with her arms tightly embracing her daughter.

"Yes, Mama. I tried not to, but I couldn't help it. He's de only man who ever loved me for *me*. He doesn't hate me 'cause ma skin is black."

"Does he love you enough ta divorce his wife 'n' face his family 'n' friends?"

"No, 'n' I love him too much ta ask him ta do dat."

"Honey, you've got ta love yourself too much ta eat crumbs from any man's table!" said Bee, holding Bay's chin up and looking deep into her soul.

"Mama, do you think I'm bad?"

"No, baby, just wounded."

Confession is indeed good for the soul. After Bay's talk with her mother that day, she felt as though a five-hundred-pound stone had been lifted off her.

CHAPTER FIFTEEN

Bay was having lunch alone in the hospital cafeteria when Roberta walked in excitedly. "Guess I have to come to my best friend's job to see her. She doesn't call me anymore or stop by the library where I work. Miss McQueen, what's going on?" asked Roberta.

"Nothing. I mean, so much has been going on."

"Even Charlotte said she had not heard from you."

"I know, I know, I know. Things are much better now."

"You've been seeing Durkston, haven't you?" asked Roberta.

"Berta, it's none of your business. Don't ride my back, okay?"

"Okay, okay, okay, your business is your business. An old friend of yours dropped by the library today. Girl, I was knocked off my feet!"

"Who?"

"Your old flame, Will," replied Roberta.

"Well, I do declare, it's a shame I wasn't there to greet him so I could have tied a rope around his balls," said Bay, smiling.

"Now you're acting like the Bay McQueen I know," said Roberta, laughing.

"Did he have his high-yella gold statue with him?"

"You mean his wife?"

"I sure do!"

"Child, that thing is so ugly, her face would cause the sun to crash. Her only asset is her light skin," cried Roberta with laughter. "Girl, you should've seen her. Ain't got no kinda figure. She is as straight as a board. No wonder Will asked about you, with lust in his eyes, while she was over in the reference section."

"That low-down dirty snake has no reason to be asking about me with his jackrabbit self. He won't ever ride this train again," said Bay proudly. She and Roberta roared with laughter. "Did he ask about Hannah?"

"He wanted to know how she looked."

"I'm sorry that Hannah won't get to know him, but I'm not goin' ta force her on that sick crew, which would do her more harm than good."

"What do you mean?"

"I don't want her to grow up thinking she's privileged cause she's light. Berta, I'd better get back to work before I'm fired," Bay said, getting up from the table.

"Bay, let's not wait so long to get together."

"I won't. Why don't you, Charlotte, and I get together real soon?" replied Bay, walking away.

"Sounds like a winner," said Roberta, walking in the opposite direction.

As Bay walked back to the business office, she couldn't believe Will showed his face in Galveston but hadn't had enough guts to face her or ask to see Hannah. *Once a coward, always a coward*, thought Bay, now entering the office.

"Bay, I need to talk to you. I don't know what to do!" whispered Marsha, desperately looking around. "I haven't told anybody, not even Sunny."

"My God, Marsha, what's wrong?"

"I'm pregnant," said Marsha softly.

"By the married guy?"

"Yes," replied Marsha, shaking her head.

"How does he feel about it? Is he going to divorce his wife?"

"Hell, no! That bastard told me to have an abortion. I never want to see him again!"

"Girl, don't you even think about havin' no back-alley abortion! You could die! Marsha, listen, let's get the group together to talk about this and come up with a solution."

"No, Bay, no, I don't want the others to know! I don't want to be judged!"

"This is the time you need support. You shouldn't handle this alone," said Bay.

Sunny walked in. "Hey, y'all, I got some really good bargains at the Fashion Shop. Look at this cute little skirt. What's wrong?" she asked, noticing Marsha's tears.

"Marsha has a small problem."

"I wish it were just a small problem," said Marsha. "Sunny, I'm pregnant."

"Pregnant? Like having a baby in nine months?" asked Sunny. "Damn, Marsha! Haven't you heard of birth control, even condoms? It's 1980!"

"I know what year it is, Sunny. Don't judge me. Guess you've never made a mistake, Miss Sunshine, have you?" shouted Marsha.

"This is not the time to throw stones, Sunny. Marsha needs our help. I bet you haven't always used birth control when you were gettin' you some. You just didn't get caught," said Bay, laughing.

"Come to think of it, there was one time. I prayed all day and night for a whole week," replied Sunny, laughing.

"Let's meet at the Grill at seven o'clock. I'll call Charlotte and Roberta," said Bay.

"Marsha, is that okay?" asked Sunny.

"Yes, I'll be there."

At seven-thirty, everybody except Marsha had arrived at the Grill. "Marsha should be here by now," said Bay, looking at her watch.

"Hope she's okay," replied Sunny.

"She's just got to decide if she's going to have the baby and make the bastard pay dearly or have an abortion," exclaimed Charlotte.

"Girl, let's not talk about having abortions. That is not a very pleasant subject. The very thought makes me hurt," said Roberta.

"She could move away for a year to live with a relative until the baby is born," Sunny suggested. "Then she could let a nice family adopt the child."

"Now that's real cold. Anyway, how in the hell is Marsha going to live for a whole year without a job? Charlotte's the only one of us who's rich," stressed Bay.

"Marsha shouldn't have to finance this problem alone. That married man shouldn't get off the hook," said Charlotte.

"I agree with Charlotte," said Roberta.

"You mean Marsha should blackmail him?" asked Sunny.

"Exactly," said Charlotte.

"Wait just a minute," said Bay. "We don't want to find Marsha in a ditch somewhere dead. Most men will do anything to cover their tracks."

"It's eight-thirty, and Marsha isn't here yet!" cried Sunny.

Bay sensed that Marsha was in trouble. "Something is wrong. Let's get over to Marsha's place!" she said, leading the way toward the exit.

"Bay, don't you think we should call first?" asked Charlotte.

"No, she's hurting. She needs us. Let's go now!"

Everybody ran and piled into Charlotte's car. "Hold on, everybody!" said Charlotte, looking at her speedometer: fifty, sixty, and then seventy-five in a fifty-five-mile-an-hour zone.

"Charlotte," cried Sunny nervously, "you're driving like you're a race driver. I think you need to slow down. Marsha will still be here while all of us are stretched out on the highway! Thank God we're almost there."

Fifteen minutes later, Sunny cried, "There's Marsha's house!"

Bay jumped out of the car, followed by the others.

"Bay, I hope you're not overreacting," said Roberta.

Bay reached the door and started knocking. "Marsha, Marsha," she cried, now ringing the bell.

"Marsha! Marsha!" yelled Charlotte.

The lady next door peeked her head out of the door. Bay said, "Ma'am, have you seen Marsha leave with anybody? Her car is here. Would you please call the police?"

"Wait," said Sunny, "she told me she always keeps an extra key above the back-door entrance." They all walked around to the back of the house.

They got to the door. Bay stood on a chair and reached for the key. "Got it!" she shouted. She opened the door, and they all followed Sunny to Marsha's bedroom. "Oh, my God! Call an ambulance!" cried Bay.

Charlotte felt Marsha's pulse and looked at Bay. "We need to get her to the hospital right away!"

"There has been a terrible accident at 121 Sunset Drive," said Sunny into the phone.

"Looks like Marsha took some sleeping pills," said Bay, picking up a bottle.

"Oh my God, she tried to kill herself!" said Sunny.

"She didn't feel as if there was any other way out," responded Roberta.

Five minutes later, the medics arrived, put Marsha into the ambulance, and rushed her off to the hospital. "Let's follow them," said Bay. "We can't go home knowing Marsha needs us. Sunny, call her parents."

"It's just her mother," replied Sunny. "I'll call when we get to the hospital."

Everybody jumped into the car, and Charlotte took off.

Sunny called Marsha's mother, who lived in Arkansas. In the meantime, Bay and the rest of her friends sat in the waiting room, anxiously awaiting the doctor's report.

"It's been three long hours," said Bay, "and nobody has told us anything. We need to know something!"

"I agree," replied Charlotte.

"We are not her relatives," said Roberta.

"We're her friends!" Bay said angrily. "I'm goin' in there to get some damn answers!"

As she and Charlotte began walking toward the door to the nurse's station, a tall, distinguished doctor appeared. "Are you the family of Miss Hunt?" he asked.

"We're like family," replied Bay.

"Yes, we are," interrupted Charlotte. "I'm Mrs. Lance Coombs. My large contributions to Galveston General are well-documented."

"Oh, yes, yes, Mrs. Coombs," replied the doctor. "Now, I can't go into detail because of confidentiality."

"Did she lose the baby?" asked Bay.

"Yes. Ah . . . she's in a coma. I don't know whether she's going to make it. We've done all we can."

Everybody became quiet. Tears were flowing from their eyes.

"Doctor, thank you so much," Bay said, wiping tears from her eyes, "but Marsha isn't going to die. I've got to tell her about all we talked about at the Grill tonight."

"Doctor, Marsha's mother should be arriving tomorrow," said Charlotte. "I don't think she knows about the pregnancy, so please handle her with care."

"I certainly will. Goodnight, ladies," he said as he walked through the double doors.

"I feel so helpless," said Sunny.

"Bay, tell me something. How did you know Marsha was in trouble?" asked Roberta.

"I felt it."

"Girl, you're sounding real spooky!" said Roberta.

"Might sound spooky, but if it hadn't been for Bay, Marsha would be gone for sure," stressed Sunny.

Bay said, "Marsha must have a strong desire to live. Things are different now. She doesn't have to worry about having the baby anymore."

"What about herself?" asked Charlotte.

"Her mind needs healing before the body will respond," said Bay.

"You sound just like Mrs. Hilda Hue," said Sunny.

"Who on earth is Hilda Hue?" asked Bay.

"She's a holy woman," replied Sunny.

"All women are holy. Didn't you know that?" asked Roberta, smiling.

"She means a woman who separates herself from people, prays all the time, and never has sex," said Charlotte, chuckling.

"Not Mrs. Hilda," said Sunny, smiling. "She knows a lot about sex and talks like she's had quite a bit of experience and still enjoys it. Course, I must admit, I've never seen a holy woman like her. She knows how to call forth the healing power of the universe. She talks about a Presence, light, and how God isn't a person but lives in us."

"You mean Mrs. Hilda knows about a light? Can I meet her?" asked Bay, curious.

"Sure, let me call her. Maybe we can ride out to her house tomorrow."

"Sounds great to me!" replied Bay.

"I'll pass on this one," said Charlotte. "She might see that not-so-pleasant side of me."

"Count me out on this one too," said Roberta. "Don't want to hear anything about a fiery hell."

"Hilda is not like that," replied Sunny. "She is very unorthodox."

Finally, they left the hospital and went their separate ways.

The next morning, Sunny picked Bay up at nine o'clock. "Morning, Bay, can't wait for you to meet Hilda."

"How did you meet her?"

"Well, she was the speaker at a women's retreat I attended two years ago."

"I see she lives a little far from the city."

"It's not that far. She lives about five miles from town. Hilda likes quietness. We're almost there," continued Sunny as she turned down a paved road. She drove another half mile and made a left turn into a dirt driveway with a huge pond to the left.

What a beautiful place, thought Bay. They reached the house. It looked like an old-fashioned cottage from a 1940s movie. "Gee, this is a very pretty house. You'd never believe a holy woman lives here," exclaimed Bay, looking around in amazement.

They walked to the door. Sunny rang the bell three times. Suddenly, the door opened. "Hello, Sunny, it's so good to see you!" cried Hilda excitedly. "Bay, welcome to my heaven on earth! Do come in. I have prepared lunch for you with vegetables from my own garden and delicious wine and yummy cake."

Gosh, thought Bay, *she's so beautiful, elegant, 'n' full of life*.

"Hilda, you didn't have to do this," said Sunny.

"I wanted to because Spirit is in you. I can't be rude to the Presence. The food should be very good. It's mixed with lots of love," continued Hilda, shaking her hips and laughing heartily.

Bay couldn't help but look at her with admiration. *Whatever she has, I want it. Dis is what I've been looking fur all ma life*, she thought.

"Hilda, Bay and I are here to ask your help for our friend Marsha," said Sunny. "She's in a coma. The doctor says there's nothing else they can do."

"She is already healed," replied Hilda confidently.

"How can that be when she is unaware of everything and everybody around her?"

"It appears to your human senses that her life is over, but it isn't. She is one with the creative life force of the universe," exclaimed Hilda, looking out the window. "We must call forth the Divine Presence within her, which is a healing presence."

"Hilda, may I come back to visit you?" asked Bay. "There are many questions I need to ask you."

"Of course! Now let's have some music and play solitaire!"

"Cards and music!" shouted Bay. "Didn't know holy folks live like this!"

"My dear, don't always believe everything you read or what you've been taught. I'm going to have a good time. I don't have visitors often!" Hilda said, getting up from the dining table. She walked through the large doorway into the beautiful foyer filled with paintings.

"Gee, I have never seen such elegance in all my life," said Bay.

Hilda opened a door to a huge, gorgeous room that was enclosed mostly with windows. "This is my sitting room. I read, study, and play here. Sometimes I even meditate here."

"I've never heard of *meditate*. What does it mean?" asked Bay.

"For me, it's sitting quietly and allowing the Presence to imbue your consciousness, consequently revealing itself through you."

"She means God," interrupted Sunny, smiling.

Bay and Sunny followed Hilda to a large table with decks of cards. They sat down. Immediately, Hilda began shuffling the cards. Bay and Sunny laughed. "Never had so much fun with a holy woman!" cried Bay joyfully.

"Mystic, my dear Bay. *Holy woman* sounds as if I'm special or different from other people, which isn't true. We are all the same in Spirit. Some of us are just not aware of it. So please don't put me on a pedestal. I don't want y'all to stomp me if I do not live up to your expectations." Hilda chuckled as she beat Bay and Sunny at the game.

"Guess we'd better go," said Sunny somberly. "We need to drop by the hospital to see Marsha."

"Sunny, I know you're feeling quite agitated because you lost the game, but cheer up. Nobody ever really loses. What did you learn from this defeat?" asked Hilda, smiling.

"I'm going to learn how to play solitaire so you won't beat me so pathetically," replied Sunny, smiling.

"Bay, what about you?"

"I desire to know the Presence. I like the peace, joy, happiness, and vitality I see in you."

"Well, you come back any time. Just call me before you come. I might have company," said Hilda, with a smile and a sparkle in her eyes.

"You mean company like a man?" asked Bay.

"I do! I do! I do!" replied Hilda, laughing.

Bay and Sunny roared with laughter as they walked to the car.

"Sunny, I had a great time!" said Bay.

"Me too. Hilda doesn't fit the traditional religious mold."

"She sure doesn't. Let me ask you a question. Does she really have a man in her life?"

"From what I've heard, she does."

"You mean they have sex?"

"Yes! What do you think they're doing, planting flowers and baking cakes?"

"Sunny, don't forget to stop by the hospital to see Marsha. Afterward, I need to get home so I can pick up my babies."

They reached the hospital parking lot. "Gosh, Charlotte is already here. She's parked in the reserved parking area with all the other big shots," said Bay, smiling.

"Hey, did you hear Charlotte remind that doctor the other night about the money she gives Galveston General?"

"I sure did. Sometimes doctors have to be reminded how to treat sick folks, and having money doesn't hurt, so I'm glad to have Charlotte on our team," said Bay as they walked into the main entrance of the hospital. "We're here to see Marsha Hunt," said Bay.

"I know who y'all here to see," said Irene, the information clerk, smiling.

"Just trying to be professional and pretend we don't work here," replied Bay jokingly.

"Have you seen Marsha's mother?" asked Sunny.

"No, I haven't."

"Thanks, we'll see you later," said Bay, walking toward the elevator with Sunny beside her.

Bay and Sunny got off the elevator on the third floor and walked over to the nurse's desk. "How is Marsha?" asked Bay as Sunny looked on.

"Well, I guess you can say she's holding her own," said the nurse.

"May we see her? We found her just in time to get her to the hospital," said Bay.

"Has her mother arrived yet?" asked Sunny.

"Yes, she's in her room now."

"Will it be all right if we see her now?" asked Bay.

"Sure."

As soon as Bay opened the door, she saw a tall, medium-complexioned Negro woman sitting next to Marsha's bed, holding her hand with her head bowed.

"Who are you?" asked Bay, curious.

"I'm Marsha's mother," replied the woman, now standing.

Well, I be damned! thought Bay. "How are you, Mrs. Hunt? Sorry to meet you under such an unpleasant situation."

Sunny was in total shock. She reached out her hand. "Ah . . . pleased to meet you," she said, as if she'd seen a ghost.

"Please sit down, ladies," said Mrs. Hunt. "I know this is a great surprise to you. The way the world is so sick about color, I convinced Marsha to pass for white. I just wanted her to be happy."

"You don't have to explain anything to me. I know exactly how painful it feels to be a product of a sick color society," replied Bay bitterly, as her mind went back to Winding River.

"Bay, Bay, are you okay?" asked Sunny.

"Yes . . . my mind wandered back to the past."

"We need to concentrate on helping Marsha realize life is worth living," said Sunny.

After visiting hours were over, Bay and Sunny left the hospital. They had plenty to talk about.

"What a bombshell!" cried Bay, while she and Sunny walked to the car. "Marsha fooled me. I never, ever would have guessed that she is colored or black, whichever one you prefer."

"I know. Marsha looks whiter than me!"

"I don't think so. You're real white!" insisted Bay.

"What is that supposed to mean?"

"I mean you're very fair. I'm not trying to be ugly."

"What on earth are Roberta and Charlotte going to think?"

"I'll call them and ask them to meet us at the Grill," said Bay.

"Don't you think it's too late?"

"Naw, child, it's never too late for some juicy information hot off the press!" Bay said, walking over to a telephone booth adjacent to the parking area. Bay opened the door and dialed Charlotte's number. "Hey, Charlotte, this is Bay. Sunny and I have something unbelievable to tell you. Can you meet us over at the Grill in ten minutes?"

"Sorry, I can't. I'm packing. Lloyd and I are going to the mountains tomorrow."

"Girl, this is so juicy. You won't ever forgive yourself if you miss this!" insisted Bay.

"Okay, Bay, you win. I'll be there shortly."

After Bay finished the conversation with Charlotte, she called Roberta.

"Hello, Roberta speaking."

"Hey, girl, Charlotte, Sunny, and I are on our way to the Grill. Why don't you join us?"

"Not tonight, maybe another time. I've undressed, so I'm in for the night."

"Berta, you can't stay home. I have some juicy news that's hot off the press. Come on, Berta. I can't wait to see your face when I tell you this!"

"You should be a lawyer. You know I'm a glutton for juicy gossip. I'll be there soon."

"This had better be good," said Charlotte, walking over to the table where Bay and Sunny were seated.

"Don't worry, it is. Sunny and I were shocked," said Bay slyly.

"Here comes Roberta," interrupted Sunny.

"Either I'm crazy or just too damn curious to say no to coming out after I was in for the night," said Roberta, sitting next to Sunny.

"Berta, do you really want me to answer that?" asked Bay, smiling. "Sunny and I met Marsha's mother. She's colored."

"Don't use *colored*, that's not proper these days," replied Roberta. "Marsha sure fooled the hell out of me. I never would've guessed that she's black."

"Charlotte, what do you think about this situation?" asked Bay.

"I don't know what to say. To be honest, I'm shocked! Of course, it doesn't make me feel any different about Marsha."

"How is Marsha doing?" asked Roberta.

"About the same," responded Sunny.

"Since I'm here, I might as well have a meal," said Roberta.

"Waiter, we're ready to order," said Bay.

They finished their dinner and left the Grill.

Bay was still astonished about Marsha's identity. After Sunny dropped her off at her house, she immediately got in her car, drove over to her mother's house, and picked up her children. *It's not easy workin' 'n' tryin' ta spend time wit' ya kids*, thought Bay. Suddenly, Bay's mind went back to her visit with Hilda, and then Bill, and then the light experience. *I've never told anybody 'bout de light I saw. They'd think I wuz crazy. Hilda wouldn't. I'll visit her soon, without Sunny,* thought Bay as she turned into Bee's driveway.

Sunday, Bay spent the whole day with Zachary and Hannah. They went to the park, bought ice cream, and went to see a movie. "Mama, can we go to the movies again tomorrow? I had a real good time," said Zack, walking behind Bay as they entered the living room.

"Not tomorrow, Zack, maybe next Saturday. Go take your clothes off so you can get your bath," said Bay, holding Hannah in her arms. The girl was sound asleep.

"Mama, I don't need a bath. I had one last night."

"Well, tonight is another night, young man," replied Bay.

"What about Hannah? She should have to take a bath too!" cried Zachary.

"Hannah is your sweet baby sister. I will give her a bath."

"Hannah isn't a baby. Emma says she's a big girl, so she should have to take a bath every night by herself," said Zack.

"Emma? I'm your mother, not Emma!" said Bay firmly. "Zachary, make sure you watch Hannah when you're outside, and don't you leave her alone," continued Bay nervously.

"Mama, Emma is nice!" replied Zack.

"Zachary, stop talking back to me before I put the paddle on your behind. Do as I say. You have to be Mama's eyes when I'm not around."

"Okay, Mama, I'll take care of Hannah."

After Bay and Sunny finished their lunch in the hospital's cafeteria, Bay decided to visit Marsha. "Bay, I started to ask you to tell Marsha that I'd see her later, but she won't hear you," said Sunny.

"How do you know that? I'll tell her anyway."

"Bay, I'd go with you, but I've got tons of work to do. I'm tired of looking at her like that," said Sunny.

"Is it because she's only half white?"

"For heaven's sake, no!"

"Just checking," replied Bay, smiling and walking in the opposite direction. *I hope dat Marsha is alone*, thought Bay as she walked to her friend's room.

Bay reached Marsha's room and pushed the door open. Mrs. Hunt was standing at the foot of the bed with her purse on her arm. "Hello, Mrs. Hunt," said Bay.

"Bay, please come in. I'm going over to Marsha's house to rest."

"I think you should. I don't intend to stay long. I really have to get back to work. Since Marsha has been out, Sunny and I have been swamped."

"Bay, do you know anything about Marsha's pregnancy?" asked Mrs. Hunt.

"Ah . . . ah . . . I knew about the baby, but I've never met the father," replied Bay. "Sunny probably knows more than me."

"Bay, women do talk to each other. I think you know a lot more than you're telling me."

"All I know is that he's married. Everything else is a mystery to me."

"If I ever find out, as the old folks used to say, his ass is grass!" said Mrs. Hunt, walking out of the room and closing the door behind her.

"She really means it," Bay said softly.

Bay walked over and stood beside Marsha's bed. "Marsha, you're surrounded by the healing Presence of light. This light is within you. It is life in you and around you," said Bay softly, now seated with bowed head. "Marsha, wake up. Everybody misses you. I want all of us to have lunch together again at the Grill, go shopping, and talk about all the men who are jackrabbits. Sunny sends love. Charlotte and Roberta miss you too." Now she prayed silently, "Oh Spirit, Divine Presence, allow Marsha's real self to come forth." She held Marsha's hand, with tears rolling down her cheeks. Suddenly, light filled the room and left just as quickly. *It's de Presence. Marsha is all right,* thought Bay, rising from her seat and walking toward the door.

"Bay, is that you? What happened? Where am I?" asked Marsha.

"Marsha! Marsha! Marsha! You're talking!" cried Bay. "Thank you, Spirit! Let me buzz the nurse!" continued Bay, pushing the button next to the bed. Two nurses entered the room immediately. Bay rushed to a telephone to call Marsha's mother and her Grill friends. After Marsha regained consciousness, her life would not be the same.

CHAPTER SIXTEEN

Marsha recovered, and her mother returned to Arkansas. Things were different—not with Bay and the rest of the crew, but with Marsha. She had to get used to living the truth. No matter how she looked on the outside to others, she had to get to know the real Marsha.

During work, Bay noticed Marsha had gotten very quiet. "Marsha, guess it's going to take some time for you to get back to normal," said Bay.

"What do you mean?"

"You don't talk much anymore."

"And you certainly don't joke or gossip," interrupted Sunny.

"I didn't think y'all cared, since I'm not really white."

"We don't have a problem with you not being white. Seems like *you* got the problem," stressed Bay.

"Marsha, you've got to get over it," said Sunny. "You've got to start liking yourself just the way you are and stop depending on your color to get you by in this world."

"It's easy for you to talk. You're white, and nobody ever called you *nigger* or killed your family because of their skin color!"

"No, they didn't. Yes, it is wrong. Still, you can't deny who you are without wounding your soul," said Sunny emotionally.

"Marsha, you are a damn coward!" exclaimed Bay. "Don't tell me about Sunny or any other white woman being privileged. Look at me! Just look at my black skin. I have been rejected all my life by my own people because I'm not as light as you or pretty enough. Only red-bones are considered beautiful. You see, y'all got good hair and light skin! So, Marsha, you need to get real and stop playing the victim! Because of the color-struck consciousness, you are embraced and adored only for the color of your skin."

"Bay, I'm sorry. It's easy to think you're the only person in the world with a problem," said Marsha, now hugging Bay and Sunny.

That same night, while Bay slept, she dreamed she was flying and saw Hilda sitting on a cloud. Suddenly, she awoke. Light filled her bedroom, and then it left. She sat up in bed. *It's de Presence! Dere's so much I need ta know*, thought Bay. *I'll call Hilda tomorrow ta find out if I kin visit her Saturday.* She lay awake the rest of the night. She could hardly wait to talk to Hilda.

Bay called Hilda the next morning, which was Saturday. However, Hilda couldn't see her until the following Saturday at ten o'clock. The week passed quickly. Bay arrived at Hilda's place about nine-fifty. She walked up on the porch and knocked on the door.

"Hello, Bay, come on in!" said Hilda joyfully. She led Bay to the same room where they'd played solitaire. "Would you like breakfast? Tea, cup of coffee, wine, lemonade?" asked Hilda, laughing.

"Lemonade will be just fine." Hilda left the room. While she was gone, Bay thought, looking around, *What a beautiful 'n' peaceful home.*

Hilda returned with a glass of wine and a glass of lemonade. "Here you are, my dear," she said, placing the lemonade on the table. Hilda noticed Bay looking at the wine. "Wine is the best medicine there is, as long as it's taken in moderation!" Hilda said, lifting the glass to her mouth and sipping contentedly with her eyes closed. "This is the best ever! Now tell me why you're burdened," continued Hilda, softly and curiously.

"I'm not really burdened. It's this dream that I've been having. While I was asleep a few nights ago, a light came into my room and left as fast as it came. Tell me, what does this mean?"

"I think it's wonderful. It's the Universe wanting you to become aware of its Presence!"

"Universe? I've never heard anything about a Presence or a Universe."

"The Universe is the same as God. I prefer using Universe. I find the word God too limiting," said Hilda.

She and Bay talked extensively about the Universal Presence. Hilda shared the book *The Wounded and the Whole* with Bay. "Bay, this book has made a profound impact on my life. Hopefully, it will do the same for you," said Hilda passionately.

"Hilda, thank you so much. I will never forget you," replied Bay, hugging her.

"I should hope not," declared Hilda. She walked Bay to the door.

"I feel that inside this book is what I've been searching for all my life," said Bay, walking down the steps and heading toward her car.

"I'm going to count on it!" Hilda said, waving good-bye.

After Bay left Hilda's house, she headed to her mother's place to pick up her children. When she arrived, Jack, Bee, and the children were working in the yard. "There's Mama!" cried Hannah, running toward Bay.

"Hey, my sweetie pie!" said Bay, sweeping her up off the grass.

"Bay, Zack is an A-1 man," said Jack, smiling.

"Jack, it's good to see you. How's Barney doing these days?" asked Bay.

"Not good, not good at all."

"Bay, guess what?" said Bee. "Mother Caine called. She wants to move to Galveston."

"I thought she had a fella in Salem."

"Mother says he's confined to the house with hip and back problems."

Bay and Jack chuckled. "Mother has to have a little more action," said Bay. "I think it's super. She's a part of our family. Mama, Jack, I'll see you tomorrow. I've got to take these two angels home."

"Ma, *angels* sounds girlish and babyish. I'm a boy and can take care of a yard as good as any man!" replied Zack proudly. "Can't I, Pawpaw?"

"You sure can!" replied Jack, smiling.

"Okay, Mr. Gardener, get in the car. Will you help me make our yard as pretty as Mama and Papa's?"

"Sure, Mom," replied Zack as he walked beside her to the car.

"Oh, Bay," cried Bee. "Mother Caine has already put her house up for sale! She's interested in buying the house down the street from us or one close to you!"

"Gee, I am so excited!" responded Bay as she drove away.

Life is like a stream. The problem is, we have to make a choice to flow with it or against it. Whichever way we decide to go determines where we end up. If we resist, we will remain wounded. But when we move with it, we become whole. Then there are some who don't feel like they have a choice in the matter. That's probably how Barney felt.

The Wounded Whole

Six months after Bay left Jack and Bee standing in their front yard, Jack's son Barney walked in front of a car and ended his life.

On a Sunday afternoon, family and friends gathered in Barney's hometown of Astoria for his funeral. Barney's mother and siblings entered the church first, and then Jack, Bee, her daughters, and Mother Caine. As Bay walked in and looked to her right, she saw all her friends: Charlotte, Marsha, Roberta, and Sunny, who was wiping away tears. *Dat's Sunny fur ya*, thought Bay. *She has a heart like a marshmallow. A long time ago, Roberta cared a lot fur Barney, but de war changed that. It's like she never knew him.*

Suddenly, Bay could hear sobbing throughout the church. She could barely contain herself when she heard Jack crying. One hour, and the funeral was over. "Thank God," said Bay softly, getting up from her seat.

First the family exited the church, and then the other attendees. Bay decided not to go to the grave site or return to the church for the repast. Instead, she pushed through the crowd to find her friends. "Thanks so much for coming. I know none of you except Roberta knew Barney," said Bay.

"You okay?" asked Charlotte, as Sunny and Marsha looked on.

"I'm okay. Today brought back old memories about Tony," answered Bay. "Berta, how you feeling?"

"I'm very sad. Back in the day, Barney never thought his life would turn out this way. Why in the hell did he have to fight a senseless war?" she asked, with tears welling up in her eyes.

"It's goin' ta be all right," replied Bay, hugging Roberta.

"Damn, don't let all of us start crying!" said Charlotte, pulling a tissue out of her purse.

Bay heard her sisters' voices. She looked around. Carrie and Sadie were walking toward them. "Sadie, Carrie, hurry! I want you to meet my circle. These are the best friends anybody could have. This is Charlotte."

"Nice to meet you," said Charlotte.

"I remember Bay mentioning you quite often," said Carrie.

"Carrie is the youngest and the lawyer in the family," interrupted Bay. "This is Sadie, my big sister, who is the best teacher in Astoria, Florida! Sisters, this is Roberta, Marsha, and Sunny."

"Marsha and I are not just part of the circle. We're Bay's coworkers," said Sunny.

"When all of you get together," said Sadie, smiling, "I'm sure there's never a dull moment."

"It's been nice meeting all of you, but my stomach is calling for food," said Carrie, walking toward Sadie's car.

"Good-bye, everybody, maybe I'll see you when I visit Galveston this summer," said Sadie, following Carrie.

Bay's friends drove back to Galveston while Bay joined her family at Sadie's house.

While Jack and Bee were still at the church, Bay and her sisters sat on the porch watching the children play. "Zack is really growing," said Carrie. "Another year, he'll be almost as tall as you, and Sara is getting tall and just as pretty as a rose."

"She has a right to be pretty. Just look at all us McQueen women!" cried Bay, putting her right hand behind her head and the other one on her hip.

"Bay, since we so fine, is there a man in your life?" asked Carrie.

"Not anymore. That's been over for some time," replied Bay softly.

"You mean it's really over?" asked Sadie.

"Yep, it really wasn't going anywhere."

"I thought you didn't want to get married," said Carrie.

"I don't, but I do want a man who is available."

"Yet you don't want to get married?" asked Sadie.

"Nope, not now or ever!" responded Bay firmly. "Baby Sister, are you getting married?"

"Naw, girls, we is shackin'," said Carrie, laughing.

"Sadie, what about you. Do you intend to marry?" asked Bay.

"I don't need a man's paycheck. I have my own money!" asserted Sadie. "Guess what? It feels pretty damn good!"

"Seems like all of us are afraid of marriage," said Bay.

"Bay, there's probably some truth to that, 'cause our parents never did anything but fight," replied Carrie.

"As much as they fought, I never could figure out how they found the time to have sex," said Bay. They laughed.

"By the way, Bay, do you ever hear from Daddy?" asked Carrie.

"Sometimes. The last time we talked he wanted me to come to his house to a cookout. His no-good brother R. Lee was visiting him. I said hell no!"

"Why?" asked Sadie and Carrie.

"I didn't want to be around him."

"There has to be another reason. That doesn't sound like you," said Sadie.

"He molested me when I was seven!" shouted Bay.

"Bay, my God, no! Did Mama know about this?" asked Sadie.

"Yes, she did," answered Bay softly.

"No wonder you were always so afraid and insecure as a child," said Sadie, pulling her off the porch and into the house. "Bay, I'm so, so sorry," she continued, crying and holding her close.

"I wish the statute of limitations hadn't expired—we could make his ass pay. One thing I hate is a low-down dirty bastard who takes advantage of innocent children!" cried Carrie.

"Gosh, this is all a shock to me. You were just seven years old. Why didn't you tell me?" asked Sadie.

"You couldn't have done anything," replied Bay.

"There's no telling how many other young girls he's molested!" replied Carrie.

"Bay, both of us have daughters we need to protect. Guess that's all we can do," said Sadie.

"Who knows, I might be having a girl too," responded Carrie.

"You pregnant?" asked Bay and Sadie excitedly.

"Yes, I am!" cried Carrie happily.

The next day, Bay did not return to Galveston to work. She remained in Astoria with her sisters. While Bee was taking a nap, Jack took Mother Caine and the children for a ride. While Bay and her sisters were seated at the table talking, Bee walked in. "That was a nice nap. Now I'm hungry," she said, stretching.

"Mama, why you never talked to me about R. Lee abusing me when I was seven years old?" said Bay.

"Honey, that was a long time ago. Don't you think you should let sleeping dogs lie? I took care of it. Didn't I put him out on the streets?" asked Bee.

"That wasn't enough! I needed you, Mama. I needed you to put your arms around me and tell me you loved me and that everything would be all right!" shouted Bay, now crying loudly.

"Bay, I'm sorry. I did all I understood how to do," said Bee sadly. "Please forgive me," she continued as she turned and walked toward the bedroom.

Sadie and Carrie walked over to comfort Bay. Suddenly she said, "I feel like a new woman. I'm so glad I released all that weight off my shoulders."

"Now you can move forward with your life," replied Sadie.

"Guess what I've been thinking about for a while?" said Bay.

"What?" asked Carrie, as she and Sadie anxiously awaited an answer.

"I've decided to go to college! I'm going to take night classes at Galveston University!" said Bay enthusiastically.

"That is super!" cried Carrie. "Bay, I think that's wonderful! I'm so proud of you!"

"Let's go out to celebrate!" shouted Sadie.

"Mama and Mother Caine will take care of the kids," said Carrie.

Two years passed. Mother Caine sold her house and moved to Galveston, down the street from Jack and Bee. Carrie added a son, Cameron, to the McQueen clan. Times were changing, so Bee sold her house in Salem and Bay became a very dedicated student in her pursuit of a degree in religion and was just as determined to earn a PhD in religion.

CHAPTER SEVENTEEN

It was now 1982. More than two years had passed since she got the book from Hilda, and Bay had not yet read it. Since Zack and Hannah were staying the weekend with Mother Caine, she decided to read it. Bay picked it up off a table in the living room that sat by the window. She walked over to the couch, sat down, and began thumbing through. *Lot of big words 'n dis book*, thought Bay. Suddenly, her eyes fell on "meditation"—stilling the mind. "I want to know more. What on earth does that mean?" she muttered softly. She started reading, and before she realized it, three hours had passed.

A few minutes later she went into her bedroom and placed a chair beside her bed. "This seems really strange and a little spooky," said Bay softly, now looking around. Suddenly she closed her eyes and became relaxed. That was not the last time. Meditation became a part of her daily ritual. The light became a constant presence, but now it was in her soul. Bay became a different person. She was quiet and confident, and her friends were concerned because she was always too busy to go to the Grill.

One day Roberta and Charlotte decided to show up unexpectedly at Bay's job to take her to lunch. They walked in. "Hi, Sunny, hi, Marsha, where's Bay?" asked Charlotte.

"She went home for lunch."

"That's not at all like Bay. Something's happened to her. She seems distant," said Marsha.

"We'll just wait until she gets back," said Roberta, now seated at Bay's desk.

Five minutes later, Bay walked in. "Hey gang, how's everybody?"

"Bay, are you seeing a man?" asked Roberta.

"No, I'm not."

"Bay McQueen, you are glowing. Nothing can do that but a man and sex!" said Charlotte, laughing.

"What about the Universe, light, God?" replied Bay.

"Universe? Bay, you don't mean to tell me that you have gone and got religious on us!" cried Roberta.

"No, just enlightened."

"That doesn't mean you're supposed to forsake your friends," exclaimed Charlotte.

"I know that. I just needed some time to myself, some solitude."

"Bay, are you ever going back to the Grill with us? It won't be the same without you," said Sunny sadly.

"Of course I'm going back to the Grill. That's our second home," answered Bay. Being confronted by her friends about her new faith was not too uncomfortable, but Bay knew it would be a horse of a different color with Bee, Jack, and Mother Caine. They were happy about Bay attending college but thought her friends and education were having a bad influence on her.

Since Mother Caine moved to Galveston, Bee and Jack had invited her and Bay over every Thursday night. That night just happened to be the time for Bee's delicious dinner. Everybody gathered in the dining room and sat around the table. Jack blessed the food. "May this meal bless and nourish us. In Your name we pray, amen."

"What a beautiful prayer!" cried Mother, throwing up one hand and reaching for a homemade roll with the other one. "Bee, child, seems like your cooking gets better every week," continued Mother, now biting down on the roll.

"Mother, now don't forget me. Save me a roll," said Bay, laughing.

"Bay, you stop it before I get choked!" said Mother, laughing. "Lord, it sure is nice being in Galveston around folks who love you and you love them," continued Mother. "Bee, I can hardly wait for church Sunday. Pastor knows how to really preach the word!"

"Yes, he does," replied Bee.

"Bay, are you going to church with us Sunday?" asked Mother.

"No, I'm not."

"Since I've been in Galveston, you haven't attended church with us. Child, all I can say is, don't get caught out there without a covering. You never know when the Lord is coming," said Mother.

"Mother, I don't know what y'all waiting on. The Spirit has already come in my life," asserted Bay. "Since we're having an open discussion about church and the Lord, I might as well inform the family that I don't intend to return to traditional Christianty. I have found something so real, something I've been looking for all my life," continued Bay, softly and calmly.

Mother, surprised, looked at Jack and then Bee. "Lord, Bay, you don't mean to tell me you done let those white folks turn your mind upside down!" said Mother.

"Mother, I thought you had changed your opinion about white people," said Bay, smiling.

"Well, I have, but when I see how you have changed because of them, it makes me upset!" said Mother, dropping food off her fork.

"I'm a big girl now. I'm a grown woman and an educated one too!" asserted Bay cheerfully.

"No matter how grown you are and educated, if you don't obey God, He will strike you down!" said Mother.

"Bay, don't get Mother all riled up," said Bee.

"Mother, God loves me. He would never strike me or anyone else down. He's on the inside of me. He's right where I am," exclaimed Bay.

"What?" said Mother, looking puzzled. "Bay, God sits on His throne up in heaven, and one day He's going to crack the sky for everyone to see!" shouted Mother.

"Just keep waiting," replied Bay, chuckling.

"Bee, I'm going to the house to go to bed. Bay done got me so upset, my head is hurting," said Mother, walking toward the foyer.

Jack stood up. "Mother, I'll walk you home."

"Jack, thank you so much. There are still some godly folks in the world," said Mother, looking over at Bay.

"Bye, Mother, I'll see you next week, same time," said Bay softly, with a smile.

After Jack and Mother left, Bay and her mother were alone. "Bay, do you really believe all that nonsense you were telling Mother Caine?"

"Of course I do. God isn't sitting on a throne up in the sky beyond the clouds. He is a living Presence that never leaves."

"Bay, I don't want to hear any more."

"Mama, it's true! I've seen it. It's light!" asserted Bay.

"Bay, if people hear you talking like this, they'd swear you've lost your mind."

"No, Mama, it's the other way around. They've lost theirs, but I have found mine," responded Bay, walking out of the dining room.

Bay returned home after having dinner with the family. Zachary and Hannah stayed with Jack and Bee. Suddenly, there was a knock at the door. *Wonder who on earth is dat? Maybe it's Roberta,* she thought. Bay walked over and opened the door. It was Bill. "Bill, how are you?" asked Bay quietly.

"Fine, how are you?"

"Great!" She became aware that he was standing. "Bill, you're walking! You're walking!" shouted Bay. "I knew you'd walk again!"

Suddenly they were in each other's arms, kissing passionately. Bay pulled away. "No, Bill, you're married. Even if you weren't, it doesn't mean we're supposed to be together."

"We could be together, if only you would forget that I'm married."

"Bill, I will not be your mistress," said Bay. She walked over to the door and opened it. "Go home to Laura. I've finally found what I've been searching for all my life, and I will not allow you or anyone to hinder me," said Bay, closing the door as she watched him walk down the steps.